$1.04

D1355478

EDITH WHARTON

(1862–1937) was born in New York, the daughter of Lucretia Rhinelander and George Frederic Jones. In 1885 she married a Boston socialite, Edward Robbins Wharton and lived with him in Newport, Rhode Island, frequently travelling to Europe where she became friendly with Henry James. But her marriage was an unhappy one and Edith turned to writing. Her first novel, *The Valley of Decision*, appeared in 1902. She went on to publish an average of more than a book a year for the rest of her life. Her first critical and popular success came with *The House of Mirth* (1905). Then followed her richest period of literary activity which included *The Fruit of the Tree* (1907), *Madame de Treymes* (1907) and *The Reef* (1912). Her husband's mental health steadily declined and in 1910, when they had moved permanently to France, the marriage finally broke up, ending in divorce in 1913.

Edith Wharton's writing was largely abandoned during the First World War. She threw herself into war work for which she was awarded the Cross of the Légion d'Honneur and the Order of Leopold. After the war she moved to an eighteenth-century villa north of Paris, and spent her winters in a converted monastery on the Riviera. *The Age of Innocence* was published in 1920, winning the Pulitzer Prize. She was the first woman to receive a Doctorate of Letters from Yale University and in 1930 she became a member of the American Academy of Arts and Letters. One of America's greatest novelists, Edith Wharton died in France at the age of seventy-five. Virago publish *The Reef, Roman Fever* (1964), *The Fruit of the Tree, Madame de Treymes, Old New York*, and *The Children* (1928). In following years *The Mother's Recompense* (1925), *Hudson River Bracketed* (1929) and *The Gods Arrive* (1932) will also be published.

VIRAGO
MODERN
CLASSIC

NUMBER

179

OLD
NEW YORK

EDITH WHARTON

With a New Introduction by
MARILYN FRENCH

First British publication by VIRAGO PRESS Limited 1985
41 William IV Street, London WC2N 4DB

First published in New York by D. Appleton and Company 1924

Copyright 1924 by William R. Tyler;
Renewal copyright 1952
Introduction Copyright © Marilyn French 1985

British Library Cataloguing in Publication Data
Wharton, Edith
  Old New York.—(Virago modern classics)
  I. Title
  813'.4[F]   PS3545.H16

  ISBN 0-86068-490-3

Printed in Great Britain by Cox and Wyman
at Reading, Berkshire

CONTENTS

INTRODUCTION

OLD NEW YORK is a set of four short novels treating the untitled aristocracy of New York in the nineteenth century. Each segment deals with one decade from the 1840s through the 1870s and the work as a whole suggests the changes in manners that occurred in that forty-year period. The novels are rich with details of setting, dress, and customs, but they also convey the ambience of a past era. Most important, they portray the people of this wealthy class in all their complacency, superiority, and insularity, their moral blindness.

Paradoxically, their morals were the ground of their pride. The men, who oversaw financial affairs, held to a high standard of probity and honour; the women were responsible for maintaining a strict sexual code. Yet, as is always true of rigid societies, it was less behaviour than appearance that really mattered; whatever people actually did, it was what other people knew and thought that determined their social standing. And social standing was the major concern of this class. If a man lost his money, or a woman her reputation for sexual "virtue", they simply fell out of society; they were treated as if they did not exist.

Since appearances were more important than reality, manners were more important than morality, and most important of all was conformity, in behaviour and taste. Good behaviour—manners—required the omission of most subjects, especially sex, money and servants; good taste required the avoidance of the pretentious, the opulent, the showy, but also of the original. It was as unacceptable for a son of this class to become an artist as to become a businessman; it was inconceivable that a daughter do anything but marry. Thus, what marked this society of wealth and leisure was what it *excluded* rather than what it permitted itself. Its morality was based in negations, narrowness, omissions and avoidances.

The four "novelettes" (as Edith Wharton called them) in this volume centre on characters who in some way are unable to abide by the restrictions of old New York society.

The first, "False Dawn", is set in the 1840s, and concerns a rich and domineering father who sends his intimidated son on the "Grand Tour" of Europe, with instructions to buy paintings by Italian artists currently fashionable in New York—Albano, Carlo Dolci, and Salvator Rosa among others. The father, Halston Raycie, wishes to create "a gallery of Heirlooms". His son, Lewis, accidentally meets John Ruskin in his travels and, under that critic's influence, buys much greater works by artists unknown to his father, who cruelly punishes what he considers Lewis's insubordination.

This novel strikes a theme that crops up throughout the volume—the ignorance and provincialism of American taste. *Old New York* was published in 1924; poets and painters were complaining of this American philistinism right up until the end of World War II. Raycie's lectures about art to his son stand in ironic counterpoint to his inability to accept the paintings of Piero della Francesca and Carpaccio, and his condemnation of an impoverished neighbour, Edgar Allen Poe. There is irony also in the fact that Lewis, who dislikes his father, spends his entire life trying to vindicate his choice, that is, symbolically trying to prove his rightness to his father even though the man is dead.

But the most interesting elements of the novel for me are the portrait of Halston Raycie, which is done delicately but very satirically, and the situation of women in this period.

Halston Raycie is called "the Commodore" because he was in the Navy during the War of 1812, and he assumes the prerogatives of such a personage, especially with his family.

> He thought well of most things related to himself by ties of blood or interest. No one had ever been quite sure that he made Mrs Raycie happy, but he was known to have the highest opinion of her. So it was with his daughters . . . no one would have sworn that they were quite at ease with their genial parent, yet everyone knew how loud he was in their praises.

He holds his family entirely in his power because he controls its money.

> Mr Raycie, the day after his marriage, had quietly taken over the management of his wife's property, and deducted, from the very moderate allowance he accorded her, all her little personal expenses, even to the postage stamps she used, and the dollar she put in the plate every Sunday. He called the allowance her "pin money," since, as he often reminded her, he paid all the household bills himself, so that Mrs Raycie's quarterly pittance could be entirely devoted, if she chose, to frills and feathers.

No one dares to oppose him. Mrs Raycie's mother only whispers the lament that her daughter "can't as much as have a drop of gruel brought up to her without his weighing the oatmeal". Food is lavish when Mr Raycie entertains, but "the ladies were supposed only to nibble". And when Lewis's generous sister, Mary Adeline, wishes to help the ill and starving Mrs Poe, she must rise before dawn and sneak to the pantry to do it. Moreover, Mr Raycie, like some wealthy people in our own period, justifies his meanness on moral grounds: it is forbidden to help the Poes because Edgar is an "Atheist" and "blasphemer".

"The Old Maid" concerns a woman of the 1850s, Charlotte Lovell, who breaks the sexual code of her class. Unmarried, she feels passion for Clem Spender, who was born to the gentry but is penniless and an artist. She conceives a child by him and secretly gives birth to it. She can conceal these acts; unfortunately for her, she loves her child and wants to raise it. Since she has no money, this is not possible. If she were rich, and a man, however, her act would have minimal consequences. Charlotte tells her cousin Delia Lovell Ralston that she is calling off her projected marriage to Joe Ralston; Delia is shocked and argues with her:

> "You don't mean to say that you're going to let any little thing in Joe's past—? Not that I've ever heard the least hint; never. But even if there were . . ." She drew a deep breath, and bravely proceeded to extremities. "Even if you've heard that he's been . . . that he's had a child—of course he would have provided for it before . . ."

Yet this same Delia, when she discovers Charlotte's true reason, insists that she is no longer worthy to be the wife of Joe Ralston.

The real focus of "The Old Maid" is the relation between Delia and Charlotte and the implicit contrast and comparison between them. Charlotte's life is narrow and grim in many ways, while Delia's seems fortunate and happy. But Delia can feel complacent about her life only by comparing it with Charlotte's, and even then, she envies her cousin—for Delia too was attracted sexually to Clem Spender, but denied that attraction and married safely, soundly, suitably, as "a nice girl in the nicest set" usually did. After Delia's marriage there were:

the large double-bed; the terror of seeing him shaving calmly the next morning, in his shirtsleeves, through the dressing-room door; the evasions, insinuations, resigned smiles and Bible texts of one's Mamma; the reminder of the phrase "to obey" in the glittering blur of the Marriage Service; a week or a month of flushed distress, confusion, embarrassed pleasure; then the growth of habit, the insidious lulling of the matter-of-course . . .

And then, the babies; the babies who were supposed to "make up for everything," and didn't—though they were such darlings, and one had no definite notion as to what it was that one had missed, and that they were to make up for.

What the babies are supposed to "make up for" is sexual pleasure, passion. "False Dawn" is a not-so-subtle condemnation of the ignorance and provincial conformity of taste in old New York society; "The Old Maid" is a subtle condemnation of the sexual mores of that class. Charlotte Lovell is never permitted fully to experience her motherhood; But Delia Lovell Ralston never experiences sexual passion and joy. Sexual constriction, a forbidden subject in 1924 (remember what happened to Joyce's *Ulysses* and D. H. Lawrence's *Lady Chatterley's Lover*: they ended up in the law courts), was even more taboo for a woman writer. But Wharton planted it firmly, if silently, in the heart of this novel.

Wharton's condemnation of New York society in "The Spark", the third in this volume, goes to the heart of its morality. For New York society is Christian, and the core virtue of Christianity is charity. "The Spark" is set in the 1860s, and is narrated by a young male from a good family who is fascinated by an older man in his parents' set, Hayley Delane. The ground of the narrator's fascination is Hayley's *difference* from other men; and in time the narrator concludes that this difference is not one of intelligence, but of moral development.

Against all advice, Hayley marries Leila Gracy. Leila is fifteen years younger than he; her father is in disgrace and has "had to resign from all his clubs"—this means Leila has no money. She is not especially beautiful, and she is not in love with Hayley. After their marriage, she engages in one flirtation after another with younger men. But Hayley loves her, and submits to her treatment of him.

His moral difference shows most clearly in discussions of social questions, problems concerning club adminstration, charity, or the relation between "gentlemen" and the community. After listening to the others argue, Hayley would say, "After all, what does it matter who makes the first move? The thing is to get the business done." The narrator is impressed by this, for,

> to everyone else, my father included, what mattered in everything, from Diocesan Meetings to Patriarch's Balls, was just what Delane seemed to be heedless of: the standing of the people who make up the committee or headed the movement. To Delane, only the movement itself counted; if the thing were worth doing, he pronounced in his slow lazy way, get it done somehow, even if its backers *were* Methodists or Congregationalists, or people who dined in the midddle of the day.

Hayley comes into conflict with his society because of his morality. Early in the novel, he horsewhips a young man for beating his horse. Since his wife is carrying on an infatuation with the young man, Hayley's behaviour appears the revenge of a jealous husband. Let stand, his act compromises his wife. Hayley is thus forced to apologise. The second conflict puts him in opposition not just to society but even to his wife. Hayley insists on taking into their home Leila's penniless, debauched, and reprobate old father. The old man's presence alienates society—people stop visiting, and they side with Leila when she leaves Hayley because of this.

The inspiration—the "spark"—for Hayley's generosity of spirit was "a queer fellow" who tended him in hospital during the Civil War, and who, Hayley claims, taught him "Christian charity" although he was an "old heathen". Our suspicion that the moral teacher was Walt Whitman is verified at the end of the tale, with an ironic twist—for Hayley neither comprehends nor likes Whitman's poetry.

It would ruin "New Year's Day" to reveal the pivot of its plot, which centres on Lizzie Hazeldean, another of the impoverished young women sprinkled through this book. Lizzie marries "up"; this makes her acceptable, but suspect. When she is suspected of having an affair, however, society ostracises her.

We may have difficulty comprehending just what ostracism meant in Wharton's day—or Austen's, or any period in which women were strictly confined to the domestic realm. In such cultures, "society" provides women's only links with life outside the family, and the arranging of social occasions provides their only occupation. Wharton dealt several times with the emptiness and despair of women cut off from society—in "Autres Temps" (*Roman Fever*), *The Mother's Recompense*, and in *The House of Mirth*. Genteel women who are ostracised may suffer also from strained finances or even poverty, but their greatest suffering arises from isolation.

Wharton never became a conscious, outspoken feminist, but she also never stopped pointing at the conditions of life for upper- and middle-class women. Given little or no education, and deprived of the right to work, they were utterly dependent for survival on marriage to a wealthy man or inherited wealth. Through a young male narrator, Wharton offers in "New

Year's Day" her most explicit protest about this situation. The narrator is looking back over Lizzie's life:

> I bent bewildered over the depths of her plight. What else, at any stage of her career, could she have done, I often wondered? Among the young women now growing up about me I find none with enough imagination to picture the helpless incapacity of the pretty girl of the 'seventies, the girl without money or vocation, seemingly put into the world only to please, and unlearned in any way of maintaining herself there by her own efforts. Marriage alone could save such a girl from starvation, unless she happened to run across an old lady who wanted her dogs exercised and her *Churchman* read aloud to her. Even the day of painting wild-roses on fans, of colouring photographs to "look like" miniatures, of manufacturing lampshades and trimming hats for more fortunate friends—even this precarious beginning of feminine independence had not dawned.

Thus, the final novel in this volume offers an indictment of a society that "regarded poverty as so distasteful that it simply took no account of it", and considers one woman's solution to her predicament. The condition of women—a theme throughout the work—completes it.

Old New York is fair-minded: the graces and luxuries of the age are there along with its cruelties and blindnesses. But the book offers more than a portrait of an age: it offers also a devastating portrait of the morals of an elite class. If many of the manners and customs described in it have vanished, these morals have not; although women are no longer so sexually circumscribed, and men no longer so honourable about money, the complacency, the assumed superiority of this class continues to appear in elite classes. A male critic once asserted that Wharton had no morality. But he was blind.

Marilyn French
New York, 1984

FALSE DAWN

(The 'Forties)

PART I

I

HAY, verbena and mignonette scented the languid July
day. Large strawberries, crimsoning through sprigs of
mint, floated in a bowl of pale yellow cup on the verandah
table: an old Georgian bowl, with complex reflections on
polygonal flanks, engraved with the Raycie arms between
lion's heads. Now and again the gentlemen, warned by a
menacing hum, slapped their cheeks, their brows or their
bald crowns; but they did so as furtively as possible, for
Mr. Halston Raycie, on whose verandah they sat, would
not admit that there were mosquitoes at High Point.

The strawberries came from Mr. Raycie's kitchen garden; the Georgian bowl came from his great-grandfather
(father of the Signer); the verandah was that of his country-house, which stood on a height above the Sound, at a
convenient driving distance from his town house in Canal
Street.

"Another glass, Commodore," said Mr. Raycie, shaking
out a cambric handkerchief the size of a table-cloth, and
applying a corner of it to his steaming brow.

Mr. Jameson Ledgely smiled and took another glass.
He was known as "the Commodore" among his intimates
because of having been in the Navy in his youth, and
having taken part, as a midshipman under Admiral
Porter, in the war of 1812. This jolly sunburnt bachelor,
whose face resembled that of one of the bronze idols he

might have brought back with him, had kept his naval air, though long retired from the service; and his white duck trousers, his gold-braided cap and shining teeth, still made him look as if he might be in command of a frigate. Instead of that, he had just sailed over a party of friends from his own place on the Long Island shore; and his trim white sloop was now lying in the bay below the point.

The Halston Raycie house overlooked a lawn sloping to the Sound. The lawn was Mr. Raycie's pride: it was mown with a scythe once a fortnight, and rolled in the spring by an old white horse specially shod for the purpose. Below the verandah the turf was broken by three rounds of rose-geranium, heliotrope and Bengal roses, which Mrs. Raycie tended in gauntlet gloves, under a small hinged sunshade that folded back on its carved ivory handle. The house, remodelled and enlarged by Mr. Raycie on his marriage, had played a part in the Revolutionary war as the settler's cottage where Benedict Arnold had had his headquarters. A contemporary print of it hung in Mr. Raycie's study; but no one could have detected the humble outline of the old house in the majestic stone-coloured dwelling built of tongued-and-grooved boards, with an angle tower, tall narrow windows, and a verandah on chamfered posts, that figured so confidently as a "Tuscan Villa" in Downing's "Landscape Gardening in America." There was the same difference between the rude lithograph of the earlier house and the fine steel engraving of its successor (with a "specimen" weeping beech on the lawn) as between the buildings themselves. Mr. Raycie had reason to think well of his architect.

He thought well of most things related to himself by ties of blood or interest. No one had ever been quite sure that he made Mrs. Raycie happy, but he was known to have the highest opinion of her. So it was with his daughters, Sarah Anne and Mary Adeline, fresher replicas of the lymphatic Mrs. Raycie; no one would have sworn that they were quite at ease with their genial parent, yet every one knew how loud he was in their praises. But the most remarkable object within the range of Mr. Raycie's self-approval was his son Lewis. And yet, as Jameson Ledgely, who was given to speaking his mind, had once observed, you wouldn't have supposed young Lewis was exactly the kind of craft Halston would have turned out if he'd had the designing of his son and heir.

Mr. Raycie was a monumental man. His extent in height, width and thickness was so nearly the same that whichever way he was turned one had an almost equally broad view of him; and every inch of that mighty circumference was so exquisitely cared for that to a farmer's eye he might have suggested a great agricultural estate of which not an acre is untilled. Even his baldness, which was in proportion to the rest, looked as if it received a special daily polish; and on a hot day his whole person was like some wonderful example of the costliest irrigation. There was so much of him, and he had so many planes, that it was fascinating to watch each runnel of moisture follow its own particular watershed. Even on his large fresh-looking hands the drops divided, trickling in different ways from the ridges of the fingers; and as for his forehead and temples, and the raised cushion of cheek beneath each of his lower lids, every one of these slopes had its own particular stream, its hollow pools and sudden cataracts; and the sight was never unpleasant, because his whole vast bubbling surface was of such a clean and hearty pink, and the exuding moisture so perceptibly flavoured with expensive eau de Cologne and the best French soap.

Mrs. Raycie, though built on a less heroic scale, had a pale amplitude which, when she put on her best watered silk (the kind that stood alone), and framed her countenance in the innumerable blonde lace ruffles and clustered purple grapes of her newest Paris cap, almost balanced her husband's bulk. Yet from this full-rigged pair, as the Commodore would have put it, had issued the lean little runt of a Lewis, a shrimp of a baby, a shaver of a boy, and now a youth as scant as an ordinary man's midday shadow.

All these things, Lewis himself mused, dangling his legs from the verandah rail, were undoubtedly passing through the minds of the four gentlemen grouped about his father's bowl of cup.

Mr. Robert Huzzard, the banker, a tall broad man, who looked big in any company but Mr. Raycie's, leaned back, lifted his glass, and bowed to Lewis.

"Here's to the Grand Tour!"

"Don't perch on that rail like a sparrow, my boy," Mr. Raycie said reprovingly; and Lewis dropped to his feet, and returned Mr. Huzzard's bow.

"I wasn't thinking," he stammered. It was his too frequent excuse.

Mr. Ambrose Huzzard, the banker's younger brother, Mr. Ledgely and Mr. Donaldson Kent, all raised their glasses and cheerily echoed: "The Grand Tour!"

Lewis bowed again, and put his lips to the glass he had forgotten. In reality, he had eyes only for Mr. Donaldson Kent, his father's cousin, a silent man with a lean hawk-like profile, who looked like a retired Revolutionary hero, and lived in daily fear of the most trifling risk or responsibility.

To this prudent and circumspect citizen had come, some years earlier, the unexpected and altogether inexcusable demand that he should look after the daughter of his only brother, Julius Kent. Julius had died in Italy—well, that was his own business, if he chose to live there. But to let his wife die before him, and to leave a minor daughter, and a will entrusting her to the guardianship of his esteemed elder brother, Donaldson Kent Esquire, of Kent's Point, Long Island, and Great Jones Street, New York—well, as Mr. Kent himself said, and as his wife said for him, there had never been anything, anything whatever, in Mr. Kent's attitude or behaviour, to justify the ungrateful Julius (whose debts he had more than once paid) in laying on him this final burden.

The girl came. She was fourteen, she was considered plain, she was small and black and skinny. Her name was Beatrice, which was bad enough, and made worse by the fact that it had been shortened by ignorant foreigners to Treeshy. But she was eager, serviceable and good-tempered, and as Mr. and Mrs. Kent's friends pointed out, her plainness made everything easy. There were two Kent boys growing up, Bill and Donald; and if this penniless cousin had been compounded of cream and roses—well, she would have taken more watching, and might have rewarded the kindness of her uncle and aunt by some act of wicked ingratitude. But this risk being obviated by her appearance, they could be goodnatured to her without afterthought, and to be goodnatured was natural to them. So, as the years passed, she gradually became the guardian of her guardians; since it was equally natural to Mr. and

Mrs. Kent to throw themselves in helpless reliance on every one whom they did not nervously fear or mistrust.

"Yes, he's off on Monday," Mr. Raycie said, nodding sharply at Lewis, who had set down his glass after one sip. "Empty it, you shirk!" the nod commanded; and Lewis, throwing back his head, gulped down the draught, though it almost stuck in his lean throat. He had already had to take two glasses, and even this scant conviviality was too much for him, and likely to result in a mood of excited volubility, followed by a morose evening and a head the next morning. And he wanted to keep his mind clear that day, and to think steadily and lucidly of Treeshy Kent.

Of course he couldn't marry her—yet. He was twenty-one that very day, and still entirely dependent on his father. And he wasn't altogether sorry to be going first on this Grand Tour. It was what he had always dreamed of, pined for, from the moment when his infant eyes had first been drawn to the prints of European cities in the long upper passage that smelt of matting. And all that Treeshy had told him about Italy had confirmed and intensified the longing. Oh, to have been going there with her—with her as his guide, his Beatrice! (For she had given him a little Dante of her father's, with a steel-engraved frontispiece of Beatrice; and his sister Mary Adeline, who had been taught Italian by one of the romantic Milanese exiles, had helped her brother out with the grammar.)

The thought of going to Italy with Treeshy was only a dream; but later, as man and wife, they would return there, and by that time, perhaps, it was Lewis who would be her guide, and reveal to her the historic marvels of her birthplace, of which after all she knew so little, except in minor domestic ways that were quaint but unimportant.

The prospect swelled her suitor's bosom, and reconciled him to the idea of their separation. After all, he secretly felt himself to be still a boy, and it was as a man that he would return: he meant to tell her that when they met the next day. When he came back his character would be formed, his knowledge of life (which he already thought considerable) would be complete; and then no one could keep them apart. He smiled in advance to think how little his father's shouting and booming would impress a man on his return from the Grand Tour. . .

The gentlemen were telling anecdotes about their own early experience in Europe. None of them—not even Mr. Raycie—had travelled as extensively as it was intended that Lewis should; but the two Huzzards had been twice to England on banking matters, and Commodore Ledgely, a bold man, to France and Belgium as well—not to speak of his early experience in the Far East. All three had kept a vivid and amused recollection, slightly tinged with disapprobation, of what they had seen— "Oh, those French wenches," the Commodore chuckled through his white teeth—but poor Mr. Kent, who had gone abroad on his honeymoon, had been caught in Paris by the revolution of 1830, had had the fever in Florence, and had nearly been arrested as a spy in Vienna; and the only satisfactory episode in this disastrous, and never repeated, adventure, had been the fact of his having been mistaken for the Duke of Wellington (as he was trying to slip out of a Viennese hotel in his courier's blue surtout) by a crowd who had been— "Well, very gratifying in their enthusiasm," Mr. Kent admitted.

"How my poor brother Julius could have lived in Europe! Well, look at the consequences—" he used to say, as if poor Treeshy's plainness gave an awful point to his moral.

"There's one thing in Paris, my boy, that you must be warned against: those gambling-hells in the Pally Royle," Mr. Kent insisted. "I never set foot in the places myself; but a glance at the outside was enough."

"I knew a feller that was fleeced of a fortune there," Mr. Henry Huzzard confirmed; while the Commodore, at his tenth glass, chuckled with moist eyes: "The trollops, oh, the trollops—"

"As for Vienna—" said Mr. Kent.

"Even in London," said Mr. Ambrose Huzzard, "a young man must be on his look-out against gamblers. Every form of swindling is practised, and the touts are always on the look-out for greenhorns; a term," he added apologetically, "which they apply to any traveller new to the country."

"In Paris," said Mr. Kent, "I was once within an ace of being challenged to fight a duel." He fetched a sigh of horror and relief, and glanced reassuredly down the Sound in the direction of his own peaceful roof-tree.

"Oh, a duel," laughed the Commodore. "A man can fight duels here. I fought a dozen when I was a young feller in New Erleens." The Commodore's mother had been a southern lady, and after his father's death had spent some years with her parents in Louisiana, so that her son's varied experiences had begun early. "'Bout women," he smiled confidentially, holding out his empty glass to Mr. Raycie.

"The ladies—!" exclaimed Mr. Kent in a voice of warning.

The gentlemen rose to their feet, the Commodore quite as prompt and steadily as the others. The drawing-room window opened, and from it emerged Mrs. Raycie, in a ruffled sarsenet dress and Point de Paris cap, followed by her two daughters in starched organdy with pink spencers. Mr. Raycie looked with proud approval at his womenkind.

"Gentlemen," said Mrs. Raycie, in a perfectly even voice, "supper is on the table, and if you will do Mr. Raycie and myself the favour—"

"The favour, ma'am," said Mr. Ambrose Huzzard, "is on your side, in so amiably inviting us."

Mrs. Raycie curtsied, the gentlemen bowed, and Mr. Raycie said: "Your arm to Mrs. Raycie, Huzzard. This little farewell party is a family affair, and the other gentlemen must content themselves with my two daughters. Sarah Anne, Mary Adeline—"

The Commodore and Mr. John Huzzard advanced ceremoniously toward the two girls, and Mr. Kent, being a cousin, closed the procession between Mr. Raycie and Lewis.

Oh, that supper-table! The vision of it used sometimes to rise before Lewis Raycie's eyes in outlandish foreign places; for though not a large or fastidious eater when he was at home, he was afterward, in lands of chestnut-flour and garlic and queer bearded sea-things, to suffer many pangs of hunger at the thought of that opulent board. In the centre stood the Raycie *épergne* of pierced silver, holding aloft a bunch of June roses surrounded by dangling baskets of sugared almonds and striped peppermints;

and grouped about this decorative "motif" were Low-
estoft platters heavy with piles of raspberries, strawberries
and the first Delaware peaches. An outer flanking of
heaped-up cookies, crullers, strawberry short-cake, piping
hot corn-bread and deep golden butter in moist blocks
still bedewed from the muslin swathings of the dairy,
led the eye to the Virginia ham in front of Mr. Raycie,
and the twin dishes of scrambled eggs on toast and broiled
blue-fish over which his wife presided. Lewis could never
afterward fit into this intricate pattern the "side-dishes"
of devilled turkeylegs and creamed chicken hash, the
sliced cucumbers and tomatoes, the heavy silver jugs of
butter-coloured cream, the floating-island, "slips" and
lemon jellies that were somehow interwoven with the
solider elements of the design; but they were all there,
either together or successively, and so were the towering
piles of waffles reeling on their foundations, and the
slender silver jugs of maple syrup perpetually escorting
them about the table as black Dinah replenished the
supply.

They ate—oh, how they all ate!—though the ladies were
supposed only to nibble; but the good things on Lewis's
plate remained untouched until, ever and again, an ad-
monishing glance from Mr. Raycie, or an entreating one
from Mary Adeline, made him insert a languid fork into
the heap.

And all the while Mr. Raycie continued to hold forth.

"A young man, in my opinion, before setting up for
himself, must see the world; form his taste; fortify his
judgment. He must study the most famous monuments,
examine the organization of foreign societies, and the

habits and customs of those older civilizations whose yoke
it has been our glory to cast off. Though he may see in
them much to deplore and to reprove—" ("Some of the
gals, though," Commodore Ledgely was heard to inter-
ject)—"much that will make him give thanks for the privilege of having been born and brought up under our own
Free Institutions, yet I believe he will also"—Mr. Raycie
conceded it with magnanimity—"be able to learn much."

"The Sundays, though," Mr. Kent hazarded warningly;
and Mrs. Raycie breathed across to her son: "Ah, that's
what *I* say!"

Mr. Raycie did not like interruption; and he met it by
growing visibly larger. His huge bulk hung a moment,
like an avalanche, above the silence which followed Mr.
Kent's interjection and Mrs. Raycie's murmur; then he
crashed down on both.

"The Sundays—the Sundays? Well, what of the Sundays? What is there to frighten a good Episcopalian in
what we call the Continental Sunday? I presume that
we're all Churchmen here, eh? No puling Methodists or
atheistical Unitarians at my table tonight, that I'm aware
of. Nor will I offend the ladies of my household by assuming that they have secretly lent an ear to the Baptist
ranter in the chapel at the foot of our lane. No? I thought
not! Well, then, I say, what's all this flutter about the
Papists? Far be it from me to approve of their heathenish
doctrines—but, damn it, they go to church, don't they?
And they have a real service as we do, don't they? And
real clergy and not a lot of nondescripts dressed like lay-
men, and damned badly at that, who chat familiarly with
the Almighty in their own vulgar lingo? No, sir"—he

swung about on the shrinking Mr. Kent—"it's not the Church I'm afraid of in foreign countries, it's the sewers, sir!"

Mrs. Raycie had grown very pale: Lewis knew that she too was deeply perturbed about the sewers. "And the night-air," she scarce-audibly sighed.

But Mr. Raycie had taken up his main theme again. "In my opinion, if a young man travels at all, he must travel as extensively as his—er—means permit; must see as much of the world as he can. Those are my son's sailing orders, Commodore; and here's to his carrying them out to the best of his powers!"

Black Dinah, removing the Virginia ham, or rather such of its bony structure as alone remained on the dish, had managed to make room for a bowl of punch from which Mr. Raycie poured deep ladlefuls of perfumed fire into the glasses ranged before him on a silver tray. The gentlemen rose, the ladies smiled and wept, and Lewis's health and the success of the Grand Tour were toasted with an eloquence which caused Mrs. Raycie, with a hasty nod to her daughters, and a covering rustle of starched flounces, to shepherd them softly from the room.

"After all," Lewis heard her murmur to them on the threshold, "your father's using such language shows that he's in the best of humour with dear Lewis."

II

IN SPITE of his enforced potations, Lewis Raycie was up the next morning before sunrise.

Unlatching his shutters without noise, he looked forth over the wet lawn merged in a blur of shrubberies, and the waters of the Sound dimly seen beneath a sky full of stars. His head ached but his heart glowed; what was before him was thrilling enough to clear a heavier brain than his.

He dressed quickly and completely (save for his shoes), and then, stripping the flowered quilt from his high mahogany bed, rolled it in a tight bundle under his arm. Thus enigmatically equipped he was feeling his way, shoes in hand, through the darkness of the upper story to the slippery oak stairs, when he was startled by a candle-gleam in the pitch-blackness of the hall below. He held his breath, and leaning over the stair-rail saw with amazement his sister Mary Adeline come forth, cloaked and bonneted, but also in stocking-feet, from the passage leading to the pantry. She too carried a double burden: her shoes and the candle in one hand, in the other a large covered basket that weighed down her bare arm.

Brother and sister stopped and stared at each other in the blue dusk: the upward slant of the candle-light distorted Mary Adeline's mild features, twisting them into a frightened grin as Lewis stole down to join her.

"Oh—" she whispered. "What in the world are you doing here? I was just getting together a few things for that poor young Mrs. Poe down the lane, who's so ill—before mother goes to the storeroom. You won't tell, will you?"

Lewis signalled his complicity, and cautiously slid open the bolt of the front door. They durst not say more till they were out of ear-shot. On the doorstep they sat down to put on their shoes; then they hastened on without a word through the ghostly shrubberies till they reached the gate into the lane.

"But you, Lewis?" the sister suddenly questioned, with an astonished stare at the rolled-up quilt under her brother's arm.

"Oh, I—. Look here, Addy—" he broke off and began to grope in his pocket—"I haven't much about me . . . the old gentleman keeps me as close as ever . . . but here's a dollar, if you think that poor Mrs. Poe could use it. . . I'd be too happy . . . consider it a privilege. . ."

"Oh, Lewis, Lewis, how noble, how generous of you! Of course I can buy a few extra things with it . . . they never see meat unless I can bring them a bit, you know . . . and I fear she's dying of a decline . . . and she and her mother are so fiery-proud. . ." She wept with gratitude, and Lewis drew a breath of relief. He had diverted her attention from the bed-quilt.

"Ah, there's the breeze," he murmured, sniffing the suddenly chilled air.

"Yes; I must be off; I must be back before the sun is up," said Mary Adeline anxiously, "and it would never do if mother knew—"

"She doesn't know of your visits to Mrs. Poe?"

A look of childish guile sharpened Mary Adeline's un-

developed face. "She *does*, of course; but yet she doesn't
. . . we've arranged it so. You see, Mr. Poe's an Atheist;
and so father—"

"I see," Lewis nodded. "Well, we part here; I'm off for
a swim," he said glibly. But abruptly he turned back and
caught his sister's arm. "Sister, tell Mrs. Poe, please, that
I heard her husband give a reading from his poems in
New York two nights ago—"

("Oh, Lewis—*you*? But father says he's a blasphemer!")

"—And that he's a great poet—a Great Poet. Tell her
that from me, will you, please, Mary Adeline?"

"Oh, brother, I couldn't . . . we never speak of him,"
the startled girl faltered, hurrying away.

In the cove where the Commodore's sloop had ridden a
few hours earlier a biggish rowing-boat took the waking
ripples. Young Raycie paddled out to her, fastened his
skiff to the moorings, and hastily clambered into the boat.

From various recesses of his pockets he produced rope,
string, a carpet-layer's needle, and other unexpected and
incongruous tackle; then, lashing one of the oars across
the top of the other, and jamming the latter upright between the forward thwart and the bow, he rigged the
flowered bed-quilt on this mast, knotted a rope to the free
end of the quilt, and sat down in the stern, one hand on
the rudder, the other on his improvised sheet.

Venus, brooding silverly above a line of pale green sky,
made a pool of glory in the sea as the dawn-breeze
plumped the lover's sail. . .

On the shelving pebbles of another cove, two or three
miles down the Sound, Lewis Raycie lowered his queer
sail and beached his boat. A clump of willows on the

shingle-edge mysteriously stirred and parted, and Treeshy Kent was in his arms.

The sun was just pushing above a belt of low clouds in the east, spattering them with liquid gold, and Venus blanched as the light spread upward. But under the willows it was still dusk, a watery green dusk in which the secret murmurs of the night were caught.

"Treeshy—Treeshy!" the young man cried, kneeling beside her—and then, a moment later: "My angel, are you sure that no one guesses—?"

The girl gave a faint laugh which screwed up her funny nose. She leaned her head on his shoulder, her round forehead and rough braids pressed against his cheek, her hands in his, breathing quickly and joyfully.

"I thought I should never get here," Lewis grumbled, "with that ridiculous bed-quilt—and it'll be broad day soon! To think that I was of age yesterday, and must come to you in a boat rigged like a child's toy on a duck-pond! If you knew how it humiliates me—"

"What does it matter, dear, since you're of age now, and your own master?"

"But am I, though? He says so—but it's only on his own terms; only while I do what he wants! You'll see. . . I've a credit of ten thousand dollars . . . ten . . . thou . . . sand . . . d'you hear? . . . placed to my name in a London bank; and not a penny here to bless myself with meanwhile. . . Why, Treeshy darling, why, what's the matter?"

She flung her arms about his neck, and through their innocent kisses he could taste her tears. "What *is* it, Treeshy?" he implored her.

"I . . . oh, I'd forgotten it was to be our last day together till you spoke of London—cruel, cruel!" she reproached him; and through the green twilight of the willows her eyes blazed on him like two stormy stars. No other eyes he knew could express such elemental rage as Treeshy's.

"You little spitfire, you!" he laughed back somewhat chokingly. "Yes, it's our last day—but not for long; at our age two years are not so very long, after all, are they? And when I come back to you I'll come as my own master, independent, free—come to claim you in face of everything and everybody! Thing of that, darling, and be brave for my sake . . . brave and patient . . . as I mean to be!" he declared heroically.

"Oh, but you—you'll see other girls; heaps and heaps of them; in those wicked old countries where they're so lovely. My uncle Kent says the European countries are all wicked, even my own poor Italy . . ."

"But *you*, Treeshy; you'll be seeing cousins Bill and Donald meanwhile—seeing them all day long and every day. And you know you've a weakness for that great hulk of a Bill. Ah, if only I stood six-foot-one in my stockings I'd go with an easier heart, you fickle child!" he tried to banter her.

"Fickle? Fickle? *Me*—oh, Lewis!"

He felt the premonitory sweep of sobs, and his untried courage failed him. It was delicious, in theory, to hold weeping beauty to one's breast, but terribly alarming, he found, in practice. There came a responsive twitching in his throat.

"No, no; firm as adamant, true as steel; that's what we both mean to be, isnt it, *cara*?"

"*Caro*, yes," she sighed appeased.

"And you'll write to me regularly, Treeshy--long, long letters? I may count on that, mayn't I, wherever I am? And they must all be numbered, every one of them, so that I shall know at once if I've missed one; remember!"

"And, Lewis, you'll wear them here?" (She touched his breast.) "Oh, not *all*," she added, laughing "for they'd make such a big bundle that you'd soon have a hump in front like Pulcinella—but always at least the last one, just the last one. Promise!"

"Always, I promise—as long as they're kind," he said, still struggling to take a spirited line.

"Oh, Lewis, they will be, as long as yours are—and long, long afterward. . ."

Venus failed and vanished in the sun's uprising.

III

THE crucial moment, Lewis had always known, would be not that of his farewell to Treeshy, but of his final interview with his father.

On that everything hung: his immediate future as well as his more distant prospects. As he stole home in the early sunlight, over the dew-drenched grass, he glanced up apprehensively at Mr. Raycie's windows, and thanked his stars that they were still tightly shuttered.

There was no doubt, as Mrs. Raycie said, that her husband's "using language" before ladies showed him to be in high good humour, relaxed and slippered, as it were— a state his family so seldom saw him in that Lewis had sometimes impertinently wondered to what awful descent from the clouds he and his two sisters owed their timorous being.

It was all very well to tell himself, as he often did, that the bulk of the money was his mother's, and that he could turn her round his little finger. What difference did that make? Mr. Raycie, the day after his marriage, had quietly taken over the management of his wife's property, and deducted, from the very moderate allowance he accorded her, all her little personal expenses, even to the postage-stamps she used, and the dollar she put in the plate every Sunday. He called the allowance her "pin-money," since, as he often reminded her, he paid all the household bills himself, so that Mrs. Raycie's quarterly pittance could be entirely devoted, if she chose, to frills and feathers.

"And will be, if you respect my wishes, my dear," he always added. "I like to see a handsome figure well set-off, and not to have our friends imagine, when they come to dine, that Mrs. Raycie is sick above-stairs, and I've replaced her by a poor relation in *allapacca*." In compliance with which Mrs. Raycie, at once flattered and terrified, spent her last penny in adorning herself and her daughters, and had to stint their bedroom fires, and the servants' meals, in order to find a penny for any private necessity.

Mr. Raycie had long since convinced his wife that this method of dealing with her, if not lavish, was suitable, and in fact "handsome"; when she spoke of the subject to her relations it was with tears of gratitude for her husband's kindness in assuming the management of her property. As he managed it exceedingly well, her hard-headed brothers (glad to have the responsibility off their hands, and convinced that, if left to herself, she would have muddled her money away in ill-advised charities) were disposed to share her approval of Mr. Raycie; though her old mother sometimes said helplessly: "When I think that Lucy Ann can't as much as have a drop of gruel brought up to her without his weighing the oatmeal. . ." But even that was only whispered, lest Mr. Raycie's mysterious faculty of hearing what was said behind his back should bring sudden reprisals on the venerable lady to whom he always alluded, with a tremor in his genial voice, as "my dear mother-in-law—unless indeed she will allow me to call her, more briefly but more truly, my dear mother."

To Lewis, hitherto, Mr. Raycie had meted the same measure as to the females of the household. He had dressed him well, educated him expensively, lauded him to the skies—and counted every penny of his allowance. Yet there was a difference and Lewis was as well aware of it as any one.

The dream, the ambition, the passion of Mr. Raycie's life, was (as his son knew) to found a Family; and he had only Lewis to found it with. He believed in primogeniture, in heirlooms, in entailed estates, in all the ritual of the English "landed" tradition. No one was louder than he in praise of the democratic institutions under which he lived; but he never thought of them as affecting that more private but more important institution, the Family; and to the Family all his care and all his thoughts were given. The result, as Lewis dimly guessed, was, that upon his own shrinking and inadequate head was centred all the passion contained in the vast expanse of Mr. Raycie's breast. Lewis was his very own, and Lewis represented what was most dear to him; and for both these reasons Mr. Raycie set an inordinate value on the boy (a quite different thing, Lewis thought from loving him).

Mr. Raycie was particularly proud of his son's taste for letters. Himself not a wholly unread man, he admired intensely what he called the "cultivated gentleman"—and that was what Lewis was evidently going to be. Could he have combined with this tendency a manlier frame, and an interest in the few forms of sport then popular among gentlemen, Mr. Raycie's satisfaction would have been complete; but whose is, in this disappointing world? Meanwhile he flattered himself that, Lewis being still young and malleable, and his health certainly mending, two years of travel and adventure might send him back a very different figure, physically as well as mentally. Mr.

Raycie had himself travelled in his youth, and was persuaded that the experience was formative; he secretly hoped for the return of a bronzed and broadened Lewis, seasoned by independence and adventure, and having discreetly sown his wild oats in foreign pastures, where they would not contaminate the home crop.

All this Lewis guessed; and he guessed as well that these two wander-years were intended by Mr. Raycie to lead up to a marriage and an establishment after Mr. Raycie's own heart, but in which Lewis's was not to have even a consulting voice.

"He's going to give me all the advantages—for his own purpose," the young man summed it up as he went down to join the family at the breakfast table.

Mr. Raycie was never more resplendent than at that moment of the day and season. His spotless white duck trousers, strapped under kid boots, his thin kerseymere coat, and drab *piqué* waistcoat crossed below a snowy stock, made him look as fresh as the morning and as appetizing as the peaches and cream banked before him.

Opposite sat Mrs. Raycie, immaculate also, but paler than usual, as became a mother about to part from her only son; and between the two was Sarah Anne, unusually pink, and apparently occupied in trying to screen her sister's empty seat. Lewis greeted them, and seated himself at his mother's right.

Mr. Raycie drew out his *guillochée* repeating watch, and detaching it from its heavy gold chain laid it on the table beside him.

"Mary Adeline is late again. It is a somewhat unusual thing for a sister to be late at the last meal she is to take— for two years—with her only brother."

"Oh, Mr. Raycie!" Mrs. Raycie faltered.

"I say, the idea is peculiar. Perhaps," said Mr. Raycie sarcastically, "I am going to be blessed with a *peculiar* daughter."

"I'm afraid Mary Adeline is beginning a sick headache, sir. She tried to get up, but really could not," said Sarah Anne in a rush.

Mr. Raycie's only reply was to arch ironic eyebrows, and Lewis hastily intervened: "I'm sorry, sir; but it may be my fault—"

Mrs. Raycie paled, Sarah Anne purpled, and Mr. Raycie echoed with punctilious incredulity: "Your—fault?"

"In being the occasion, sir, of last night's too-sumptuous festivity—"

"Ha—ha—ha!" Mr. Raycie laughed, his thunders instantly dispelled.

He pushed back his chair and nodded to his son with a smile; and the two, leaving the ladies to wash up the teacups (as was still the habit in genteel families) betook themselves to Mr. Raycie's study,

What Mr. Raycie studied in this apartment—except the accounts, and ways of making himself unpleasant to his family—Lewis had never been able to discover. It was a small bare formidable room; and the young man, who never crossed the threshold but with a sinking of his heart, felt it sink lower than ever. *"Now!"* he thought.

Mr. Raycie took the only easy-chair, and began.

"My dear fellow, our time is short, but long enough for what I have to say. In a few hours you will be setting out on your great journey: an important event in the life of any young man. Your talents and character—combined with your means of improving the opportunity—make me hope that in your case it will be decisive. I expect you to come home from this trip a man—"

So far, it was all to order, so to speak; Lewis could have recited it beforehand. He bent his head in acquiescence.

"A man," Mr. Raycie repeated, "prepared to play a part, a considerable part, in the social life of the community. I expect you to be a figure in New York; and I shall give you the means to be so." He cleared his throat. "But means are not enough—though you must never forget that they are essential. Education, polish, experience of the world; these are what so many of our men of standing lack. What do they know of Art or Letters? We have had little time here to produce either as yet—you spoke?" Mr. Raycie broke off with a crushing courtesy.

"I—oh, no," his son stammered.

"Ah; I thought you might be about to allude to certain blasphemous penny-a-liners whose poetic ravings are said to have given them a kind of pothouse notoriety."

Lewis reddened at the allusion but was silent, and his father went on:

"Where is our Byron—our Scott—our Shakespeare? And in painting it is the same. Where are our Old Masters? We are not without contemporary talent; but for works of genius we must still look to the past; we must, in most cases, content ourselves with copies. . . Ah, here, I know, my dear boy, I touch a responsive chord! Your love of the arts has not passed unperceived; and I mean, I desire, to do all I can to encourage it. Your future position in the world—your duties and obligations as a gentleman and a man of fortune—will not permit you to become, yourself, an eminent painter or a famous sculptor; but I shall raise no objection to your dabbling in these arts as an amateur —at least while you are travelling abroad. It will form your taste, strengthen your judgment, and give you, I hope, the discernment necessary to select for me a few masterpieces which shall *not* be copies. Copies," Mr. Raycie pursued with a deepening emphasis, "are for the less discriminating, or for those less blessed with this world's goods. Yes, my dear Lewis, I wish to create a gallery: a gallery of Heirlooms. Your mother participates in this ambition—she desires to see on our walls a few original specimens of the Italian genius. Raphael, I fear, we can hardly aspire to; but a Domenichino, an Albano, a Carlo Dolci, a Guercino, a Carlo Maratta—one or two of Salvator Rosa's noble landscapes . . . you see my idea? There shall be a Raycie Gallery; and it shall be your mission to get together its nucleus." Mr. Raycie paused, and mopped his flowing forehead. "I believe I could have given my son no task more to his liking."

"Oh, no, sir, none indeed!" Lewis cried, flushing and paling. He had in fact never suspected this part of his father's plan, and his heart swelled with the honour of so unforeseen a mission. Nothing, in truth, could have made him prouder or happier. For a moment he forgot love, forgot Treeshy, forgot everything but the rapture of moving among the masterpieces of which he had so long dreamed, moving not as a mere hungry spectator, but as one whose privilege it should at least be to single out and carry away some of the lesser treasures. He could hardly take in what had happened, and the shock of the announcement left him, as usual, inarticulate.

He heard his father booming on, developing the plan, explaining with his usual pompous precision that one of

the partners of the London bank in which Lewis's funds
were deposited was himself a noted collector, and had
agreed to provide the young traveller with letters of introduction to other connoisseurs, both in France and
Italy, so that Lewis's acquisitions might be made under
the most enlightened guidance.

"It is," Mr. Raycie concluded, "in order to put you on
a footing of equality with the best collectors that I have
placed such a large sum at your disposal. I reckon that for
ten thousand dollars you can travel for two years in the
very best style; and I mean to place another five thousand
to your credit"—he paused, and let the syllables drop
slowly into his son's brain: "five thousand dollars for the
purchase of works of art, which eventually—remember—
will be yours; and will be handed on, I trust, to your sons'
sons as long as the name of Raycie survives"—a length of
time, Mr. Raycie's tone seemed to imply, hardly to be
measured in periods less extensive than those of the
Egyptian dynasties.

Lewis heard him with a whirling brain. *Five thousand
dollars!* The sum seemed so enormous, even in dollars,
and so incalculably larger when translated into any continental currency, that he wondered why his father, in
advance, had given up all hope of a Raphael. . . "If I
travel economically," he said to himself, "and deny myself
unnecessary luxuries, I may yet be able to surprise him
by bringing one back. And my mother—how magnanimous, how splendid! Now I see why she has consented to
all the little economies that sometimes seemed so paltry
and so humiliating. . ."

The young man's eyes filled with tears, but he was still
silent, though he longed as never before to express his

gratitude and admiration to his father. He had entered the study expecting a parting sermon on the subject of thrift, coupled with the prospective announcement of a "suitable establishment" (he could even guess the particular Huzzard girl his father had in view); and instead he had been told to spend his princely allowance in a princely manner, and to return home with a gallery of masterpieces. "At least," he murmured to himself, "it shall contain a Correggio."

"Well, sir?" Mr. Raycie boomed.

"Oh, sir—" his son cried, and flung himself on the vast slope of the parental waistcoat.

Amid all these accumulated joys there murmured deep down in him the thought that nothing had been said or done to interfere with his secret plans about Treeshy. It seemed almost as if his father had tacitly accepted the idea of their unmentioned engagement; and Lewis felt half guilty at not confessing to it then and there. But the gods are formidable even when they unbend; never more so, perhaps, than at such moments. . .

PART II

IV

LEWIS RAYCIE stood on a projecting rock and surveyed the sublime spectacle of Mont Blanc.

It was a brilliant August day, and the air, at that height, was already so sharp that he had had to put on his fur-lined pelisse. Behind him, at a respectful distance, was the travelling servant who, at a signal, had brought it up to him; below, in the bend of the mountain road, stood the light and elegant carriage which had carried him thus far on his travels.

Scarcely more than a year had passed since he had waved a farewell to New York from the deck of the packet-ship headed down the bay; yet, to the young man confidently facing Mont Blanc, nothing seemed left in him of that fluid and insubstantial being, the former Lewis Raycie, save a lurking and abeyant fear of Mr. Raycie senior. Even that, however, was so attenuated by distance and time, so far sunk below the horizon, and anchored on the far side of the globe, that it stirred in its sleep only when a handsomely folded and wafered letter in his parent's writing was handed out across the desk of some continental counting-house. Mr. Raycie senior did not write often, and when he did it was in a bland and stilted strain. He felt at a disadvantage on paper, and his natural sarcasm was swamped in the rolling periods which it cost him hours of labour to bring forth; so that the dreaded quality lurked for his son only in the curve of certain letters, and in a positively awful way of writing out, at full length, the word *Esquire*.

It was not that Lewis had broken with all the memories of his past of a year ago. Many still lingered in him, or rather had been transferred to the new man he had become—as for instance his tenderness for Treeshy Kent, which, somewhat to his surprise, had obstinately resisted all the assaults of English keep-sake beauties and almond-eyed houris of the East. It startled him, at times to find Treeshy's short dusky face, with its round forehead, the widely spaced eyes and the high cheek-bones, starting out at him suddenly in the street of some legendary town, or in a landscape of languid beauty, just as he had now and again been arrested in an exotic garden by the very scent of the verbena under the verandah at home. His travels had confirmed rather than weakened the family view of Treeshy's plainness; she could not be made to fit into any of the patterns of female beauty so far submitted to him; yet there she was, ensconced in his new heart and mind as deeply as in the old, though her kisses seemed less vivid, and the peculiar rough notes of her voice hardly reached him. Sometimes, half irritably, he said to himself that with an effort he could disperse her once for all; yet she lived on in him, unseen yet ineffaceable, like the image on a daguerreotype plate, no less there because so often invisible.

To the new Lewis, however, the whole business was less important than he had once thought it. His suddenly acquired maturity made Treeshy seem a petted child rather than the guide, the Beatrice, he had once considered her; and he promised himself, with an elderly smile, that as soon as he got to Italy he would write her the long letter for which he was now considerably in her debt.

His travels had first carried him to England. There he spent some weeks in collecting letters and recommendations for his tour, in purchasing his travelling-carriage and its numerous appurtenances, and in driving in it from cathedral town to storied castle, omitting nothing, from Abbotsford to Kenilworth, which deserved the attention of a cultivated mind. From England he crossed to Calais, moving slowly southward to the Mediterranean; and there, taking ship for the Piræus, he plunged into pure romance, and the tourist became a Giaour.

It was the East which had made him into a new Lewis Raycie; the East, so squalid and splendid, so pestilent and so poetic, so full of knavery and romance and fleas and nightingales, and so different, alike in its glories and its dirt, from what his studious youth had dreamed. After Smyrna and the bazaars, after Damascus and Palmyra, the Acropolis, Mytilene and Sunium, what could be left in his mind of Canal Street and the lawn above the Sound? Even the mosquitoes, which seemed at first the only connecting link, were different, because he fought with them in scenes so different; and a young gentleman who had journeyed across the desert in Arabian dress, slept under goats'-hair tents, been attacked by robbers in the Peloponnesus and despoiled by his own escort at Baalbek, and by customs' officials everywhere, could not but look with a smile on the terrors that walk New York and the Hudson river. Encased in security and monotony, that other Lewis Raycie, when his little figure bobbed up to the surface, seemed like a new-born babe preserved in alcohol. Even

Mr. Raycie senior's thunders were now no more than the far-off murmur of summer lightning on a perfect evening. Had Mr. Raycie ever really frightened Lewis? Why, now he was not even frightened by Mont Blanc!

He was still gazing with a sense of easy equality at its awful pinnacles when another travelling-carriage paused near his own, and a young man, eagerly jumping from it, and also followed by a servant with a cloak, began to mount the slope. Lewis at once recognized the carriage, and the light springing figure of the young man, his blue coat and swelling stock, and the scar slightly distorting his handsome and eloquent mouth. It was the Englishman who had arrived at the Montanvert inn the night before with a valet, a guide, and such a cargo of books, maps and sketching-materials as threatened to overshadow even Lewis's outfit.

Lewis, at first, had not been greatly drawn to the newcomer, who, seated aloof in the dining-room, seemed not to see his fellow-traveller. The truth was that Lewis was dying for a little conversation. His astonishing experiences were so tightly packed in him (with no outlet save the meagre trickle of his nightly diary) that he felt they would soon melt into the vague blur of other people's travels unless he could give them fresh reality by talking them over. And the stranger with the deep-blue eyes that matched his coat, the scarred cheek and eloquent lip, seemed to Lewis a worthy listener. The Englishman appeared to think otherwise. He preserved an air of moody abstraction, which Lewis's vanity imagined him to have put on as the gods becloud themselves for their secret errands; and the curtness of his goodnight was (Lewis flattered himself) surpassed only by the young New Yorker's.

But today all was different. The stranger advanced affably, raised his hat from his tossed statue-like hair, and enquired with a smile: "Are you by any chance interested in the forms of cirrous clouds?"

His voice was as sweet as his smile, and the two were reinforced by a glance so winning that it made the odd question seem not only pertinent but natural. Lewis, though surprised, was not disconcerted. He merely coloured with the unwonted sense of his ignorance, and replied ingenuously: "I believe, sir, I am interested in everything."

"A noble answer!" cried the other, and held out his hand.

"But I must add," Lewis continued with courageous honesty, "that I have never as yet had occasion to occupy myself particularly with the forms of cirrous clouds."

His companion looked at him merrily. "That," said he, "is no reason why you shouldn't begin to do so now!" To which Lewis as merrily agreed. "For in order to be interested in things," the other continued more gravely, "it is only necessary to see them; and I believe I am not wrong in saying that you are one of the privileged beings to whom the seeing eye has been given."

Lewis blushed his agreement, and his interlocutor continued: "You are one of those who have been on the road to Damascus."

"On the road? I've been to the place itself!" the wanderer exclaimed, bursting with the particulars of his travels; and then blushed more deeply at the perception that the other's use of the name had of course been figurative.

The young Englishman's face lit up. "You've been to Damascus—literally been there yourself? But that may be almost as interesting, in its quite different way, as the formation of clouds or lichens. For the present," he continued with a gesture toward the mountain, "I must devote myself to the extremely inadequate rendering of some of these delicate *aiguilles*; a bit of drudgery not likely to interest you in the face of so sublime a scene. But perhaps this evening—if, as I think, we are staying in the same inn—you will give me a few minutes of your society, and tell me something of your travels. My father," he added with his engaging smile, "has had packed with my paint-brushes a few bottles of a wholly trustworthy Madeira; and if you will favour me with your company at dinner. . ."

He signed to his servant to undo the sketching materials, spread his cloak on the rock, and was already lost in his task as Lewis descended to the carriage.

The Madeira proved as trustworthy as his host had promised. Perhaps it was its exceptional quality which threw such a golden lustre over the dinner; unless it were rather the conversation of the blue-eyed Englishman which made Lewis Raycie, always a small drinker, feel that in his company every drop was nectar.

When Lewis joined his host it had been with the secret hope of at last being able to talk; but when the evening was over (and they kept it up to the small hours) he perceived that he had chiefly listened. Yet there had been no sense of suppression, of thwarted volubility; he had been given all the openings he wanted. Only, whenever he produced a little fact it was instantly overflowed by the other's imagination till it burned like a dull pebble tossed into a rushing stream. For whatever Lewis said was seen by his companion from a new angle, and suggested a new train of thought; each commonplace item of experience became a many-faceted crystal flashing with unexpected fires. The young Englishman's mind moved in a world of associations and references far more richly peopled than Lewis's; but his eager communicativeness, his directness of speech and manner, instantly opened its gates to the simpler youth. It was certainly not the Madeira which sped the hours and flooded them with magic; but the magic gave the Madeira—excellent, and reputed of its kind, as Lewis afterward learned—a taste no other vintage was to have for him.

"Oh, but we must meet again in Italy—there are many things there that I could perhaps help you to see," the young Englishman declared as they swore eternal friendship on the stairs of the sleeping inn.

V

IT WAS in a tiny Venetian church, no more than a chapel, that Lewis Raycie's eyes had been unsealed—in a dull-looking little church not even mentioned in the guide-books. But for his chance encounter with the young Englishman in the shadow of Mont Blanc, Lewis would never have heard of the place; but then what else that was worth knowing would he ever have heard of, he wondered?

He had stood a long time looking at the frescoes, put off at first——he could admit it now—by a certain stiffness in the attitudes of the people, by the childish elaboration of their dress (so different from the noble draperies which Sir Joshua's Discourses on Art had taught him to admire in the great painters), and by the innocent inexpressive look in their young faces—for even the gray-beards seemed young. And then suddenly his gaze had lit on one of these faces in particular: that of a girl with round cheeks, high cheek-bones and widely set eyes under an intricate head-dress of pearl-woven braids. Why, it was Treeshy—Treeshy Kent to the life! And so far from being thought "plain," the young lady was no other than the peerless princess about whom the tale revolved. And what a fairy-land she lived in—full of lithe youths and round-faced pouting maidens, rosy old men and burnished black-amoors, pretty birds and cats and nibbling rabbits—and all involved and enclosed in golden balustrades, in colon-

nades of pink and blue, laurel-garlands festooned from
ivory balconies, and domes and minarets against summer
seas! Lewis's imagination lost itself in the scene; he forgot
to regret the noble draperies, the exalted sentiments, the
fuliginous backgrounds, of the artists he had come to Italy
to admire—forgot Sassoferrato, Guido Reni, Carlo Dolce,
Lo Spagnoletto, the Carracci, and even the Transfigura-
tion of Raphael, though he knew it to be the greatest picture in the world.

After that he had seen almost everything else that
Italian art had to offer; had been to Florence, Naples,
Rome; to Bologna to study the Eclectic School, to Parma
to examine the Correggios and the Giulio Romanos. But
that first vision had laid a magic seed between his lips;
the seed that makes you hear what the birds say and the
grasses whisper. Even if his English friend had not continued at his side, pointing out, explaining, inspiring,
Lewis Raycie flattered himself that the round face of the
little Saint Ursula would have led him safely and confidently past all her rivals. She had become his touchstone,
his star: how insipid seemed to him all the sheep-faced
Virgins draped in red and blue paint after he had looked
into her wondering girlish eyes and traced the elaborate
pattern of her brocades! He could remember now, quite
distinctly, the day when he had given up even Beatrice
Cenci . . . and as for that fat naked Magdalen of Carlo
Dolce's lolling over the book she was not reading, and
ogling the spectator in the good old way . . . faugh!
Saint Ursula did not need to rescue him from *her*. . .

His eyes had been opened to a new world of art. And
this world it was his mission to reveal to others—he, the
insignificant and ignorant Lewis Raycie, as "but for the

grace of God," and that chance encounter on Mont Blanc, he might have gone on being to the end! He shuddered to think of the army of Neapolitan beggar-boys, bituminous monks, whirling prophets, languishing Madonnas and pink-rumped *amorini* who might have been travelling home with him in the hold of the fast new steam-packet.

His excitement had something of the apostle's ecstasy. He was not only, in a few hours, to embrace Treeshy, and be reunited to his honoured parents; he was also to go forth and preach the new gospel to them that sat in the darkness of Salvator Rosa and Lo Spagnoletto . . .

The first thing that struck Lewis was the smallness of the house on the Sound, and the largeness of Mr. Raycie.

He had expected to receive the opposite impression. In his recollection the varnished Tuscan villa had retained something of its impressiveness, even when compared to its supposed originals. Perhaps the very contrast between their draughty distances and naked floors, and the expensive carpets and bright fires of High Point, magnified his memory of the latter—there were moments when the thought of its groaning board certainly added to the effect. But the image of Mr. Raycie had meanwhile dwindled. Everything about him, as his son looked back, seemed narrow, juvenile, almost childish. His bluster about Edgar Poe, for instance—true poet still to Lewis, though he had since heard richer notes; his fussy tyranny of his womenkind; his unconscious but total ignorance of most of the things, books, people, ideas, that now filled his son's mind; above all, the arrogance and incompetence of his artistic judgments. Beyond a narrow range of reading—mostly, Lewis suspected, culled in drowsy after-dinner snatches

from Knight's "Half-hours with the Best Authors"—Mr.
Raycie made no pretence to book-learning; left *that*, as he
handsomely said, "to the professors." But on matters of art
he was dogmatic and explicit, prepared to justify his
opinions by the citing of eminent authorities and of
market-prices, and quite clear, as his farewell talk with
his son had shown, as to which Old Masters should be
privileged to figure in the Raycie collection.

The young man felt no impatience of these judgments.
America was a long way from Europe, and it was many
years since Mr. Raycie had travelled. He could hardly be
blamed for not knowing that the things he admired were
no longer admirable, still less for not knowing why. The
pictures before which Lewis had knelt in spirit had been
virtually undiscovered, even by art-students and critics, in
his father's youth. How was an American gentleman, filled
with his own self-importance, and paying his courier the
highest salary to show him the accredited "Masterpieces"
—how was he to guess that whenever he stood rapt before
a Sassoferrato or a Carlo Dolce one of those unknown
treasures lurked near by under dust and cobwebs?

No; Lewis felt only tolerance and understanding. Such
a view was not one to magnify the paternal image; but
when the young man entered the study where Mr. Raycie
sat immobilized by gout, the swathed leg stretched along
his sofa seemed only another reason for indulgence . . .

Perhaps, Lewis thought afterward, it was his father's
prone position, the way his great bulk billowed over the
sofa, and the lame leg reached out like a mountain-ridge,
that made him suddenly seem to fill the room; or else the
sound of his voice booming irritably across the threshold,
and scattering Mrs. Raycie and the girls with a fierce:

"And now, ladies, if the hugging and kissing are over, I should be glad of a moment with my son." But it was odd that, after mother and daughters had withdrawn with all their hoops and flounces, the study seemed to grow even smaller, and Lewis himself to feel more like a David without the pebble.

"Well, my boy," his father cried, crimson and puffing, "here you are at home again, with many adventures to relate, no doubt; and a few masterpieces to show me, as I gather from the drafts on my exchequer."

"Oh, as to the masterpieces, sir, certainly," Lewis simpered, wondering why his voice sounded so fluty, and his smile was produced with such a conscious muscular effort.

"Good—good," Mr. Raycie approved, waving a violet hand which seemed to be ripening for a bandage. "Reedy carried out my orders, I presume? Saw to it that the paintings were deposited with the bulk of your luggage in Canal Street?"

"Oh, yes, sir; Mr. Reedy was on the dock with precise instructions. You know he always carries out your orders," Lewis ventured with a faint irony.

Mr. Raycie stared. "Mr. Reedy," he said, "does what I tell him, if that's what you mean; otherwise he would hardly have been in my employ for over thirty years."

Lewis was silent, and his father examined him critically. "You appear to have filled out: your health is satisfactory? Well . . . well . . . Mr. Robert Huzzard and his daughters are dining here this evening, by the way, and will no doubt be expecting to see the latest French novelties in stocks and waistcoats. Malvina has become a very elegant figure, your sisters tell me." Mr. Raycie chuckled, and

Lewis thought: "I *knew* it was the oldest Huzzard girl!"
while a slight chill ran down his spine.

"As to the pictures," Mr. Raycie pursued with growing
animation, "I am laid low, as you see, by this cursèd affliction, and till the doctors get me up again, here must I lie
and try to imagine how your treasures will look in the
new gallery. And meanwhile, my dear boy, I need hardly
say that no one is to be admitted to see them till they
have been inspected by me and suitably hung. Reedy shall
begin unpacking at once; and when we move to town
next month Mrs. Raycie, God willing, shall give the handsomest evening party New York has yet seen, to show my
son's collection, and perhaps . . . eh, well? . . . to cele-
brate another interesting event in his history."

Lewis met this with a faint but respectful gurgle, and
before his blurred eyes rose the wistful face of Treeshy
Kent.

"Ah, well, I shall see her tomorrow," he thought, taking
heart again as soon as he was out of his father's presence.

VI

Mr. Raycie stood silent for a long time after making the round of the room in the Canal Street house where the unpacked pictures had been set out.

He had driven to town alone with Lewis, sternly rebuffing his daughters' timid hints, and Mrs. Raycie's mute but visible yearning to accompany him. Though the gout was over he was still weak and irritable, and Mrs. Raycie, fluttered at the thought of "crossing him," had swept the girls away at his first frown.

Lewis's hopes rose as he followed his parent's limping progress. The pictures, though standing on chairs and tables, and set clumsily askew to catch the light, bloomed out of the half-dusk of the empty house with a new and persuasive beauty. Ah, how right he had been—how inevitable that his father should own it!

Mr. Raycie halted in the middle of the room. He was still silent, and his face, so quick to frown and glare, wore the calm, almost expressionless look known to Lewis as the mask of inward perplexity. "Oh, of course it will take a little time," the son thought, tingling with the eagerness of youth.

At last, Mr. Raycie woke the echoes by clearing his throat; but the voice which issued from it was as inexpressive as his face. "It is singular," he said, "how little the best copies of the Old Masters resemble the originals.

For these *are* Originals?" he questioned, suddenly swinging about on Lewis.

"Oh, absolutely, sir! Besides—" The young man was about to add: "No one would ever have taken the trouble to copy them"—but hastily checked himself.

"Besides—?"

"I meant, I had the most competent advice obtainable."

"So I assume; since it was the express condition on which I authorized your purchases."

Lewis felt himself shrinking and his father expanding; but he sent a glance along the wall, and beauty shed her reviving beam on him.

Mr. Raycie's brows projected ominously; but his face remained smooth and dubious. Once more he cast a slow glance about him.

"Let us," he said pleasantly, "begin with the Raphael." And it was evident that he did not know which way to turn.

"Oh, sir, a Raphael nowadays—I warned you it would be far beyond my budget."

Mr. Raycie's face fell slightly. "I had hoped nevertheless . . . for an inferior specimen. . ." Then, with an effort: "The Sassoferrato, then."

Lewis felt more at his ease; he even ventured a respectful smile. "Sassoferrato is *all* inferior, isn't he? The fact is, he no longer stands . . . quite as he used to. . ."

Mr. Raycie stood motionless: his eyes were vacuously fired on the nearest picture.

"Sassoferrato . . . no longer . . . ?"

"Well, sir, *no;* not for a collection of this quality."

Lewis saw that he had at last struck the right note. Something large and uncomfortable appeared to struggle in Mr. Raycie's throat; then he gave a cough which might almost have been said to cast out Sassoferrato.

There was another pause before he pointed with his stick to a small picture representing a snub-nosed young woman with a high forehead and jewelled coif, against a background of delicately interwoven columbines. "Is *that*," he questioned, "your Carlo Dolce? The style is much the same, I see; but it seems to me lacking in his peculiar sentiment."

"Oh, but it's not a Carlo Dolce: it's a Piero della Francesca, sir!" burst in triumph from the trembling Lewis.

His father sternly faced him. "It's a *copy*, you mean? I thought so!"

"No, no; not a copy; it's by a great painter . . . a much greater . . ."

Mr. Raycie had reddened sharply at his mistake. To conceal his natural annoyance he assumed a still more silken manner. "In that case," he said, "I think I should like to see the inferior painters first. Where *is* the Carlo Dolce?"

"There *is* no Carlo Dolce," said Lewis, white to the lips.

The young man's next distinct recollection was of standing, he knew not how long afterward, before the armchair in which his father had sunk down, almost as white and shaken as himself.

"This," stammered Mr. Raycie, "this is going to bring back my gout. . ." But when Lewis entreated: "Oh, sir, do let us drive back quietly to the country, and give me a chance later to explain . . . to put my case" . . . the old gentleman had struck through the pleading with a furious wave of his stick.

"Explain later? Put your case later? It's just what I insist upon doing here and now!" And Mr. Raycie added hoarsely, and as if in actual physical anguish: "I understand that young John Huzzard returned from Rome last week with a Raphael."

After that, Lewis heard himself—as if with the icy detachment of a spectator—marshalling his arguments, pleading the cause he hoped his pictures would have pleaded for him, dethroning the old Powers and Principalities, and setting up these new names in their place. It was first of all the names that stuck in Mr. Raycie's throat: after spending a life-time in committing to memory the correct pronunciation of words like Lo Spagnoletto and Giulio Romano, it was bad enough, his wrathful eyes seemed to say, to have to begin a new set of verbal gymnastics before you could be sure of saying to a friend with careless accuracy: "And *this* is my Giotto da Bondone."

But that was only the first shock, soon forgotten in the rush of greater tribulation. For one might conceivably learn how to pronounce Giotto da Bondone, and even enjoy doing so, provided the friend in question recognized the name and bowed to its authority. But to have your effort received by a blank stare, and the playful request: "You'll have to say that over again, please"—to know that, in going the round of the gallery (the Raycie Gallery!) the same stare and the same request were likely to be repeated before each picture; the bitterness of this was so great that Mr. Raycie, without exaggeration, might have likened his case to that of Agag.

"God! God! God! Carpatcher, you say this other fellow's called? Kept him back till the last because it's the

gem of the collection, did you? Carpatcher—well he'd have
done better to stick to his trade. Something to do with
those new European steam-cars, I suppose eh?" Mr. Raycie
was so incensed that his irony was less subtle than usual.
"And Angelico you say did that kind of Noah's Ark soldier in pink armour on gold-leaf? Well *there* I've caught
you tripping, my boy. Not Angelic*o*, Angelic*a;* Angelica
Kauffman was a lady. And the damned swindler who
foisted that barbarous daub on you as a picture of hers
deserves to be drawn and quartered—and shall be, sir, by
God, if the law can reach him! He shall disgorge every
penny he's rooked you out of, or my name's not Halston
Raycie! A bargain . . . you say the thing was a *bargain?*
Why, the price of a clean postage stamp would be too dear
for it! God—my son; do you realize you had a *trust* to
carry out?"

"Yes, sir, yes; and it's just because—"

"You might have written; you might at least have
placed your views before me . . ."

How could Lewis say: "If I had, I knew you'd have re-
fused to let me buy the pictures?" He could only stammer:
"I *did* allude to the revolution in taste . . . new names
coming up . . . you may remember . . ."

"Revolution! New names! Who says so? I had a letter
last week from the London dealers to whom I especially
recommended you, telling me than an undoubted Guido
Reni was coming into the market this summer."

"Oh, the dealers—*they* don't know!"

"The dealers . . . don't? . . . Who does . . . except
yourself?" Mr. Raycie pronounced in a white sneer.

Lewis, as white, still held his ground. "I wrote you, sir,

about my friends; in Italy, and afterward in England."

"Well, God damn it, I never heard of one of *their* names before, either; no more'n of these painters of yours here. I supplied you with the names of all the advisers you needed, and all the painters, too; I all but made the collection for you myself, before you started . . . I was explicit enough, in all conscience, wasn't I?"

Lewis smiled faintly. "That's what I hoped the pictures would be . . ."

"What? Be what? What'd you mean?"

"Be explicit. . . Speak for themselves . . . make you see that their painters are already superseding some of the better-known . . ."

Mr. Raycie gave an awful laugh. "They are, are they?" In whose estimation? Your friends', I suppose. What's the name, again, of that fellow you met in Italy who picked 'em out for you?"

"Ruskin—John Ruskin," said Lewis.

Mr. Raycie's laugh, prolonged, gathered up into itself a fresh shower of expletives. "Ruskin—Ruskin—just plain John Ruskin, eh? And who *is* this great John Ruskin, who sets God A'mighty right in his judgments? Who'd you say John Ruskin's father was, now?"

"A respected wine-merchant in London, sir."

Mr. Raycie ceased to laugh: he looked at his son with an expression of unutterable disgust.

"Retail?"

"I . . . believe so . . ."

"Faugh!" said Mr. Raycie.

"It wasn't only Ruskin, father. . . I told you of those other friends in London, whom I met on the way home.

They inspected the pictures, and all of them agreed that
. . . that the collection would some day be very valu-
able."

"*Some day*—did they give you a date . . . the month
and the year? Ah, those other friends; yes. You said there
was a Mr. Brown and a Mr. Hunt and a Mr. Rossiter, was
it? Well, I never heard of any of those names, either—except perhaps in a trades' directory."

"It's not Rossiter, father: Dante Rossetti."

"Excuse me: Rossetti. And what does Mr. Dante Rossetti's father do? Sell macaroni, I presume?"

Lewis was silent, and Mr. Raycie went on, speaking
now with a deadly steadiness: "The friends I sent you to
were judges of art, sir; men who know what a picture's
worth; not one of 'em but could pick out a genuine
Raphael. Couldn't you find 'em when you got to England?
Or hadn't they the time to spare for you? You'd better
not," Mr. Raycie added, "tell me *that*, for I know how
they'd have received your father's son."

"Oh, most kindly . . . they did indeed, sir . . ."

"Ay; but that didn't suit you. You didn't *want* to be
advised. You wanted to show off before a lot of ignora-
muses like yourself. You wanted—how'd I know what you
wanted? It's as if I'd never given you an instruction or
laid a charge on you! And the money—God! Where'd it
go to? Buying *this*? Nonsense—." Mr. Raycie raised himself heavily on his stick and fixed his angry eyes on his
son. "Own up, Lewis; tell me they got it out of you at
cards. Professional gamblers the lot, I make no doubt;
your Ruskin and your Morris and your Rossiter. Make a
business to pick up young American greenhorns on their
travels, I daresay. . . No? Not that, you say? Then—

women? . . . God A'mighty, Lewis," gasped Mr. Raycie, tottering toward his son with outstretched stick, "I'm no blue-nosed Puritan, sir, and I'd a damn sight rather you told me you'd spent it on a woman, every penny of it, than let yourself be fleeced like a simpleton, buying these things that look more like cuts out o' Foxe's Book of Martyrs than Originals of the Old Masters for a Gentleman's Gallery. . . Youth's youth. . . Gad, sir, I've been young myself . . . a fellow's got to go through his apprenticeship. . . Own up now: women?"

"Oh, not women—"

"Not even!" Mr. Raycie groaned. "All in pictures, then? Well, say no more to me now. . . I'll get home, I'll get home. . ." He cast a last apoplectic glance about the room. "The Raycie Gallery! That pack of bones and mummers' finery! . . . Why, let alone the rest, there's not a full-bodied female among 'em. . . Do you know what those Madonnas of yours are like, my son? Why, there ain't one of 'em that don't remind me of a bad likeness of poor Treeshy Kent. . . I should say you'd hired half the sign-painters of Europe to do her portrait for you—if I could imagine your wanting it. . . No, sir! I don't need your arm," Mr. Raycie snarled, heaving his great bulk painfully across the hall. He withered Lewis with a last look from the doorstep. "And to buy *that* you overdrew your account?—No, I'll drive home alone."

VII

Mr. Raycie did not die till nearly a year later; but New York agreed it was the affair of the pictures that had killed him.

The day after his first and only sight of them he sent for his lawyer, and it became known that he had made a new will. Then he took to his bed with a return of the gout, and grew so rapidly worse that it was thought "only proper" to postpone the party Mrs. Raycie was to have given that autumn to inaugurate the gallery. This enabled the family to pass over in silence the question of the works of art themselves; but outside of the Raycie house, where they were never mentioned, they formed, that winter, a frequent and fruitful topic of discussion.

Only two persons besides Mr. Raycie were known to have seen them. One was Mr. Donaldson Kent, who owed the privilege to the fact of having once been to Italy; the other, Mr. Reedy, the agent, who had unpacked the pictures. Mr. Reedy, beset by Raycie cousins and old family friends, had replied with genuine humility: "Why, the truth is, I never was taught to see any difference between one picture and another, except as regards the size of them; and these struck me as smallish . . . on the small side, I would say. . ."

Mr. Kent was known to have unbosomed himself to Mr. Raycie with considerable frankness—he went so far, it was rumoured, as to declare that he had never seen any pictures in Italy like those brought back by Lewis, and begged to doubt if they really came from there. But in public he maintained that noncommittal attitude which passed for prudence, but proceeded only from timidity; no one ever got anything from him but the guarded statement: "The subjects are wholly inoffensive."

It was believed that Mr. Raycie dared not consult the Huzzards. Young John Huzzard had just brought home a Raphael; it would have been hard not to avoid comparisons which would have been too galling. Neither to them, nor to any one else, did Mr. Raycie ever again allude to the Raycie Gallery. But when his will was opened it was found that he had bequeathed the pictures to his son. The rest of his property was left absolutely to his two daughters. The bulk of the estate was Mrs. Raycie's; but it was known that Mrs. Raycie had had her instructions, and among them, perhaps, was the order to fade away in her turn after six months of widowhood. When she had been laid beside her husband in Trinity church-yard her will (made in the same week as Mr. Raycie's, and obviously at his dictation) was found to allow five thousand dollars a year to Lewis during his lifetime; the residue of the fortune, which Mr. Raycie's thrift and good management had made into one of the largest in New York, was divided between the daughters. Of these, the one promptly married a Kent and the other a Huzzard; and the latter, Sarah Anne (who had never been Lewis's favourite), was wont to say in later years: "Oh, no, I never grudged my poor brother those funny old pictures. You see, we have a Raphael."

The house stood on the corner of Third Avenue and

Tenth Street. It had lately come to Lewis Raycie as his share in the property of a distant cousin, who had made an "old New York will" under which all his kin benefited in proportion to their consanguinity. The neighbourhood was unfashionable, and the house in bad repair; but Mr. and Mrs. Lewis Raycie, who, since their marriage, had been living in retirement at Tarrytown, immediately moved into it.

Their arrival excited small attention. Within a year of his father's death, Lewis had married Treeshy Kent. The alliance had not been encouraged by Mr. and Mrs. Kent, who went so far as to say that their niece might have done better; but as that one of their sons who was still unmarried had always shown a lively sympathy for Treeshy, they yielded to the prudent thought that, after all, it was better than having her entangle Bill.

The Lewis Raycies had been four years married, and during that time had dropped out of the memory of New York as completely as if their exile had covered half a century. Neither of them had ever cut a great figure there. Treeshy had been nothing but the Kents' Cinderella, and Lewis's ephemeral importance, as heir to the Raycie millions, had been effaced by the painful episode which resulted in his being deprived of them.

So secluded was their way of living, and so much had it come to be a habit, that when Lewis announced that he had inherited Uncle Ebenezer's house his wife hardly looked up from the baby-blanket she was embroidering.

"Uncle Ebenezer's house in New York?"

He drew a deep breath. "Now I shall be able to show the pictures."

"Oh, Lewis—" She dropped the blanket. "Are we going to live there?"

"Certainly. But the house is so large that I shall turn the two corner rooms on the ground floor into a gallery. they are very suitably lighted. It was there that Cousin Ebenezer was laid out."

"Oh, Lewis—"

If anything could have made Lewis Raycie believe in his own strength of will it was his wife's attitude. Merely to hear that unquestioning murmur of submission was to feel something of his father's tyrannous strength arise in him; but with the wish to use it more humanely.

"You'll like that, Treeshy? It's been dull for you here, I know."

She flushed up. "Dull? With *you*, darling? Besides, I like the country. But I shall like Tenth Street too. Only —you said there were repairs?"

He nodded sternly. "I shall borrow money to make them. If necessary—" he lowered his voice—"I shall mortgage the pictures."

He saw her eyes fill. "Oh, but it won't be! There are so many ways still in which I can economize."

He laid his hand on hers and turned his profile toward her, because he knew it was so much stronger than his full face. He did not feel sure that she quite grasped his intention about the pictures; was not even certain that he wished her to. He went in to New York every week now, occupying himself mysteriously and importantly with plans, specifications and other business transactions with long names; while Treeshy, through the hot summer months, sat in Tarrytown and waited for the baby.

A little girl was born at the end of the summer and christened Louisa; and when she was a few weeks old the Lewis Raycies left the country for New York.

"*Now!*" thought Lewis, as they bumped over the cobblestones of Tenth Street in the direction of Cousin Ebenezer's house.

The carriage stopped, he handed out his wife, the nurse followed with the baby, and they all stood and looked up at the house-front.

"Oh, Lewis—" Treeshy gasped; and even little Louisa set up a sympathetic wail.

Over the door—over Cousin Ebenezer's respectable, conservative and intensely private front-door—hung a large sign-board bearing, in gold letters on a black ground, the inscription:

GALLERY OF CHRISTIAN ART
OPEN ON WEEK-DAYS FROM 2 TO 4
ADMISSION 25 CENTS.   CHILDREN 10 CENTS

Lewis saw his wife turn pale, and pressed her arm in his. "Believe me, it's the only way to make the pictures known. And they *must* be made known," he said with a thrill of his old ardour.

"Yes, dear, of course. But . . . to every one? Publicly?"

"If we showed them only to our friends, of what use would it be? Their opinion is already formed."

She sighed her acknowledgment. "But the . . . the entrance fee . . ."

"If we can afford it later, the gallery will be free. But meanwhile—"

"Oh, Lewis, I quite understand!" And clinging to him,

the still-protesting baby in her wake, she passed with a dauntless step under the awful sign-board.

"At last I shall see the pictures properly lighted!" she exclaimed, and turned in the hall to fling her arms about her husband.

"It's all they need . . . to be appreciated," he answered, aglow with her encouragement.

Since his withdrawal from the world it had been a part of Lewis's system never to read the daily papers. His wife eagerly conformed to his example, and they lived in a little air-tight circle of aloofness, as if the cottage at Tarrytown had been situated in another and happier planet.

Lewis, nevertheless, the day after the opening of the Gallery of Christian Art, deemed it his duty to derogate from this attitude, and sallied forth secretly to buy the principal journals. When he reentered his house he went straight up to the nursery where he knew that, at that hour, Treeshy would be giving the little girl her bath. But it was later than he supposed. The rite was over, the baby lay asleep in its modest cot, and the mother sat crouched by the fire, her face hidden in her hands. Lewis instantly guessed that she too had seen the papers.

"Treeshy—you mustn't . . . consider this of any consequence. . . ," he stammered.

She lifted a tear-stained face. "Oh, my darling! I thought you never read the papers."

"Not usually. But I thought it my duty—"

"Yes; I see. But, as you say, what earthly consequence—?"

"None whatever; we must just be patient and persist."

She hesitated, and then, her arms about him, her head

on his breast: "Only, dearest, I've been counting up again, ever so carefully; and even if we give up fires everywhere but in the nursery, I'm afraid the wages of the doorkeeper and the guardian . . . especially if the gallery's open to the public every day . . ."

"I've thought of that already, too; and I myself shall hereafter act as doorkeeper and guardian."

He kept his eyes on hers as he spoke. "This is the test," he thought. Her face paled under its brown glow, and the eyes dilated in her effort to check her tears. Then she said gaily: "That will be . . . very interesting, won't it, Lewis? Hearing what the people say. . . Because, as they begin to know the pictures better, and to understand them, they can't fail to say very interesting things . . . can they?" She turned and caught up the sleeping Louisa. "Can they . . . oh, you darling—darling?"

Lewis turned away too. Not another woman in New York would have been capable of that. He could hear all the town echoing with this new scandal of his showing the pictures himself—and she, so much more sensitive to ridicule, so much less carried away by apostolic ardour, how much louder must that mocking echo ring in her ears! But his pang was only momentary. The one thought that possessed him for any length of time was that of vindicating himself by making the pictures known; he could no longer fix his attention on lesser matters. The derision of illiterate journalists was not a thing to wince at; once let the pictures be seen by educated and intelligent people, and they would speak for themselves—especially if he were at hand to interpret them.

VIII

FOR a week or two a great many people came to the gallery; but, even with Lewis as interpreter, the pictures failed to make themselves heard. During the first days, indeed, owing to the unprecedented idea of holding a paying exhibition in a private house, and to the mockery of the newspapers, the Gallery of Christian Art was thronged with noisy curiosity-seekers; once the astonished metropolitan police had to be invited in to calm their comments and control their movements. But the name of "Christian Art" soon chilled this class of sightseer, and before long they were replaced by a dumb and respectable throng, who roamed vacantly through the rooms and out again, grumbling that it wasn't worth the money. Then these too diminished; and once the tide had turned, the ebb was rapid. Every day from two to four Lewis still sat shivering among his treasures, or patiently measured the length of the deserted gallery: as long as there was a chance of any one coming he would not admit that he was beaten. For the next visitor might always be the one who understood.

One snowy February day he had thus paced the rooms in unbroken solitude for above an hour when carriage-wheels stopped at the door. He hastened to open it, and in a great noise of silks his sister Sarah Anne Huzzard entered.

Lewis felt for a moment as he used to under his father's glance. Marriage and millions had given the moon-faced Sarah something of the Raycie awfulness; but her brother looked into her empty eyes, and his own kept their level.

"Well, Lewis," said Mrs. Huzzard with a simpering sternness, and caught her breath.

"Well, Sarah Anne—I'm happy that you've come to take a look at my pictures."

"I've come to see you and your wife." She gave another nervous gasp, shook out her flounces, and added in a rush: "And to ask you how much longer this . . . this spectacle is to continue. . ."

"The exhibition?" Lewis smiled. She signed a flushed assent.

"Well, there has been a considerable falling-off lately in the number of visitors—"

"Thank heaven!" she interjected.

"But as long as I feel that any one wishes to come . . . I shall be here . . . to open the door, as you see."

She sent a shuddering glance about her. "Lewis—I wonder if you realize . . . ?"

"Oh, fully."

"Then *why* do you go on? Isn't it enough—aren't you satisfied?"

"With the effect they have produced?"

"With the effect *you* have produced—on your family and on the whole of New York. With the slur on poor Papa's memory."

"Papa left me the pictures, Sarah Anne."

"Yes. But not to make yourself a mountebank about them."

Lewis considered this impartially. "Are you sure? Perhaps, on the contrary, he did it for that very reason."

"Oh, don't heap more insults on our father's memory! Things are bad enough without that. How your wife can allow it I can't see. Do you ever consider the humiliation to *her*?"

Lewis gave another dry smile. "She's used to being humiliated. The Kents accustomed her to that."

Sarah Anne reddened. "I don't know why I should stay to be spoken to in this way. But I came with my husband's approval."

"Do you need that to come and see your brother?"

"I need it to—to make the offer I am about to make; and which he authorizes."

Lewis looked at her in surprise, and she purpled up to the lace ruffles inside her satin bonnet.

"Have you come to make an offer for my collection?" he asked her, humorously.

"You seem to take pleasure in insinuating preposterous things. But anything is better than this public slight on our name." Again she ran a shuddering glance over the pictures. "John and I," she announced, "are prepared to double the allowance mother left you on condition that this . . . this ends . . . for good. That that horrible sign is taken down tonight."

Lewis seemed mildly to weigh the proposal. "Thank you very much, Sarah Anne," he said at length. "I'm touched . . . touched and . . . and surprised . . . that you and John should have made this offer. But perhaps, before I decline it, you will accept *mine*: simply to show you my pictures. When once you've looked at them I think you'll understand—"

Mrs. Huzzard drew back hastily, her air of majesty collapsing. "Look at the pictures? Oh, thank you . . . but I can see them very well from here. And besides, I don't pretend to be a judge . . ."

"Then come up and see Treeshy and the baby," said Lewis quietly.

She stared at him, embarrassed. "Oh, thank you," she stammered again; and as she prepared to follow him: "Then it's *no*, really no, Lewis? Do consider, my dear! You say yourself that hardly any one comes. What harm can there be in closing the place?"

"What—when tomorrow the man may come who understands?"

Mrs. Huzzard tossed her plumes despairingly and followed him in silence.

"What—Mary Adeline?" she exclaimed, pausing abruptly on the threshold of the nursery. Treeshy, as usual, sat holding her baby by the fire; and from a low seat opposite her rose a lady as richly furred and feathered as Mrs. Huzzard, but with far less assurance to carry off her furbelows. Mrs. Kent ran to Lewis and laid her plump cheek against his, while Treeshy greeted Sarah Anne.

"I had no idea you were here, Mary Adeline," Mrs. Huzzard murmured. It was clear that she had not imparted her philanthropic project to her sister, and was disturbed at the idea that Lewis might be about to do so. "I just dropped in for a minute," she continued, "to see that darling little pet of an angel child—" and she enveloped the astonished baby in her ample rustlings and flutterings.

"I'm very glad to see you here, Sarah Anne," Mary Adeline answered with simplicity.

"Ah, it's not for want of wishing that I haven't come before! Treeshy knows that, I hope. But the cares of a household like mine . . ."

"Yes; and it's been so difficult to get about in the bad weather," Treeshy suggested sympathetically.

Mrs. Huzzard lifted the Raycie eyebrows. "Has it really? With two pairs of horses one hardly notices the weather. . . Oh, the pretty, pretty, *pretty* baby! . . . Mary Adeline," Sarah Anne continued, turning severely to her sister, "I shall be happy to offer you a seat in my carriage if you're thinking of leaving."

But Mary Adeline was a married woman too. She raised her mild head and her glance crossed her sister's quietly. "My own carriage is at the door, thank you kindly, Sarah Anne," she said; and the baffled Sarah Anne withdrew on Lewis's arm. But a moment later the old habit of subordination reasserted itself. Mary Adeline's gentle countenance grew as timorous as a child's, and she gathered up her cloak in haste.

"Perhaps I was too quick. . . I'm sure she meant it kindly," she exclaimed, overtaking Lewis as he turned to come up the stairs; and with a smile he stood watching his two sisters drive off together in the Huzzard coach.

He returned to the nursery, where Treeshy was still crooning over her daughter.

"Well, my dear," he said, "what do you suppose Sarah Anne came for?" And, in reply to her wondering gaze: "To buy me off from showing the pictures!"

His wife's indignation took just the form he could have wished. She simply went on with her rich cooing laugh and hugged the baby tighter. But Lewis felt the perverse desire to lay a still greater strain upon her loyalty.

"Offered to double my allowance, she and John, if only I'll take down the sign!"

"No one shall touch the sign!" Treeshy flamed.

"Not till I do," said her husband grimly.

She turned about and scanned him with anxious eyes. "Lewis . . . *you?*"

"Oh, my dear . . . they're right. . . It can't go on forever . . ." He went up to her, and put his arm about her and the child. "You've been braver than an army of heroes; but it won't do. The expenses have been a good deal heavier than I was led to expect. And I . . . I can't raise a mortgage on the pictures. Nobody will touch them."

She met this quickly. "No; I know. That was what Mary Adeline came about."

The blood rushed angrily to Lewis's temples. "Mary Adeline—how the devil did *she* hear of it?"

"Through Mr. Reedy, I suppose. But you must not be angry. She was kindness itself: she doesn't want you to close the gallery, Lewis . . . that is, not as long as you really continue to believe in it. . . She and Donald Kent will lend us enough to go on with for a year longer. That is what she came to say."

For the first time since the struggle had begun, Lewis Raycie's throat was choked with tears. His faithful Mary Adeline! He had a sudden vision of her, stealing out of the house at High Point before daylight to carry a basket of scraps to the poor Mrs. Edgar Poe who was dying of a decline down the lane. . . He laughed aloud in his joy.

"Dear old Mary Adeline! How magnificent of her! Enough to give me a whole year more . . ." He pressed his wet cheek against his wife's in a long silence. "Well, dear," he said at length, "it's for you to say—do we accept?"

He held her off, questioningly, at arm's length, and her wan little smile met his own and mingled with it.

"Of course we accept!"

IX

OF THE Raycie family, which prevailed so powerfully in the New York of the 'forties, only one of the name survived in my boyhood, half a century later. Like so many of the descendants of the proud little Colonial society, the Raycies had totally vanished, forgotten by everyone but a few old ladies, one or two genealogists and the sexton of Trinity Church, who kept the record of their graves.

The Raycie blood was of course still to be traced in various allied families: Kents, Huzzards, Cosbys and many others, proud to claim cousinship with a "Signer," but already indifferent or incurious as to the fate of his progeny. These old New Yorkers, who lived so well and spent their money so liberally, vanished like a pinch of dust when they disappeared from their pews and their dinner-tables.

If I happen to have been familiar with the name since my youth, it is chiefly because its one survivor was a distant cousin of my mother's whom she sometimes took me to see on days when she thought I was likely to be good because I had been promised a treat for the morrow.

Old Miss Alethea Raycie lived in a house I had always heard spoken of as "Cousin Ebenezer's." It had evidently, in its day, been an admired specimen of domestic architecture; but was now regarded as the hideous though venerable relic of a bygone age. Miss Raycie, being crippled by rheumatism, sat above stairs in a large cold room, meagrely furnished with beadwork tables, rosewood étagères and portraits of pale sad-looking people in odd clothes. She herself was large and saturnine, with a battlemented black lace cap, and so deaf that she seemed a survival of forgotten days, a Rosetta Stone to which the clue was lost. Even to my mother, nursed in that vanished tradition, and knowing instinctively to whom Miss Raycie alluded when she spoke of Mary Adeline, Sarah Anne or Uncle Doctor, intercourse with her was difficult and languishing, and my juvenile interruptions were oftener encouraged than reproved.

In the course of one of these visits my eyes, listlessly roaming, singled out among the pallid portraits a three-crayon drawing of a little girl with a large forehead and dark eyes, dressed in a plaid frock and embroidered pantalettes, and sitting on a grass-bank. I pulled my mother's sleeve to ask who she was, and my mother answered: "Ah, that was poor little Louisa Raycie, who died of a decline. How old was little Louisa when she died, Cousin Alethea?"

To batter this simple question into Cousin Alethea's brain was the affair of ten laborious minutes; and when the job was done, and Miss Raycie, with an air of mysterious displeasure, had dropped a deep "Eleven," my mother was too exhausted to continue. So she turned to me to add, with one of the private smiles we kept for each other: "It was the poor child who would have inherited the Raycie Gallery." But to a little boy of my age this item of information lacked interest, nor did I understand my mother's surreptitious amusement.

This far-off scene suddenly came back to me last year, when, on one of my infrequent visits to New York, I went to dine with my old friend, the banker, John Selwyn, and came to an astonished stand before the mantelpiece in his new library.

"Hal*lo!*" I said, looking up at the picture above the chimney.

My host squared his shoulders, thrust his hands into his pockets, and affected the air of modesty which people think it proper to assume when their possessions are admired. "The Macrino d'Alba? Y—yes . . . it was the only thing I managed to capture out of the Raycie collection."

"The only thing? Well—"

"Ah, but you should have seen the Mantegna; *and* the Giotto; *and* the Piero della Francesca—hang it, one of the most beautiful Piero della Francescas in the world. . . A girl in profile, with her hair in a pearl net, against a background of columbines; *that* went back to Europe—the National Gallery, I believe. And the Carpaccio, the most exquisite little St. George . . . that went to California . . . *Lord!*" He sat down with the sigh of a hungry man turned away from a groaning board. "Well, it nearly broke me buying *this!*" he murmured, as if at least that fact were some consolation.

I was turning over my early memories in quest of a clue to what he spoke of as the Raycie collection, in a tone which implied that he was alluding to objects familiar to all art-lovers.

Suddenly: "They weren't poor little Louisa's pictures, by any chance?" I asked, remembering my mother's cryptic smile.

Selwyn looked at me perplexedly. "Who the deuce is

poor little Louisa?" And, without waiting for my answer, he went on: "They were that fool Netta Cosby's until a year ago—and she never even knew it."

We looked at each other interrogatively, my friend perplexed at my ignorance, and I now absorbed in trying to run down the genealogy of Netta Cosby. I did so finally. "Netta Cosby—you don't mean Netta Kent, the one who married Jim Cosby?"

"That's it. The were cousins of the Raycies', and she inherited the pictures."

I continued to ponder. "I wanted awfully to marry her, the year I left Harvard," I said presently, more to myself than to my hearer.

"Well, if you had you'd have annexed a prize fool; *and* one of the most beautiful collections of Italian Primitives in the world."

"In the world?"

"Well—you wait till you see them; if you haven't already. And I seem to make out that you haven't—that you can't have. How long have you been in Japan? Four years? I thought so. Well, it was only last winter that Netta found out."

"Found out what?"

"What there was in old Alethea Raycie's attic. You must remember the old Miss Raycie who lived in that hideous house in Tenth Street when we were children. She was a cousin of your mother's, wasn't she? Well, the old fool lived there for nearly half a century, with five milllions' worth of pictures shut up in the attic over her head. It seems they'd been there ever since the death of a poor young Raycie who collected them in Italy years and years ago. I don't know much about the story; I never was strong on genealogy, and the Raycies have always been rather dim to me. They were everybody's cousins, of course; but as far as one can make out that seems to have been their principal if not their only function. Oh—and I suppose the Raycie Building was called after them; only *they* didn't build it!

"But there was this one young fellow—I wish I could find out more about him. All that Netta seems to know (or to care, for that matter) is that when he was very young—barely out of college—he was sent to Italy by his father to buy Old Masters—in the 'forties, it must have been—and came back with this extraordinary, this unbelievable collection . . . a boy of that age! . . . and was disinherited by the old gentleman for bringing home such rubbish. The young fellow and his wife died ever so many years ago, both of them. It seems he was so laughed at for buying such pictures that they went away and lived like hermits in the depths of the country. There were some funny spectral portraits of them that old Alethea had up in her bedroom. Netta showed me one of them the last time I went to see her: a pathetic drawing of the only child, an anæmic little girl with a big forehead. Jove, but that must have been your little Louisa!"

I nodded. "In a plaid frock and embroidered pantalettes?"

"Yes, something of the sort. Well, when Louisa and her parents died, I suppose the pictures went to old Miss Raycie. At any rate, at some time or other—and it must have been longer ago than you or I can remember—the old lady inherited them with the Tenth Street house; and when *she* died, three or four years ago, her relations found she'd never even been upstairs to look at them."

"Well—?"

"Well, she died intestate, and Netta Kent—Netta Cosby —turned out to be the next of kin. There wasn't much to be got out of the estate (or so they thought) and, as the Cosbys are always hard up, the house in Tenth Street had to be sold, and the pictures were very nearly sent off to the auction room with all the rest of the stuff. But nobody supposed they would bring anything, and the auctioneer said that if you tried to sell pictures with carpets and bedding and kitchen furniture it always depreciated the whole thing; and so, as the Cosbys had some bare walls to cover, they sent for the lot—there were about thirty—and decided to have them cleaned and hang them up. 'After all,' Netta said, 'as well as I can make out through the cobwebs, some of them look like rather jolly copies of early Italian things.' But as she was short of cash she decided to clean them at home instead of sending them to an expert; and one day, while she was operating on this very one before you, with her sleeves rolled up, the man called who always *does* call on such occasions; the man who knows. In the given case, it was a quiet fellow connected with the Louvre, who'd brought her a letter from Paris, and whom she'd invited to one of her stupid dinners. He was announced, and she thought it would be a joke to let him see what she was doing; she has pretty arms, you may remember. So he was asked into the dining-room, where he found her with a pail of hot water and soap-suds, and *this* laid out on the table; and the first thing he did was to grab her pretty arm so tight that it was black and blue, while he shouted out: 'God in heaven! Not *hot* water!' "

My friend leaned back with a sigh of mingled resentment and satisfaction, and we sat silently looking up at the lovely "Adoration" above the mantelpiece.

"That's how I got it a little cheaper—most of the old varnish was gone for good. But luckily for her it was the first picture she has attacked; and as for the others—you must see them, that's all I can say. . . Wait; I've got the catalogue somewhere about . . ."

He began to rummage for it, and I asked, remembering how nearly I had married Netta Kent: "Do you mean to say she didn't keep a single one of them?"

"Oh, yes—in the shape of pearls and Rolls-Royces. And you've seen their new house in Fifth Avenue?" He ended with a grin of irony: "The best of the joke is that Jim was just thinking of divorcing her when the pictures were discovered."

"Poor little Louisa!" I sighed.

THE OLD MAID

(The 'Fifties)

PART I

I

In the old New York of the 'fifties a few families ruled, in simplicity and affluence. Of these were the Ralstons.

The sturdy English and the rubicund and heavier Dutch had mingled to produce a prosperous, prudent and yet lavish society. To "do things handsomely" had always been a fundamental principle in this cautious world, built up on the fortunes of bankers, India merchants, ship-builders and ship-chandlers. Those well-fed slow-moving people, who seemed irritable and dyspeptic to European eyes only because the caprices of the climate had stripped them of superfluous flesh, and strung their nerves a little tighter, lived in a genteel monotony of which the surface was never stirred by the dumb dramas now and then enacted underground. Sensitive souls in those days were like muted key-boards, on which Fate played without a sound.

In this compact society, built of solidly welded blocks, one of the largest areas was filled by the Ralstons and their ramifications. The Ralstons were of middle-class English stock. They had not come to the colonies to die for a creed but to live for a bank-account. The result had been beyond their hopes, and their religion was tinged by their success. An edulcorated Church of England which, under the conciliatory name of the "Episcopal Church of the United States of America," left out the coarser allusions in the Marriage Service, slid over the comminatory passages in the Athanasian Creed, and thought it more respectful to say "Our Father *who*" than "*which*" in the Lord's Prayer, was exactly suited to the spirit of compromise whereon the Ralstons had built themselves up. There was in all the tribe the same instinctive recoil from new religions as from unaccounted-for people. Institutional to the core, they represented the conservative element that holds new societies together as seaplants bind the seashore.

Compared with the Ralstons, even such traditionalists as the Lovells, the Halseys or the Vandergraves appeared careless, indifferent to money, almost reckless in their impulses and indecisions. Old John Frederick Ralston, the stout founder of the race, had perceived the difference, and emphasized it to his son, Frederick John, in whom he had scented a faint leaning toward the untried and unprofitable.

"You let the Lannings and the Dagonets and the Spenders take risks and fly kites. It's the county-family blood in 'em: we've nothing to do with that. Look how they're petering out already—the men, I mean. Let your boys marry their girls, if you like (they're wholesome and handsome); though I'd sooner see my grandsons take a Lovell or a Vandergrave, or any of our own kind. But don't let your sons go mooning around after their young fellows, horse-racing, and running down south to those d——d Springs, and gambling at New Orleans, and all the rest of it. That's how you'll build up the family, and keep the weather out. The way we've always done it."

Frederick John listened, obeyed, married a Halsey, and passively followed in his father's steps. He belonged to the cautious generation of New York gentlemen who revered Hamilton and served Jefferson, who longed to lay out

New York like Washington, and who laid it out instead like a gridiron, lest they should be thought "undemocratic" by people they secretly looked down upon. Shopkeepers to the marrow, they put in their windows the wares there was most demand for, keeping their private opinions for the back-shop, where through lack of use, they gradually lost substance and colour.

The fourth generation of Ralstons had nothing left in the way of convictions save an acute sense of honour in private and business matters; on the life of the community and the state they took their daily views from the newspapers, and the newspapers they already despised. The Ralstons had done little to shape the destiny of their country, except to finance the Cause when it had become safe to do so. They were related to many of the great men who had built the Republic; but no Ralston had so far committed himself as to be great. As old John Frederick said, it was safer to be satisfied with three per cent: they regarded heroism as a form of gambling. Yet by merely being so numerous and so similar they had come to have a weight in the community. People said: "The Ralstons" when they wished to invoke a precedent. This attribution of authority had gradually convinced the third generation of its collective importance, and the fourth, to which Delia Ralston's husband belonged, had the ease and simplicity of a ruling class.

Within the limits of their universal caution, the Ralstons fulfilled their obligations as rich and respected citizens. They figured on the boards of all the old-established charities, gave handsomely to thriving institutions, had the best cooks in New York, and when they travelled abroad ordered statuary of the American sculptors in

Rome whose reputation was already established. The first Ralston who had brought home a statue had been regarded as a wild fellow; but when it became known that the sculptor had executed several orders for the British aristocracy it was felt in the family that this too was a three per cent investment.

Two marriages with the Dutch Vandergraves had consolidated these qualities of thrift and handsome living, and the carefully built-up Ralston character was now so congenital that Delia Ralston sometimes asked herself whether, were she to turn her own little boy loose in a wilderness, he would not create a small New York there, and be on all its boards of directors.

Delia Lovell had married James Ralston at twenty. The marriage, which had taken place in the month of September, 1840, had been solemnized, as was then the custom, in the drawing-room of the bride's country home, at what is now the corner of Avenue A and Ninety-first Street, overlooking the Sound. Thence her husband had driven her (in Grandmamma Lovell's canary-coloured coach with a fringed hammer-cloth) through spreading suburbs and untidy elm-shaded streets to one of the new houses in Gramercy Park, which the pioneers of the younger set were just beginning to affect; and there, at five-and-twenty, she was established, the mother of two children, the possessor of a generous allowance of pin-money, and, by common consent, one of the handsomest and most popular "young matrons" (as they were called) of her day.

She was thinking placidly and gratefully of these things as she sat one afternoon in her handsome bedroom in Gramercy Park. She was too near to the primitive Ralstons to have as clear a view of them as, for instance, the son in question might one day command: she lived under them as unthinkingly as one lives under the laws of one's country. Yet that tremor of the muted key-board, that secret questioning which sometimes beat in her like wings, would now and then so divide her from them that for a fleeting moment she could survey them in their relation to other things. The moment was always fleeting; she dropped back from it quickly, breathless and a little pale, to her children, her house-keeping, her new dresses and her kindly Jim.

She thought of him today with a smile of tenderness, remembering how he had told her to spare no expense on her new bonnet. Though she was twenty-five, and twice a mother, her image was still surprisingly fresh. The plumpness then thought seemly in a young wife stretched the grey silk across her bosom, and caused her heavy gold watch-chain—after it left the anchorage of the brooch of St. Peter's in mosaic that fastened her low-cut Cluny collar—to dangle perilously in the void above a tiny waist buckled into a velvet waist-band. But the shoulders above sloped youthfully under her Cashmere scarf, and every movement was as quick as a girl's.

Mrs. Jim Ralston approvingly examined the rosy-cheeked oval set in the blonde ruffles of the bonnet on which, in compliance with her husband's instructions, she had spared no expense. It was a cabriolet of white velvet tied with wide satin ribbons and plumed with a crystal-spangled marabout—a wedding bonnet ordered for the marriage of her cousin, Charlotte Lovell, which was to take place that week at St. Mark's-in-the-Bouwerie. Charlotte was making a match exactly like Delia's own: marrying a Ralston, of the Waverly Place branch, than which nothing could be safer, sounder or more—well, usual. Delia did not know why the word had occurred to her, for it could hardly be postulated, even of the young women of her own narrow clan, that they "usually" married Ralstons; but the soundness, safeness, suitability of the arrangement, did make it typical of the kind of alliance which a nice girl in the nicest set would serenely and blushingly forecast for herself.

Yes—and afterward?

Well—what? And what did this new question mean? Afterward: why, of course, there was the startled puzzled surrender to the incomprehensible exigencies of the young man to whom one had at most yielded a rosy cheek in return for an engagement ring; there was the large double-bed; the terror of seeing him shaving calmly the next morning, in his shirt-sleeves, through the dressing-room door; the evasions, insinuations, resigned smiles and Bible texts of one's Mamma; the reminder of the phrase "to obey" in the glittering blur of the Marriage Service; a week or a month of flushed distress, confusion, embarrassed pleasure; then the growth of habit, the insidious lulling of the matter-of-course, the dreamless double slumbers in the big white bed, the early morning discussions and consultations through that dressing-room door which had once seemed to open into a fiery pit scorching the brow of innocence.

And then, the babies; the babies who were supposed to "make up for everything," and didn't—though they were such darlings, and one had no definite notion as to what it was that one had missed, and that they were to make up for.

Yes: Charlotte's fate would be just like hers. Joe Ralston was so like his second cousin Jim (Delia's James), that Delia could see no reason why life in the squat brick house in Waverly Place should not exactly resemble life in the tall brown-stone house in Gramercy Park. Only Charlotte's bedroom would certainly not be as pretty as hers.

She glanced complacently at the French wall-paper that reproduced a watered silk, with a "valanced" border, and tassels between the loops. The mahogany bedstead, covered with a white embroidered counterpane, was symmetrically reflected in the mirror of a wardrobe which matched it. Coloured lithographs of the "Four Seasons" by Léopold Robert surmounted groups of family daguerreotypes in deeply-recessed gilt frames. The ormolu clock represented a shepherdess sitting on a fallen trunk, a basket of flowers at her feet. A shepherd, stealing up, surprised her with a kiss, while her little dog barked at him from a clump of roses. One knew the profession of the lovers by their crooks and the shape of their hats. This frivolous time-piece had been a wedding-gift from Delia's aunt, Mrs. Manson Mingott, a dashing widow who lived in Paris and was received at the Tuileries. It had been entrusted by Mrs. Mingott to young Clement Spender, who had come back from Italy for a short holiday just after Delia's marriage; the marriage which might never have been, if Clem Spender could have supported a wife, or if he had consented to give up painting and Rome for New York and the law. The young man (who looked, already, so odd and foreign and sarcastic) had laughingly assured the bride that her aunt's gift was "the newest thing in the Palais Royal"; and the family, who admired

Mrs. Manson Mingott's taste though they disapproved of her "foreignness," had criticized Delia's putting the clock in her bedroom instead of displaying it on the drawing-room mantel. But she liked, when she woke in the morning to see the bold shepherd stealing his kiss.

Charlotte would certainly not have such a pretty clock in her bedroom; but then she had not been used to pretty things. Her father, who had died at thirty of lung-fever, was one of the "poor Lovells." His widow, burdened with a young family, and living all the year round "up the River," could not do much for her eldest girl; and Charlotte had entered society in her mother's turned garments, and shod with satin sandals handed down from a defunct aunt who had "opened a ball" with General Washington. The old-fashioned Ralston furniture, which Delia already saw herself banishing, would seem sumptuous to Chatty; very likely she would think Delia's gay French time-piece somewhat frivolous, or even not "quite nice." Poor Charlotte had become so serious, so prudish almost, since she had given up balls and taken to visiting the poor! Delia remembered, with ever-recurring wonder, the abrupt change in her: the precise moment at which it had been privately agreed in the family that, after all, Charlotte Lovell was going to be an old maid.

They had not thought so when she came out. Though her mother could not afford to give her more than one new tarlatan dress, and though nearly everything in her appearance was regrettable, from the too bright red of her hair to the too pale brown of her eyes—not to mention the rounds of brick-rose on her cheek-bones, which almost (preposterous thought!) made her look as if she painted— yet these defects were redeemed by a slim waist, a light

foot and a gay laugh; and when her hair was well oiled
and brushed for an evening party, so that it looked almost
brown, and lay smoothly along her delicate cheeks under
a wreath of red and white camellias, several eligible young
men (Joe Ralston among them) were known to have
called her pretty.

Then came her illness. She caught cold on a moonlight
sleighing-party, the brick-rose circles deepened, and she
began to cough. There was a report that she was "going
like her father," and she was hurried off to a remote
village in Georgia, where she lived alone for a year with
an old family governess. When she came back everyone
felt at once that there was a change in her. She was pale,
and thinner than ever, but with an exquisitely transparent
cheek, darker eyes and redder hair; and the oddness of
her appearance was increased by plain dresses of Quak-
erish cut. She had left off trinkets and watch-chains, always wore the same grey cloak and small close bonnet,
and displayed a sudden zeal for visiting the indigent. The
family explained that during her year in the south she
had been shocked by the hopeless degradation of the
"poor whites" and their children, and that this revelation
of misery had made it impossible for her to return to the
light-hearted life of her young friends. Everyone agreed,
with significant glances, that this unnatural state of mind
would "pass off in time"; and meanwhile old Mrs. Lovell,
Chatty's grandmother, who understood her perhaps better
than the others, gave her a little money for her paupers,
and lent her a room in the Lovell stables (at the back of
the old lady's Mercer Street house) where she gathered
about her, in what would afterward have been called a
"day-nursery," some of the destitute children of the neigh-

bourhood. There was even, among them, the baby girl whose origin had excited such intense curiosity two or three years earlier, when a veiled lady in a handsome cloak had brought it to the hovel of Cyrus Washington, the Negro handy-man whose wife Jessamine took in Dr. Lanskell's washing. Dr. Lanskell, the chief medical practitioner of the day, was presumably versed in the secret history of every household from the Battery to Union Square; but, though beset by inquisitive patients, he had invariably declared himself unable to identify Jessamine's "veiled lady," or to hazard a guess as to the origin of the hundred dollar bill pinned to the baby's bib.

The hundred dollars were never renewed, the lady never reappeared, but the baby lived healthily and happily with Jessamine's piccaninnies, and as soon as it could toddle was brought to Chatty Lovell's day-nursery, where it appeared (like its fellow paupers) in little garments cut down from her old dresses, and socks knitted by her untiring hands. Delia, absorbed in her own babies, had nevertheless dropped in once or twice at the nursery, and had come away wishing that Chatty's maternal instinct might find its normal outlet in marriage. The married cousin confusedly felt that her own affection for her handsome children was a mild and measured sentiment compared with Chatty's fierce passion for the waifs in Grandmamma Lovell's stable.

And then, to the general surprise, Charlotte Lovell engaged herself to Joe Ralston. It was known that Joe had "admired her" the year she came out. She was a graceful dancer, and Joe, who was tall and nimble, had footed it with her through many a reel and *Schottische*. By the end of the winter all the match-makers were predicting that something would come of it; but when Delia sounded her cousin, the girl's evasive answer and burning brow seemed to imply that her suitor had changed his mind, and no further questions could be asked. Now it was clear that there had, in fact, been an old romance between them, probably followed by that exciting incident, a "misunderstanding"; but at last all was well, and the bells of St. Mark's were preparing to ring in happier days for Charlotte. "Ah, when she has her first baby," the Ralston mothers chorused . . .

"Chatty!" Delia exclaimed, pushing back her chair as she saw her cousin's image reflected in the glass over her shoulder.

Charlotte Lovell had paused in the doorway. "They told me you were here—so I ran up."

"Of course, darling. How handsome you do look in your poplin! I always said you needed rich materials. I'm so thankful to see you out of grey cashmere." Delia, lifting her hands, removed the white bonnet from her dark polished head, and shook it gently to make the crystals glitter.

"I hope you like it? It's for your wedding," she laughed.

Charlotte Lovell stood motionless. In her mother's old dove-coloured poplin, freshly banded with narrow rows of crimson velvet ribbon, an ermine tippet crossed on her bosom, and a new beaver bonnet with a falling feather, she had already something of the assurance and majesty of a married woman.

"And you know your hair certainly *is* darker, darling," Delia added, still hopefully surveying her.

"Darker? It's grey," Charlotte suddenly broke out in her

deep voice. She pushed back one of the pommaded bands that framed her face, and showed a white lock on her temple. "You needn't save up your bonnet; I'm not going to be married," she added, with a smile that showed her small white teeth in a fleeting glare.

Delia had just enough presence of mind to lay down the bonnet, marabout-up, before she flung herself on her cousin.

"Not going to be married? Charlotte, are you perfectly crazy?"

"Why is it crazy to do what I think right?"

"But people said you were going to marry him the year you came out. And no one understood what happened then. And now—how can it possibly be right? You simply *can't!*" Delia incoherently cried.

"Oh—people!" said Charlotte Lovell wearily.

Her married cousin looked at her with a start. Something thrilled in her voice that Delia had never heard in it, or in any other human voice, before. Its echo seemed to set their familiar world rocking, and the Axminster carpet actually heaved under Delia's shrinking slippers.

Charlotte Lovell stood staring ahead of her with strained lids. In the pale brown of her eyes Delia noticed the green specks that floated there when she was angry or excited.

"Charlotte—where on earth have you come from?" she questioned, drawing the girl down to the sofa.

"Come from?"

"Yes. You look as if you had seen a ghost—an army of ghosts."

The same snarling smile drew up Charlotte's lip. "I've seen Joe," she said.

"Well?—Oh, Chatty," Delia exclaimed abruptly illuminated, "you don't mean to say that you're going to let
any little thing in Joe's past—? Not that I've ever heard
the last hint; never. But even if there were. . ." She drew
a deep breath, and bravely proceeded to extremities.
"Even if you've heard that he's been . . . that he's had a
child—of course he would have provided for it before . . ."

The girl shook her head. "I know: you needn't go on.
'Men will be men'; but it's not that."

"Tell me what it is."

Charlotte Lovell looked about the sunny prosperous
room as if it were the image of her world, and that world
were a prison she must break out of. She lowered her
head. "I want—to get away," she panted.

"Get away? From Joe?"

"From his ideas—the Ralston ideas."

Delia bridled—after all, she was a Ralston! "The Ralston ideas? I haven't found them—so unbearably unpleasant to live with," she smiled a little tartly.

"No. But it was different with you: they didn't ask you
to give up things."

"What things?" What in the world (Delia wondered)
had poor Charlotte that any one could want her to give
up? She had always been in the position of taking rather
than of having to surrender. "Can't you explain to me,
dear?" Delia urged.

"My poor children—he says I'm to give them up," cried
the girl in a stricken whisper.

"Give them up? Give up helping them?"

"Seeing them—looking after them. Give them up altogether. He got his mother to explain to me. After—after

we have children . . . he's afraid . . . afraid our children might catch things. . . He'll give me money, of
course, to pay some one . . . a hired person, to look after
them. He thought that handsome," Charlotte broke out
with a sob. She flung off her bonnet and smothered her
prostrate weeping in the cushions.

Delia sat perplexed. Of all unforeseen complications
this was surely the least imaginable. And with all the
acquired Ralston that was in her she could not help seeing
the force of Joe's objection, could almost find herself
agreeing with him. No one in New York had forgotten the
death of the poor Henry van der Luydens' only child, who
had caught small-pox at the circus to which an unprin-
cipled nurse had surreptitiously taken him. After such a
warning as that, parents felt justified in every precaution
against contagion. And poor people were so ignorant and
careless, and their children, of course, so perpetually exposed to everything catching. No, Joe Ralston was certainly right, and Charlotte almost insanely unreasonable.
But it would be useless to tell her so now. Instinctively,
Delia temporized.

"After all," she whispered to the prone ear, "if it's only
after you have children—you may not have any—for some
time."

"Oh, yes, I shall!" came back in anguish from the
cushions.

Delia smiled with matronly superiority. "Really,
Chatty, I don't quite see how you can know. You don't
understand."

Charlotte Lovell lifted herself up. Her collar of Brussels
lace had come undone and hung in a wisp on her
crumpled bodice, and through the disorder of her hair the

white lock glimmered haggardly. In her pale brown eyes the little green specks floated like leaves in a trout-pool.

"Poor girl," Delia thought, "how old and ugly she looks! More than ever like an old maid; and she doesn't seem to realize in the least that she'll never have another chance."

"You must try to be sensible, Chatty dear. After all, one's own babies have the first claim."

"That's just it." The girl seized her fiercely by the wrists. "How can I give up my own baby?"

"Your—your—?" Delia's world again began to waver under her. "Which of the poor little waifs, dearest, do you call your own baby?" she questioned patiently.

Charlotte looked her straight in the eyes. "I call my own baby my own baby."

"Your own—? Take care—you're hurting my wrists, Chatty!" Delia freed herself, forcing a smile. "Your own—?"

"My own little girl. The one that Jessamine and Cyrus—"

"Oh—" Delia Ralston gasped.

The two cousins sat silent, facing each other; but Delia looked away. It came over her with a shudder of repugnance that such things, even if they had to be said, should not have been spoken in her bedroom, so near the spotless nursery across the passage. Mechanically she smoothed the organ-like folds of her silk skirt, which her cousins's embrace had tumbled. Then she looked again at Charlotte's eyes, and her own melted.

"Oh, poor Chatty—my poor Chatty!" She held out her arms to her cousin.

II

THE shepherd continued to steal his kiss from the shepherdess, and the clock in the fallen trunk continued to tick out the minutes.

Delia, petrified, sat unconscious of their passing, her cousin clasped to her. She was dumb with the horror and amazement of learning that her own blood ran in the veins of the anonymous foundling, the "hundred dollar baby" about whom New York had so long furtively jested and conjectured. It was her first contact with the nether side of the smooth social surface, and she sickened at the thought that such things were, and that she, Delia Ralston, should be hearing of them in her own house, and from the lips of the victim! For Chatty of course was a victim—but whose? She had spoken no name, and Delia could put no question: the horror of it sealed her lips. Her mind had instantly raced back over Chatty's past; but she saw no masculine figure in it but Joe Ralston's. And to connect Joe with the episode was obviously unthinkable. Some one in the south, then—? But no: Charlotte had been ill when she left—and in a flash Delia understood the real nature of that illness, and of the girl's disappearance. But from such speculations too her mind recoiled, and instinctively she fastened on something she could still grasp: Joe Ralstons attitude about Chatty's paupers. Of course Joe could not let his wife risk bringing contagion into their home—that was safe ground to dwell on. Her own Jim would have felt in the same way; and she would certainly have agreed with him.

Her eyes travelled back to the clock. She always thought of Clem Spender when she looked at the clock, and suddenly she wondered—if things had been different—what *he* would have said if she had made such an appeal to him as Charlotte had made to Joe. The thing was hard to imagine; yet in a flash of mental readjusment Delia saw herself as Clem's wife, she saw her children as his, she pictured herself asking him to let her go on caring for the poor waifs in the Mercer Street stable, and she distinctly heard his laugh and his light answer: "Why on earth did you ask, you little goose? Do you take me for such a Pharisee as that?"

Yes, that was Clem Spender all over—tolerant, reckless, indifferent to consequences, always doing the kind thing at the moment, and too often leaving others to pay the score. "There's something cheap about Clem," Jim had once said in his heavy way. Delia Ralston roused herself and pressed her cousin closer. "Chatty, tell me," she whispered.

"There's nothing more."

"I mean, about yourself . . . this thing . . . this. . ." Clem Spender's voice was still in her ears. "You loved some one," she breathed.

"Yes, that's over—. Now it's only the child. . . And I could love Joe—in another way." Chatty Lovell straightened herself, wan and frowning.

"I need the money—I must have it for my baby. Or else they'll send it to an Institution." She paused. "But that's not all. I want to marry—to be a wife, like all of you. I

should have loved Joe's children—our children. Life
doesn't stop . . ."

"No; I suppose not. But you speak as if . . . as if . . .
the person who took advantage of you . . ."

"No one took advantage of me. I was lonely and unhappy. I met some one who was lonely and unhappy.
People don't all have your luck. We were both too poor
to marry each other . . . and mother would never have
consented. And so one day . . . one day before he said
goodbye . . ."

"He said goodbye?"

"Yes. He was going to leave the country."

"He left the country—knowing?"

"How was he to know? He doesn't live here. He'd just
come back—come back to see his family—for a few
weeks . . ." She broke off, her thin lips pressed together
upon her secret.

There was a silence. Blindly Delia stared at the bold
shepherd.

"Come back from where?" she asked at length in a low
tone.

"Oh, what does it matter? You wouldn't understand,"
Charlotte broke off, in the very words her married cousin
had compassionately addressed to her virginity.

A slow blush rose to Delia's cheek: she felt oddly
humiliated by the rebuke conveyed in that contemptuous
retort. She seemed to herself shy, ineffectual, as incapable
as an ignorant girl of dealing with the abominations that
Charlotte was thrusting on her. But suddenly some fierce
feminine intuition struggled and woke in her. She forced
her eyes upon her cousin's.

"You won't tell me who it was?"

"What's the use? I haven't told anybody."

"Then why have you come to me?"

Charlotte's stony face broke up in weeping. "It's for my baby . . . my baby . . ."

Delia did not heed her. "How can I help you if I don't know?" she insisted in a harsh dry voice: her heart-beats were so violent that they seemed to send up throttling hands to her throat.

Charlotte made no answer.

"Come back from where?" Delia doggedly repeated; and at that, with a long wail, the girl flung her hands up, screening her eyes. "He always thought you'd wait for him," she sobbed out, "and then, when he found you hadn't . . . and that you were marrying Jim. . . He heard it just as he was sailing. . . He didn't know it till Mrs. Mingott asked him to bring the clock back for your wedding . . ."

"Stop—stop," Delia cried, springing to her feet. She had provoked the avowal, and now that it had come she felt that it had been gratuitously and indecently thrust upon her. Was this New York, *her* New York, her safe friendly hypocritical New York, was this James Ralston's house, and this his wife listening to such revelations of dishonour?

Charlotte Lovell stood up in her turn. "I knew it—I knew it! You think worse of my baby now, instead of better. . . Oh, why did you make me tell you? I knew you'd never understand. I'd always cared for him, ever since I came out; that was why I wouldn't marry any one else. But I knew there was no hope for me . . . he never looked at anybody but you. And then, when he came back four years ago, and there was no *you* for him any more, he began to notice me, to be kind, to talk to me about his life and his painting. . ." She drew a deep breath, and her voice cleared. "That's over—all over. It's as if I couldn't either hate him or love him. There's only the child now—my child. He doesn't even know of it—why should he? It's none of his business; it's nobody's business but mine. But surely you must see that I can't give up my baby."

Delia Ralston stood speechless, looking away from her cousin in a growing horror. She had lost all sense of reality, all feeling of safety and self-reliance. Her impulse was to close her ears to the other's appeal as a child buries its head from midnight terrors. At last she drew herself up, and spoke with dry lips.

"But what do you mean to do? Why have you come to me? Why have you told me all this?"

"Because he loved you!" Charlotte Lovell stammered out; and the two women stood and faced each other.

Slowly the tears rose to Delia's eyes and rolled down her cheeks, moistening her parched lips. Through the tears she saw her cousin's haggard countenance waver and droop like a drowning face under water. Things half-guessed, obscurely felt, surged up from unsuspected depths in her. It was almost as if, for a moment, this other woman were telling her of her own secret past, putting into crude words all the trembling silences of her own heart.

The worst of it was, as Charlotte said, that they must act now; there was not a day to lose. Chatty was right—it was impossible that she should marry Joe if to do so meant giving up the child. But, in any case, how could she marry him without telling him the truth? And was it conceivable that, after hearing it, he should repudiate her? All these questions spun agonizingly through Delia's brain, and through them glimmered the persistent vision of the child—Clem Spender's child—growing up on charity in a Negro hovel, or herded in one of the plague-houses they called Asylums. No: the child came first—she felt it in every fibre of her body. But what should she do, of whom take counsel, how advise the wretched creature who had come to her in Clement's name? Delia glanced about her desperately, and then turned back to her cousin.

"You must give me time. I must think. You ought not to marry him—and yet all the arrangements are made; and the wedding presents. . . There would be a scandal . . . it would kill Granny Lovell . . ."

Charlotte answered in a low voice: "There *is* no time. I must decide now."

Delia pressed her hands against her breast. "I tell you I must think. I wish you would go home.—Or, no: stay here: your mother mustn't see your eyes. Jim's not coming home till late; you can wait in this room till I come back." She had opened the wardrobe and was reaching up for a plain bonnet and heavy veil.

"Stay here? But where are you going?"

"I don't know. I want to walk—to get the air. I think I want to be alone." Feverishly, Delia unfolded her Paisley shawl, tied on bonnet and veil, thrust her mittened hands into her muff. Charlotte, without moving, stared at her dumbly from the sofa.

"You'll wait," Delia insisted, on the threshold.

"Yes: I'll wait."

Delia shut the door and hurried down the stairs.

III

SHE had spoken the truth in saying that she did not know where she was going. She simply wanted to get away from Charlotte's unbearable face, and from the immediate atmosphere of her tragedy. Outside, in the open, perhaps it would be easier to think.

As she skirted the park-rails she saw her rosy children playing, under their nurse's eyes, with the pampered progeny of other square-dwellers. The little girl had on her new plaid velvet bonnet and white tippet, and the boy his Highland cap and broad-cloth spencer. How happy and jolly they looked! The nurse spied her, but she shook her head, waved at the group and hurried on.

She walked and walked through the familiar streets decked with bright winter sunshine. It was early afternoon, an hour when the gentlemen had just returned to their offices, and there were few pedestrians in Irving Place and Union Square. Delia crossed the Square to Broadway.

The Lovell house in Mercer Street was a sturdy old-fashioned brick dwelling. A large stable adjoined it, opening on an alley such as Delia, on her honey-moon trip to England, had heard called a "mews." She turned into the alley, entered the stable court, and pushed open a door. In a shabby white-washed room a dozen children, gathered about a stove, were playing with broken toys. The Irishwoman who had charge of them was cutting out small garments on a broken-legged deal table. She raised a friendly face, recognizing Delia as the lady who had once or twice been to see the children with Miss Charlotte.

Delia paused, embarrassed.

"I—I came to ask if you need any new toys," she stammered.

"That we do, ma'am. And many another thing too, though Miss Charlotte tells me I'm not to beg of the ladies that comes to see our poor darlin's."

"Oh, you may beg of me, Bridget," Mrs. Ralston answered, smiling. "Let me see your babies—it's so long since I've been here."

The children had stopped playing and, huddled against their nurse, gazed up open-mouthed at the rich rustling lady. One little girl with pale brown eyes and scarlet cheeks was dressed in a plaid alpaca frock trimmed with imitation coral buttons that Delia remembered. Those buttons had been on Charlotte's "best dress" the year she came out. Delia stopped and took up the child. Its curly hair was brown, the exact colour of the eyes—thank heaven! But the eyes had the same little green spangles floating in their transparency. Delia sat down, and the little girl, standing on her knee, gravely fingered her watch-chain.

"Oh, ma'am—maybe her shoes'll soil your skirt. The floor here ain't none too clean."

Delia shook her head, and pressed the child against her. She had forgotten the other gazing babies and their wardress. The little creature on her knee was made of different stuff—it had not needed the plaid alpaca and coral buttons to single her out. Her brown curls grew in points on her high forehead, exactly as Clement Spender's did. Delia laid a burning cheek against the forehead.

"Baby want my lovely yellow chain?"

Baby did.

Delia unfastened the gold chain and hung it about the child's neck. The other babies clapped and crowed, but the little girl, gravely dimpling, continued to finger the links in silence.

"Oh, ma'am, you can't leave that fine chain on little Teeny. When she has to go back to those blacks . . ."

"What is her name?"

"Teena they call her, I believe. It don't seem a Christian name, har'ly."

Delia was silent.

"What I say is, her cheeks is too red. And she coughs too easy. Always one cold and another. Here, Teeny, leave the lady go."

Delia stood up, loosening the tender arms.

"She doesn't want to leave go of you, ma'am. Miss Chatty ain't been in today, and the little thing's kinder lonesome without her. She don't play like the other children, somehow. . . Teeny, you look at that lovely chain you've got . . . there, there now . . ."

"Goodbye, Clementina," Delia whispered below her breath. She kissed the pale brown eyes, the curly crown, and dropped her veil on rushing tears. In the stable-yard she dried them on her large embroidered handkerchief, and stood hesitating. Then with a decided step she turned toward home.

The house was as she had left it, except that the children had come in; she heard them romping in the nursery as she went down the passage to her bedroom. Charlotte

Lovell was seated on the sofa, upright and rigid, as Delia had left her.

"Chatty—Chatty, I've thought it out. Listen. Whatever happens, the baby shan't stay with those people. I mean to keep her."

Charlotte stood up, tall and white. The eyes in her thin face had grown so dark that they seemed like spectral hollows in a skull. She opened her lips to speak, and then, snatching at her handkerchief, pressed it to her mouth, and sank down again. A red trickle dripped through the handkerchief onto her poplin skirt.

"Charlotte—Charlotte," Delia screamed, on her knees beside her cousin. Charlotte's head slid back against the cushions and the trickle ceased. She closed her eyes, and Delia, seizing a vinaigrette from the dressing-table, held it to her pinched nostrils. The room was filled with an acrid aromatic scent.

Charlotte's lids lifted. "Don't be frightened. I still spit blood sometimes—not often. My lung is nearly healed. But it's the terror—"

"No, no: there's to be no terror. I tell you I've thought it all out. Jim is going to let me take the baby."

The girl raised herself haggardly. "Jim? Have you told him? Is that where you've been?"

"No, darling. I've only been to see the baby."

"Oh," Charlotte moaned, leaning back again. Delia took her own handkerchief, and wiped away the tears that were raining down her cousin's cheeks.

"You mustn't cry, Chatty; you must be brave. Your little girl and his—how could you think? But you must give me time: I must manage it in my own way. . . Only trust me . . ."

Charlotte's lips stirred faintly.

"The tears . . . don't dry them, Delia. . . . I like to feel them . . ."

The two cousins continued to lean against each other without speaking. The ormolu clock ticked out the measure of their mute communion in minutes, quarters, a half-hour, then an hour: the day declined and darkened, the shadows lengthened across the garlands of the Axminster and the broad white bed. There was a knock.

"The children's waiting to say their grace before supper, ma'am."

"Yes, Eliza. Let them say it to you. I'll come later." As the nurse's steps receded Charlotte Lovell disengaged herself from Delia's embrace.

"Now I can go," she said.

"You're not too weak, dear? I can send for a coach to take you home."

"No, no; it would frighten mother. And I shall like walking now, in the darkness. Sometimes the world used to seem all one awful glare to me. There were days when I thought the sun would never set. And then there was the moon at night." She laid her hands on her cousin's shoulders. "Now it's different. Bye and bye I shan't hate the light."

The two women kissed each other, and Delia whispered: "Tomorrow."

IV

THE Ralstons gave up old customs reluctantly, but once they had adopted a new one they found it impossible to understand why everyone else did not immediately do likewise.

When Delia, who came of the laxer Lovells, and was naturally inclined to novelty, had first proposed to her husband to dine at six o'clock instead of two, his malleable young face had become as relentless as that of the old original Ralston in his grim Colonial portrait. But after a two days' resistance he had come round to his wife's view, and now smiled contemptuously at the obstinacy of those who clung to a heavy mid-day meal and high tea.

"There's nothing I hate like narrow-mindedness. Let people eat when they like, for all I care; it's their narrow-mindedness that I can't stand."

Delia was thinking of this as she sat in the drawing-room (her mother would have called it the parlour) waiting for her husband's return. She had just had time to smooth her glossy braids, and slip on the black-and-white striped moire with cherry pipings which was his favourite dress. The drawing-room, with its Nottingham lace curtains looped back under florid gilt cornices, its marble centre-table on a carved rosewood foot, and its old-fashioned mahogany armchairs covered with one of the new French silk damasks in a tart shade of apple-green, was one for any young wife to be proud of. The rosewood what-nots on each side of the folding doors that led into the dining-room were adorned with tropical shells, feldspar vases, an alabaster model of the Leaning Tower of Pisa, a pair of obelisks made of scraps of porphyry and serpentine picked up by the young couple in the Roman Forum, a bust of Clytie in chalk-white biscuit de Sèvres, and four old-fashioned figures of the Seasons in Chelsea ware, that had to be left among the newer ornaments because they had belonged to great-grandmamma Ralston. On the walls hung large dark steel-engravings of Cole's "Voyage of Life," and between the windows stood the life-size statue of "A Captive Maiden" executed for Jim Ralston's father by the celebrated Harriet Hosmer, immortalized in Hawthorne's novel of the Marble Faun. On the table lay handsomely tooled copies of Turner's Rivers of France, Drake's Culprit Fay, Crabbe's Tales, and the Book of Beauty containing portraits of the British peeresses who had participated in the Earl of Eglinton's tournament.

As Delia sat there, before the hard-coal fire in its arched opening of black marble, her citron-wood work-table at her side, and one of the new French lamps shedding a pleasant light on the centre-table from under a crystal-fringed shade, she asked herself how she could have passed, in such a short time, so completely out of her usual circle of impressions and convictions—so much farther than ever before beyond the Ralston horizon. Here it was, closing in on her again, as if the very plaster ornaments of the ceiling, the forms of the furniture, the cut of her dress, had been built out of Ralston prejudices, and turned to adamant by the touch of Ralston hands.

She must have been mad, she thought, to have committed herself so far to Charlotte; yet, turn about as she would in the ever-tightening circle of the problem, she could still find no other issue. Somehow, it lay with her to save Clem Spender's baby.

She heard the sound of the latch-key (her heart had never beat so high at it), and the putting down of a tall hat on the hall console—or of two tall hats, was it? The drawing-room door opened, and two high-stocked and ample-coated young men came in: two Jim Ralstons, so to speak. Delia had never before noticed how much her husband and his cousin Joe were alike; it made her feel how justified she was in always thinking of the Ralstons collectively.

She would not have been young and tender, and a happy wife, if she had not thought Joe but an indifferent copy of her Jim; yet, allowing for defects in the reproduction, there remained a striking likeness between the two tall athletic figures, the short sanguine faces with straight noses, straight whiskers, straight brows, candid blue eyes and sweet selfish smiles. Only, at the present moment, Joe looked like Jim with a tooth-ache.

"Look here, my dear: here's a young man who's asked to take pot-luck with us," Jim smiled, with the confidence of a well-nourished husband who knows that he can always bring a friend home.

"How nice of you, Joe!—Do you suppose he can put up with oyster soup and a stuffed goose?" Delia beamed upon her husband.

"I knew it! I told you so, my dear chap! He said you wouldn't like it—that you'd be fussed about the dinner. Wait till you're married, Joseph Ralston—." Jim brought down a genial paw on his cousin's bottle-green shoulder, and Joe grimaced as if the tooth had stabbed him.

"It's excessively kind of you, cousin Delia, to take me in this evening. The fact is—"

"Dinner first, my boy, if you don't mind! A bottle of Burgundy will brush away the blue devils. Your arm to your cousin, please; I'll just go and see that the wine is brought up."

Oyster soup, broiled bass, stuffed goose, apple fritters and green peppers, followed by one of Grandmamma Ralston's famous caramel custards: through all her mental anguish, Delia was faintly aware of a secret pride in her achievement. Certainly it would serve to confirm the rumour that Jim Ralston could always bring a friend home to dine without notice. The Ralston and Lovell wines rounded off the effect, and even Joe's drawn face had mellowed by the time the Lovell Madeira started westward. Delia marked the change when the two young men rejoined her in the drawing-room.

"And now, my dear fellow, you'd better tell her the whole story," Jim counselled, pushing an armchair toward his cousin.

The young woman, bent above her wool-work, listened with lowered lids and flushed cheeks. As a married woman —as a mother—Joe hoped she would think him justified in speaking to her frankly: he had her husband's authority to do so.

"Oh, go ahead, go ahead," chafed the exuberant after-dinner Jim from the hearth-rug.

Delia listened, considered, let the bride-groom flounder on through his embarrassed exposition. Her needle hung

like a sword of Damocles above the canvas; she saw at once
that Joe depended on her trying to win Charlotte over
to his way of thinking. But he was very much in love:
at a word from Delia, she understood that he would yield,
and Charlotte gain her point, save the child, and marry
him . . .

How easy it was, after all! A friendly welcome, a good
dinner, a ripe wine, and the memory of Charlotte's eyes—
so much the more expressive for all that they had looked
upon. A secret envy stabbed the wife who had lacked this
last enlightenment.

How easy it was—and yet it must not be! Whatever happened, she could not let Charlotte Lovell marry Joe Ralston. All the traditions of honour and probity in which
she had been brought up forbade her to connive at such
a plan. She could conceive—had already conceived—of
high-handed measures, swift and adroit defiances of precedent, subtle revolts against the heartlessness of the social
routine. But a lie she could never connive at. The idea
of Charlotte's marrying Joe Ralston—her own Jim's cousin
—without revealing her past to him, seemed to Delia as
dishonourable as it would have seemed to any Ralston.
And to tell him the truth would at once put an end to
the marriage; of that even Chatty was aware. Social tolerance was not dealt in the same measure to men and to
women, and neither Delia nor Charlotte had ever wondered why: like all the young women of their class they
simply bowed to the ineluctable.

No; there was no escape from the dilemma. As clearly
as it was Delia's duty to save Clem Spender's child, so
clearly, also, she seemed destined to sacrifice his mistress.
As the thought pressed on her she remembered Charlotte's

wistful cry: "I want to be married, like all of you," and her heart tightened. But yet it must not be.

"I make every allowance" (Joe was droning on) "for my sweet girl's ignorance and inexperience—for her lovely purity. How could a man wish his future wife to be—to be otherwise? You're with me, Jim? And Delia? I've told her, you understand, that she shall always have a special sum set apart for her poor children—in addition to her pin-money; on that she may absolutely count. God! I'm willing to draw up a deed, a settlement, before a lawyer, if she says so. I admire, I appreciate her generosity. But I ask you, Delia, as a mother—mind you, now, I want your frank opinion. If you think I can stretch a point—can let her go on giving her personal care to these children until . . . until . . ." A flush of pride suffused the potential father's brow . . . "till nearer duties claim her, why, I'm more than ready . . . if you'll tell her so. I undertake," Joe proclaimed, suddenly tingling with the memory of his last glass, "to make it right with my mother, whose prejudices, of course, while I respect them, I can never allow to—to come between me and my own convictions." He sprang to his feet, and beamed on his dauntless double in the chimney-mirror. "My convictions," he flung back at it.

"Hear, hear!" cried Jim emotionally.

Delia's needle gave the canvas a sharp prick, and she pushed her work aside.

"I think I understand you both, Joe. Certainly, in Charlotte's place, I could never give up those children."

"There you are, my dear fellow!" Jim triumphed, as proud of this vicarious courage as of the perfection of the dinner.

"Never," said Delia. "Especially, I mean, the foundlings —there are two, I think. Those children always die if they are sent to asylums. That is what is haunting Chatty."

"Poor innocents! How I love her for loving them! That there should be such scoundrels upon this earth unpunished—. Delia, will you tell her that I'll do whatever—"

"Gently, old man, gently," Jim admonished him, with a flash of Ralston caution.

"Well, that is to say, whatever—in reason—"

Delia lifted an arresting hand. "I'll tell her, Joe: she will be grateful. But it's of no use—"

"No use? What more—?"

"Nothing more: except this. Charlotte has had a return of her old illness. She coughed blood here today. You must not marry her."

There: it was done. She stood up, trembling in every bone, and feeling herself pale to the lips. Had she done right? Had she done wrong? And would she ever know?

Poor Joe turned on her a face as wan as hers: he clutched the back of his armchair, his head drooping forward like an old man's. His lips moved, but made no sound.

"My God!" Jim stammered. "But you know you've got to buck up, old boy."

"I'm—I'm so sorry for you, Joe. She'll tell you herself tomorrow," Delia faltered, while her husband continued to proffer heavy consolations.

"Take it like a man, old chap. Think of yourself—your future. Can't be, you know. Delia's right; she always *is*. Better get it over—better face the music now than later."

"Now than later," Joe echoed with a tortured grin; and it occurred to Delia that never before in the course of his

easy good-natured life had he had—any more than her Jim—
to give up anything his heart was set on. Even the vocab-
ulary of renunciation, and its conventional gestures, were
unfamiliar to him.

"But I don't understand. I can't give her up," he declared, blinking away a boyish tear.

"Think of the children, my dear fellow; it's your duty,"
Jim insisted, checking a glance of pride at Delia's wholesome comeliness.

In the long conversation that followed between the
cousins—argument, counter-argument, sage counsel and
hopeless protest—Delia took but an occasional part. She
knew well enough what the end would be. The bride-
groom who had feared that his bride might bring home
contagion from her visits to the poor would not know-
ingly implant disease in his race. Nor was that all. Too
many sad instances of mothers prematurely fading, and
leaving their husbands alone with a young flock to rear,
must be pressing upon Joe's memory. Ralstons, Lovells,
Lannings, Archers, van der Luydens—which one of them
had not some grave to care for in a distant cemetery:
graves of young relatives "in a decline," sent abroad to be
cured by balmy Italy? The Protestant grave-yards of Rome
and Pisa were full of New York names; the vision of that
familiar pilgrimage with a dying wife was one to turn the
most ardent Ralston cold. And all the while, as she listened with bent head, Delia kept repeating to herself:
"This is easy; but how am I going to tell Charlotte?"

When poor Joe, late that evening, wrung her hand
with a stammered farewell, she called him back abruptly
from the threshold.

"You must let me see her first, please; you must wait till

she sends for you—" and she winced a little at the alacrity of his acceptance. But no amount of rhetorical bolstering-up could make it easy for a young man to face what lay ahead of Joe; and her final glance at him was one of compassion . . .

The front door closed upon Joe, and she was roused by her husband's touch on her shoulder.

"I never admired you more, darling. My wise Delia!"

Her head bent back, she took his kiss, and then drew apart. The sparkle in his eyes she understood to be as much an invitation to her bloom as a tribute to her sagacity.

She held him at arms' length. "What should you have done, Jim, if I'd had to tell you about myself what I've just told Joe about Chatty?"

A slight frown showed that he thought the question negligible, and hardly in her usual taste. "Come," his strong arm entreated her.

She continued to stand away from him, with grave eyes. "Poor Chatty! Nothing left now—"

His own eyes grew grave, in instant sympathy. At such moments he was still the sentimental boy whom she could manage.

"Ah, poor Chatty, indeed!" He groped for the readiest panacea. "Lucky, now, after all, that she has those paupers, isn't it? I suppose a woman *must* have children to love——somebody else's if not her own." It was evident that the thought of the remedy had already relieved his pain.

"Yes," Delia agreed, "I see no other comfort for her. I'm sure Joe will feel that too. Between us, darling—" and now she let him have her hands—"between us, you and I must see to it that she keeps her babies."

"Her babies?" He smiled at the possessive pronoun. "Of course, poor girl! Unless indeed she's sent to Italy?"

"Oh, she won't be that—where's the money to come from? And, besides, she'd never leave Aunt Lovell. But I thought, dear, if I might tell her tomorrow—you see, I'm not exactly looking forward to my talk with her—if I might tell her that you would let me look after the baby she's most worried about, the poor little foundling girl who has no name and no home—if I might put aside a fixed sum from my pin-money . . ."

Their hands flowed together, she lifted her flushing face to his. Manly tears were in his eyes; ah, how he triumphed in her health, her wisdom, her generosity!

"Not a penny from your pin-money—never!"

She feigned discouragement and wonder. "Think, dear —if I'd had to give you up!"

"Not a penny from your pin-money, I say—but as much more as you need, to help poor Chatty's pauper. There —will that content you?"

"Dearest! When I think of our own, upstairs!" They held each other, awed by that evocation.

V

CHARLOTTE LOVELL, at the sound of her cousin's step, lifted a fevered face from the pillow.

The bedroom, dim and close, smelt of eau de Cologne and fresh linen. Delia, blinking in from the bright winter sun, had to feel her way through a twilight obstructed by dark mahogany.

"I want to see your face, Chatty: unless your head aches too much?"

Charlotte signed "No," and Delia drew back the heavy window curtains and let in a ray of light. In it she saw the girl's head, livid against the bed-linen, the brick-rose circles again visible under darkly shadowed lids. Just so, she remembered, poor cousin So-and-so had looked the week before she sailed for Italy!

"Delia!" Charlotte breathed.

Delia drew near the bed, and stood looking down at her cousin with new eyes. Yes: it had been easy enough, the night before, to dispose of Chatty's future as if it were her own. But now?

"Darling—"

"Oh, begin, please," the girl interrupted, "or I shall know that what's coming is too dreadful!"

"Chatty, dearest, if I promised you too much—"

"Jim won't let you take my child? I knew it! Shall I always go on dreaming things that can never be?"

Delia, her tears running down, knelt by the bed and gave her fresh hand into the other's burning clutch.

"Don't think that, dear: think only of what you'd like best . . ."

"Like best?" The girl sat up sharply against her pillows, alive to the hot fingertips.

"You can't marry Joe, dear—can you—and keep little Tina?" Delia continued.

"Not keep her with me, no: but somewhere where I could slip off to see her—oh, I had hoped such follies!"

"Give up follies, Charlotte. Keep her where? See your own child in secret? Always in dread of disgrace? Of wrong to your other children? Have you ever thought of that?"

"Oh, my poor head won't think! You're trying to tell me that I must give her up?"

"No, dear; but that you must not marry Joe."

Charlotte sank back on the pillow, her eyes half-closed. "I tell you I must make my child a home. Delia, you're too blest to understand!"

"Think yourself blest too, Chatty. You shan't give up your baby. She shall live with you: you shall take care of her—for me."

"For you?"

"I promised you I'd take her, didn't I? But not that you should marry Joe. Only that I would make a home for your baby. Well, that's done; you two shall be always together."

Charlotte clung to her and sobbed. "But Joe—I can't tell him, I can't!" She put back Delia suddenly. "You haven't told him of my—of my baby? I couldn't bear to hurt him as much as that."

"I told him that you coughed blood yesterday. He'll see you presently: he's dreadfully unhappy. He has been given to understand that, in view of your bad health, the engagement is broken by your wish—and he accepts your decision; but if he weakens, or if you weaken, I can do nothing for you or for little Tina. For heaven's sake remember that!"

Delia released her hold, and Charlotte leaned back silent, with closed eyes and narrowed lips. Almost like a corpse she lay there. On a chair near the bed hung the poplin with red velvet ribbons which had been made over in honour of her betrothal. A pair of new slippers of bronze kid peeped from beneath it. Poor Chatty! She had hardly had time to be pretty . . .

Delia sat by the bed motionless, her eyes on her cousin's closed face. They followed the course of a tear that forced a way between Charlotte's tight lids, hung on the lashes, glittered slowly down the cheeks. As the tear reached the narrowed lips they spoke.

"Shall I live with her somewhere, do you mean? Just she and I together?"

"Just you and she."

"In a little house?"

"In a little house . . ."

"You're sure, Delia?"

"Sure, my dearest."

Charlotte once more raised herself on her elbow and sent a hand groping under the pillow. She drew out a narrow ribbon on which hung a diamond ring.

"I had taken it off already," she said simply, and handed it to Delia.

PART II

You could always have told, every one agreed afterward,
that Charlotte Lovell was meant to be an old maid. Even
before her illness it had been manifest: there was something prim about her in spite of her fiery hair. Lucky
enough for her, poor girl, considering her wretched health
in her youth: Mrs. James Ralston's contemporaries, for
instance, remembered Charlotte as a mere ghost, coughing
her lungs out—that, of course, had been the reason for her
breaking her engagement with Joe Ralston.

True, she had recovered very rapidly, in spite of the
peculiar treatment she was given. The Lovells, as every
one knew, couldn't afford to send her to Italy; the previous experiment in Georgia had been unsuccessful; and
so she was packed off to a farm-house on the Hudson—a
little place on the James Ralstons' property—where she
lived for five or six years with an Irish servant-woman and
a foundling baby. The story of the foundling was another
queer episode in Charlotte's history. From the time of her
first illness, when she was only twenty-two or three, she
has developed an almost morbid tenderness for children,
especially for the children of the poor. It was said—Dr.
Lanskell was understood to have said—that the baffled
instinct of motherhood was peculiarly intense in cases
where lung-disease prevented marriage. And so, when it
was decided that Chatty must break her engagement to

Joe Ralston and go to live in the country, the doctor had told her family that the only hope of saving her lay in not separating her entirely from her pauper children, but in letting her choose one of them, the youngest and most pitiable, and devote herself to its care. So the James Ralstons had lent her their little farm-house, and Mrs. Jim, with her extraordinary gift of taking things in at a glance, had at once arranged everything, and even pledged herself to look after the baby if Charlotte died.

Charlotte did not die. She lived to grow robust and middle-aged, energetic and even tyrannical. And as the transformation in her character took place she became more and more like the typical old maid: precise, methodical, absorbed in trifles, and attaching an exaggerated importance to the smallest social and domestic observances. Such was her reputation as a vigilant house-wife that, when poor Jim Ralston was killed by a fall from his horse, and left Delia, still young, with a boy and girl to bring up, it seemed perfectly natural that the heart-broken widow should take her cousin to live with her and share her task. But Delia Ralston never did things quite like other people. When she took Charlotte she took Charlotte's foundling too: a dark-haired child with pale brown eyes, and the odd incisive manner of children who have lived too much with their elders. The little girl was called Tina Lovell: it was vaguely supposed that Charlotte had adopted her. She grew up on terms of affectionate equality with her young Ralston cousins, and almost as much so—it might be said—with the two women who mothered her. But, impelled by an instinct of imitation which no one took the trouble to correct, she always called Delia Ralston "Mamma" and Charlotte Lovell "Aunt Chatty." She was a brilliant and engaging creature, and people marvelled at poor Chatty's luck in having chosen so interesting a specimen among her foundlings (for she was by this time supposed to have had a whole asylum-full to choose from).

The agreeable elderly bachelor, Sillerton Jackson, returning from a prolonged sojourn in Paris (where he was understood to have been made much of by the highest personages) was immensely struck by Tina's charms when he saw her at her coming-out ball, and asked Delia's permission to come some evening and dine alone with her and her young people. He complimented the widow on the rosy beauty of her own young Delia; but the mother's keen eye perceived that all the while he was watching Tina, and after dinner he confided to the older ladies that there was something "very French" in the girl's way of doing her hair, and that in the capital of all the Elegances she would have been pronounced extremely stylish.

"Oh—" Delia deprecated, beamingly, while Charlotte Lovell sat bent over her work with pinched lips; but Tina, who had been laughing with her cousins at the other end of the room, was around upon her elders in a flash.

"I heard what Mr. Sillerton said! Yes, I did, Mamma: he says I do my hair stylishly. Didn't I always tell you so? I *know* it's more becoming to let it curl as it wants to than to plaster it down with bandoline like Aunty's—"

"Tina, Tina—you always think people are admiring you!" Miss Lovell protested.

"Why shouldn't I, when they do?" the girl laughingly

challenged; and, turning her mocking eyes on Sillerton Jackson: "Do tell Aunt Charlotte not to be so dreadfully old-maidish!"

Delia saw the blood rise to Charlotte Lovell's face. It no longer painted two brick-rose circles on her thin cheek-bones, but diffused a harsh flush over her whole countenance, from the collar fastened with an old-fashioned garnet brooch to the pepper-and-salt hair (with no trace of red left in it) flattened down over her hollow temples.

That evening, when they went up to bed, Delia called Tina into her room.

"You ought not to speak to your Aunt Charlotte as you did this evening, dear. It's disrespectful—you must see that it hurts her."

The girl overflowed with compunction. "Oh, I'm so sorry! Because I said she was an old maid? But she *is*, isn't she, Mamma? In her inmost soul, I mean. I don't believe she's ever been young—ever thought of fun or admiration or falling in love—do you? That's why she never understands me, and you always do, you darling dear Mamma." With one of her light movements, Tina was in the widow's arms.

"Child, child," Delia softly scolded, kissing the dark curls planted in five points on the girl's forehead.

There was a soft foot-fall in the passage, and Charlotte Lovell stood in the door. Delia, without moving, sent her a glance of welcome over Tina's shoulder.

"Come in, Charlotte, I'm scolding Tina for behaving like a spoilt baby before Sillerton Jackson. What will he think of her?"

"Just what she deserves, probably," Charlotte returned with a cold smile. Tina went toward her, and her thin lips touched the girl's proffered forehead just where Delia's warm kiss had rested. "Goodnight, child," she said in her dry tone of dismissal.

The door closed on the two women, and Delia signed to Charlotte to take the armchair opposite to her own.

"Not so near the fire," Miss Lovell answered. She chose a straight-backed seat, and sat down with folded hands. Delia's eyes rested absently on the thin ringless fingers: she wondered why Charlotte never wore her mother's jewels.

"I overheard what you were saying to Tina, Delia. You were scolding her because she called me an old maid."

It was Delia's turn to colour. "I scolded her for being disrespectful, dear; if you heard what I said you can't think that I was too severe."

"Not too severe: no. I've never thought you too severe with Tina; on the contrary."

"You think I spoil her?"

"Sometimes."

Delia felt an unreasoning resentment. "What was it I said that you object to?"

Charlotte returned her glance steadily. "I would rather she thought me an old maid than—"

"Oh—" Delia murmured. With one of her quick leaps of intuition she had entered into the other's soul, and once more measured its shuddering loneliness.

"What else," Charlotte inexorably pursued, "*can* she possibly be allowed to think me—ever?"

"I see . . . I see . . ." the widow faltered.

"A ridiculous narrow-minded old maid—nothing else," Charlotte Lovell insisted, getting to her feet, "or I shall never feel safe with her."

"Goodnight, my dear," Delia said compassionately. There were moment when she almost hated Charlotte for being Tina's mother, and others, such as this, when her heart was wrung by the tragic spectacle of that unavowed bond.

Charlotte seemed to have divined her thought.

"Oh, but don't pity me! She's mine," she murmured, going.

VII

DELIA RALSTON sometimes felt that the real events of
her life did not begin until both her children had contracted—so safely and suitably—their irreproachable New
York alliances. The boy had married first, choosing a
Vandergrave in whose father's bank at Albany he was to
have an immediate junior partnership; and young Delia
(as her mother had foreseen she would) had selected John
Junius, the safest and soundest of the many young
Halseys, and followed him to his parents' house the year
after her brother's marriage.

After young Delia had left the house in Gramercy
Park it was inevitable that Tina should take the centre
front of its narrow stage. Tina had reached the marriage-
able age, she was admired and sought after; but what hope
was there of her finding a husband? The two watchful
women did not propound this question to each other;
but Delia Ralston, brooding over it day by day, and taking it up with her when she mounted at night to her bedroom, knew that Charlotte Lovell, at the same hour,
carried the same problem with her to the floor above.

The two cousins, during their eight years of life together, had seldom openly disagreed. Indeed, it might
almost have been said that there was nothing open in
their relation. Delia would have had it otherwise: after
they had once looked so deeply into each other's souls it

seemed unnatural that a veil should fall between them. But she understood that Tina's ignorance of her origin must at all costs be preserved, and that Charlotte Lovell, abrupt, passionate and inarticulate, knew of no other security than to wall herself up in perpetual silence.

So far had she carried this self-imposed reticence that Mrs. Ralston was surprised at her suddenly asking, soon after young Delia's marriage, to be allowed to move down into the small bedroom next to Tina's that had been left vacant by the bride's departure.

"But you'll be so much less comfortable there, Chatty. Have you though of that? Or is it on account of the stairs?"

"No; it's not the stairs," Charlotte answered with her usual bluntness. How could she avail herself of the pretext Delia offered her, when Delia knew that she still ran up and down the three flights like a girl? "It's because I should be next to Tina," she said, in a low voice that jarred like an untuned string.

"Oh—very well. As you please." Mrs. Ralston could not tell why she felt suddenly irritated by the request, unless it were that she had already amused herself with the idea of fitting up the vacant room as a sitting-room for Tina. She had meant to do it in pink and pale green, like an opening flower.

"Of course, if there is any reason—" Charlotte suggested, as if reading her thought.

"None whatever; except that—well, I'd meant to surprise Tina by doing the room up as a sort of little boudoir where she could have her books and things, and see her girl friends."

"You're too kind, Delia; but Tina mustn't have boudoirs," Miss Lovell answered ironically, the green specks showing in her eyes.

"Very well: as you please," Delia repeated, in the same irritated tone. "I'll have your things brought down tomorrow."

Charlotte paused in the doorway. "You're sure there's no other reason?"

"Other reason? Why should there be?" The two women looked at each other almost with hostility, and Charlotte turned to go.

The talk once over, Delia was annoyed with herself for having yielded to Charlotte's wish. Why must it always be she who gave in, she who, after all, was the mistress of the house, and to whom both Charlotte and Tina might almost be said to owe their very existence, or at least all that made it worth having? Yet whenever any question arose about the girl it was invariably Charlotte who gained her point, Delia who yielded: it seemed as if Charlotte, in her mute obstinate way, were determined to take every advantage of the dependence that made it impossible for a woman of Delia's nature to oppose her.

In truth, Delia had looked forward more than she knew to the quiet talks with Tina to which the little boudoir would have lent itself. While her own daughter inhabited the room, Mrs. Ralston had been in the habit of spending an hour there every evening, chatting with the two girls while they undressed, and listening to their comments on the incidents of the day. She always knew beforehand exactly what her own girl would say; but Tina's views and opinions were a perpetual delicious shock to her. Not that they were strange or unfamiliar; there were moments when they seemed to well straight up from the dumb depths of Delia's own past. Only they expressed feelings she had never uttered, ideas she had hardly avowed to herself: Tina sometimes said things which Delia Ralston, in far-off self-communions, had imagined herself saying to Clement Spender.

And now there would be an end to these evening talks: if Charlotte had asked to be lodged next to her daughter, might it not conceivably be because she wished them to end? It had never before occurred to Delia that her influence over Tina might be resented; now the discovery flashed a light far down into the abyss which had always divided the two women. But a moment later Delia reproached herself for attributing feelings of jealousy to her cousin. Was it not rather to herself that she should have ascribed them? Charlotte, as Tina's mother, had every right to wish to be near her, near her in all senses of the word; what claim had Delia to oppose to that natural privilege? The next morning she gave the order that Charlotte's things should be taken down to the room next to Tina's.

That evening, when bedtime came, Charlotte and Tina went upstairs together; but Delia lingered in the drawing-room, on the pretext of having letters to write. In truth, she dreaded to pass the threshold where, evening after evening, the fresh laughter of the two girls used to waylay her while Charlotte Lovell already slept her old-maid sleep on the floor above. A pang went through Delia at the thought that henceforth she would be cut off from this means of keeping her hold on Tina.

An hour later, when she mounted the stairs in her turn,

she was guiltily conscious of moving as noiselessly as she could along the heavy carpet of the corridor, and of pausing longer than was necessary over the putting out of the gas-jet on the landing. As she lingered she strained her ears for the sound of voices from the adjoining doors behind which Charlotte and Tina slept; she would have been secretly hurt at hearing talk and laughter from within. But none came, nor was there any light beneath the doors. Evidently Charlotte, in her hard methodical way, had said goodnight to her daughter, and gone straight to bed as usual. Perhaps she had never approved of Tina's vigils, of the long undressing punctuated with mirth and confidences; she might have asked for the room next to her daughter's simply because she did not want the girl to miss her "beauty sleep."

Whenever Delia tried to explore the secret of her cousin's actions she returned from the adventure humiliated and abashed by the base motives she found herself attributing to Charlotte. How was it that she, Delia Ralston, whose happiness had been open and avowed to the world, so often found herself envying poor Charlotte the secret of her scanted motherhood? She hated herself for this movement of envy whenever she detected it, and tried to atone for it by a softened manner and a more anxious regard for Charlotte's feelings; but the attempt was not always successful, and Delia sometimes wondered if Charlotte did not resent any show of sympathy as an indirect glance at her misfortune. The worst of suffering such as hers was that it left one sore to the gentlest touch . . .

Delia, slowly undressing before the same lace-draped toilet-glass which had reflected her bridal image, was turning over these thoughts when she heard a light knock. She opened the door, and there stood Tina, in a dressing-gown, her dark curls falling over her shoulders.

With a happy heart-beat Delia held out her arms.

"I had to say goodnight, Mamma," the girl whispered.

"Of course, dear." Delia pressed a long kiss on her lifted forehead. "Run off now, or you might disturb your aunt. You know she sleeps badly, and you must be as quiet as a mouse now she's next to you."

"Yes, I know," Tina acquiesced, with a grave glance that was almost of complicity.

She asked no further question, she did not linger: lifting Delia's hand she held it a moment against her cheek, and then stole out as noiselessly as she had come.

VIII

"But you must see," Charlotte Lovell insisted, laying aside the *Evening Post*, "that Tina has changed. You do see that?"

The two women were sitting alone by the drawing-room fire in Gramercy Park. Tina had gone to dine with her cousin, young Mrs. John Junius Halsey, and was to be taken afterward to a ball at the Vandergraves', from which the John Juniuses had promised to see her home. Mrs. Ralston and Charlotte, their early dinner finished, had the long evening to themselves. Their custom, on such occasions, was for Charlotte to read the news aloud to her cousin, while the latter embroidered; but tonight, all through Charlotte's conscientious progress from column to column, without a slip or an omission, Delia had felt her, for some special reason, alert to take advantage of her daughter's absence.

To gain time before answering, Mrs. Ralston bent over a stitch in her delicate white embroidery.

"Tina changed? Since when?" she questioned.

The answer flashed out instantly. "Since Lanning Halsey has been coming here so much."

"Lanning? I used to think he came for Delia," Mrs. Ralston mused, speaking at random to gain still more time.

"It's natural you should suppose that every one came

for Delia," Charlotte rejoined dryly; "but as Lanning continues to seek every chance of being with Tina—"

Mrs. Ralston raised her head and stole a swift glance at her cousin. She had in truth noticed that Tina had changed, as a flower changes at the mysterious moment when the unopened petals flush from within. The girl had grown handsomer, shyer, more silent, at times more irrelevantly gay. But Delia had not associated these variations of mood with the presence of Lanning Halsey, one of the numerous youths who had haunted the house before young Delia's marriage. There had, indeed, been a moment when Mrs. Ralston's eye had been fixed, with a certain apprehension, on the handsome Lanning. Among all the sturdy and stolid Halsey cousins he was the only one to whom a prudent mother might have hesitated to entrust her daughter; it would have been hard to say why, except that he was handsomer and more conversable than the rest, chronically unpunctual, and totally unperturbed by the fact. Clem Spender had been like that; and what if young Delia—?

But young Delia's mother was speedily reassured. The girl, herself arch and appetizing, took no interest in the corresponding graces except when backed by more solid qualities. A Ralston to the core, she demanded the Ralston virtues, and chose the Halsey most worthy of a Ralston bride.

Mrs. Ralston felt that Charlotte was waiting for her to speak. "It will be hard to get used to the idea of Tina's marrying," she said gently. "I don't know what we two old women shall do, alone in this empty house—for it will be an empty house then. But I suppose we ought to face the idea."

"I *do* face it," said Charlotte Lovell gravely.

"And you dislike Lanning? I mean, as a husband for Tina?"

Miss Lovell folded the evening paper, and stretched out a thin hand for her knitting. She glanced across the citron-wood work-table at her cousin. "Tina must not be too difficult—" she began.

"Oh—" Delia protested, reddening.

"Let us call things by their names," the other evenly pursued. "That's my way, when I speak at all. Usually, as you know, I say nothing."

The widow made a sign of assent, and Charlotte went on: "It's better so. But I've always known a time would come when we should have to talk this thing out."

"Talk this thing out? You and I? What thing?"

"Tina's future."

There was a silence. Delia Ralston, who always responded instantly to the least appeal to her sincerity, breathed a deep sigh of relief. At last the ice in Charlotte's breast was breaking up!

"My dear," Delia murmured, "you know how much Tina's happiness concerns me. If you disapprove of Lanning Halsey as a husband, have you any other candidate in mind?"

Miss Lovell smiled one of her faint hard smiles. "I am not aware that there is a queue at the door. Nor do I disapprove of Lanning Halsey as a husband. Personally, I find him very agreeable; I understand his attraction for Tina."

"Ah—Tina *is* attracted?"

"Yes."

Mrs. Ralston pushed aside her work and thoughtfully

considered her cousin's sharp-lined face. Never had Charlotte Lovell more completely presented the typical image of the old maid than as she sat there, upright on her straight-backed chair, with narrowed elbows and clicking needles, and imperturbably discussed her daughter's marriage.

"I don't understand, Chatty. Whatever Lanning's faults are—and I don't believe they're grave—I share your liking for him. After all—" Mrs. Ralston paused—"what is it that people find so reprehensible in him? Chiefly, as far as I can hear, that he can't decide on the choice of a profession. The New York view about that is rather narrow, as we know. Young men may have other tastes . . . artistic . . . literary . . . they may even have difficulty in deciding . . ."

Both women coloured slightly, and Delia guessed that the same reminiscence which shook her own bosom also throbbed under Charlotte's strait bodice.

Charlotte spoke. "Yes: I understand that. But hesitancy about a profession may cause hesitancy about . . . other decisions . . ."

"What do you mean? Surely not that Lanning—?"

"Lanning has not asked Tina to marry him."

Charlotte paused. The steady click of her needles punctuated the silence as once, years before, it had been punctuated by the tick of the Parisian clock on Delia's mantel. As Delia's memory fled back to that scene she felt its mysterious tension in the air.

Charlotte spoke. "Lanning is not hesitating any longer: he has decided *not* to marry Tina. But he has also decided—not to give up seeing her."

Delia flushed abruptly; she was irritated and bewildered

by Charlotte's oracular phrases, doled out betweeen parsimonious lips.

"You don't mean that he has offered himself and then drawn back? I can't think him capable of such an insult to Tina."

"He has not insulted Tina. He has simply told her that he can't afford to marry. Until he chooses a profession his father will allow him only a few hundred dollars a year; and that may be suppressed if—if he marries against his parents' wishes."

It was Delia's turn to be silent. The past was too overwhelmingly resuscitated in Charlotte's words. Clement Spender stood before her, irresolute, impecunious, persuasive. Ah, if only she had let herself be persuaded!

"I'm very sorry that this should have happened to Tina. But as Lanning appears to have behaved honourably, and withdrawn without raising false expectations, we must hope . . . we must hope. . ." Delia paused, not knowing what they must hope.

Charlotte Lovell laid down her knitting. "You know as well as I do, Delia, that every young man who is inclined to fall in love with Tina will find as good reasons for not marrying her."

"Then you think Lanning's excuses are a pretext?"

"Naturally. The first of many that will be found by his successors—for of course he will have successors. Tina—attracts."

"Ah," Delia murmured.

Here they were at last face to face with the problem which, through all the years of silence and evasiveness, had lain as close to the surface as a corpse too hastily buried! Delia drew another deep breath, which again was

almost one of relief. She had always known that it would
be difficult, almost impossible, to find a husband for Tina;
and much as she desired Tina's happiness, some inmost
selfishness whispered how much less lonely and purpose-
less the close of her own life would be should the girl be
forced to share it. But how say this to Tina's mother?

"I hope you exaggerate, Charlotte. There may be dis-
interested characters. . . But, in any case, surely Tina
need not be unhappy here, with us who love her so
dearly."

"Tina an old maid? Never!" Charlotte Lovell rose
abruptly, her closed hand crashing down on the slender
work-table. "My child shall have her life . . . her own
life . . . whatever it costs me . . ."

Delia's ready sympathy welled up. "I understand your
feeling. I should want also . . . hard as it will be to let
her go. But surely there is no hurry—no reason for looking
so far ahead. The child is not twenty. Wait."

Charlotte stood before her, motionless, perpendicular.
At such moments she made Delia think of lava struggling
through granite: there seemed no issue for the fires within.

"Wait? But if *she* doesn't wait?"

"But if he has withdrawn—what do you mean?"

"He has given up marrying her—but not seeing her."

Delia sprang up in her turn, flushed and trembling.

"Charlotte! Do you know what you're insinuating?"

"Yes: I know."

"But it's too outrageous. No decent girl—"

The words died on Delia's lips. Charlotte Lovell held
her eyes inexorably. "Girls are not always what you call
decent," she declared.

Mrs. Ralston turned slowly back to her seat. Her tambour frame had fallen to the floor; she stooped heavily to pick it up. Charlotte's gaunt figure hung over her, relentless as doom.

"I can't imagine, Charlotte, what is gained by saying such things—even by hinting them. Surely you trust your own child."

Charlotte laughed. "My mother trusted me," she said.

"How dare you—how dare you?' Delia began; but her eyes fell, and she felt a tremor of weakness in her throat.

"Oh, I dare anything for Tina, even to judging her as she is," Tina's mother murmured.

"As she is? She's perfect!"

"Let us say then that she must pay for my imperfections. All I want is that she shouldn't pay too heavily."

Mrs. Ralston sat silent. It seemed to her that Charlotte spoke with the voice of all the dark destinies coiled under the safe surface of life; and that to such a voice there was no answer but an awed acquiescence.

"Poor Tina!" she breathed.

"Oh, I don't intend that she shall suffer! It's not for that I've waited . . . waited. Only I've made mistakes: mistakes that I understand now, and must remedy. You've been too good to us—and we must go."

"Go?" Delia gasped.

"Yes. Don't think me ungrateful. You saved my child once—do you suppose I can forget? But now it's my turn—it's I who must save her. And it's only by taking her away from everything here—from everything she's known till now—that I can do it. She's lived too long among unrealities: and she's like me. They won't content her."

"Unrealities?" Delia echoed vaguely.

"Unrealities for her. Young men who make love to her and can't marry her. Happy households where she's welcomed till she's suspected of designs on a brother or a husband—or else exposed to their insults. How could we ever have imagined, either of us, that the child could escape disaster? I thought only of her present happiness—of all the advantages, for both of us, of being with you. But this affair with young Halsey has opened my eyes. I must take Tina away. We must go and live somewhere where we're not known, where we shall be among plain people, leading plain lives. Somewhere where she can find a husband, and make herself a home."

Charlotte paused. She had spoken in a rapid monotonous tone, as if by rote; but now her voice broke and she repeated painfully: "I'm not ungrateful."

"Oh, don't let's speak of gratitude! What place has it between you and me?"

Delia had risen and begun to move uneasily about the room. She longed to plead with Charlotte, to implore her not to be in haste, to picture to her the cruelty of severing Tina from all her habits and associations, of carrying her inexplicably away to lead "a plain life among plain people." What chance was there, indeed, that a creature so radiant would tamely submit to such a fate, or find an acceptable husband in such conditions? The change might only precipitate a tragedy. Delia's experience was too limited for her to picture exactly what might happen to a girl like Tina, suddenly cut off from all that sweetened life for her; but vague visions of revolt and flight—of a "fall" deeper and more irretrievable than Charlotte's—flashed through her agonized imagination.

"It's too cruel—it's too cruel," she cried, speaking to herself rather than to Charlotte.

Charlotte, instead of answering, glanced abruptly at the clock.

"Do you know what time it is? Past midnight. I mustn't keep you sitting up for my foolish girl."

Delia's heart contracted. She saw that Charlotte wished to cut the conversation short, and to do so by reminding her that only Tina's mother had a right to decide what Tina's future should be. At that moment, though Delia had just protested that there could be no question of gratitude between them, Charlotte Lovell seemed to her a monster of ingratitude, and it was on the tip of her tongue to cry out: "Have all the years then given me no share in Tina?" But at the same instant she had put herself once more in Charlotte's place, and was feeling the mother's fierce terrors for her child. It was natural enough that Charlotte should resent the faintest attempt to usurp in private the authority she could never assert in public. With a pang of compassion Delia realized that she herself was literally the one being on earth before whom Charlotte could act the mother. "Poor thing—ah, let her!" she murmured inwardly.

"But why should you sit up for Tina? She has the key, and Delia is to bring her home."

Charlotte Lovell did not immediately answer. She rolled up her knitting, looked severely at one of the candelabra on the mantelpiece, and crossed over to straighten it. Then she picked up her work-bag.

"Yes, as you say—why should any one sit up for her?" She moved about the room, putting out the lamps, covering the fire, assuring herself that the windows were bolted, while Delia passively watched her. Then the two cousins lit their bedroom candles and walked upstairs through the darkened house. Charlotte seemed determined to make no further allusion to the subject of their talk. On the landing she paused, bending her head toward Delia's nightly kiss.

"I hope they've kept up your fire," she said, with her capable housekeeping air; and on Delia's hasty reassurance the two murmured a simultaneous "Goodnight," and Charlotte turned down the passage to her room.

IX

DELIA's fire had been kept up, and her dressing-gown was warming on an arm-chair near the hearth. But she neither undressed nor yet seated herself. Her conversation with Charlotte had filled her with a deep unrest.

For a few moments she stood in the middle of the floor, looking slowly about her. Nothing had ever been changed in the room which, even as a bride, she had planned to modernize. All her dreams of renovation had faded long ago. Some deep central indifference had gradually made her regard herself as a third person, living the life meant for another woman, a woman totally unrelated to the vivid Delia Lovell who had entered that house so full of plans and visions. The fault, she knew, was not her husband's. With a little managing and a little wheedling she would have gained every point as easily as she had gained the capital one of taking the foundling baby under her wing. The difficulty was that, after that victory, nothing else seemed worth trying for. The first sight of little Tina had somehow decentralized Delia Ralston's whole life, making her indifferent to everything else, except indeed the welfare of her own husband and children. Ahead of her she saw only a future full of duties, and these she had gaily and faithfully accomplished. But her own life was over; she felt as detached as a cloistered nun.

The change in her was too deep not to be visible. The

Ralstons openly gloried in dear Delia's conformity. Each acquiescence passed for a concession, and the family doctrine was fortified by such fresh proofs of its durability. Now, as Delia glanced about her at the Léopold Robert lithographs, the family daguerreotypes, the rosewood and mahogany, she understood that she was looking at the walls of her own grave.

The change had come on the day when Charlotte Lovell, cowering on that very lounge, had made her terrible avowal. Then for the first time Delia, with a kind of fearful exaltation, had heard the blind forces of life groping and crying underfoot. But on that day also she had known herself excluded from them, doomed to dwell among shadows. Life had passed her by, and left her with the Ralstons.

Very well, then! She would make the best of herself, and of the Ralstons. The vow was immediate and unflinching; and for nearly twenty years she had gone on observing it. Once only had she been not a Ralston but herself; once only had it seemed worth while. And now perhaps the same challenge had sounded again; again, for a moment, it might be worth while to live. Not for the sake of Clement Spender—poor Clement, married years ago to a plain determined cousin, who had hunted him down in Rome, and enclosing him in an unrelenting domesticity, had obliged all New York on the grand tour to buy his pictures with a resigned grimace. No, not for Clement Spender, hardly for Charlotte or even for Tina; but for her own sake, hers, Delia Ralston's, for the sake of her one missed vision, her forfeited reality, she would once more break down the Ralston barriers and reach out into the world.

A faint sound through the silent house disturbed her meditation. Listening, she heard Charlotte Lovell's door open and her stiff petticoats rustle toward the landing. A light glanced under the door and vanished; Charlotte had passed Delia's threshold on her way downstairs.

Without moving, Delia continued to listen. Perhaps the careful Charlotte had gone down to make sure that the front door was not bolted, or that she had really covered up the fire. If that were her object, her step would presently be heard returning. But no step sounded; and it became gradually evident that Charlotte had gone down to wait for her daughter. Why?

Delia's bedroom was at the front of the house. She stole across the heavy carpet, drew aside the curtains and cautiously folded back the inner shutters. Below her lay the empty square, white with moonlight, its tree-trunks patterned on a fresh sprinkling of snow. The houses opposite slept in darkness; not a footfall broke the white surface, not a wheel-track marred the brilliant street. Overhead a heaven full of stars swam in the moonlight.

Of the households around Gramercy Park Delia knew that only two others had gone to the ball: the Petrus Vandergraves and their cousins the young Parmly Ralstons. The Lucius Lannings had just entered on their three years of mourning for Mrs. Lucius's mother (it was hard on their daughter Kate, just eighteen, who would be unable to "come out" till she was twenty-one); young Mrs. Marcy Mingott was "expecting her third," and consequently secluded from the public eye for nearly a year; and the other denizens of the square belonged to the undifferentiated and uninvited.

Delia pressed her forehead against the pane. Before

long carriages would turn the corner, the sleeping square ring with hoof-beats, fresh laughter and young farewells mount from the door-steps. But why was Charlotte waiting for her daughter downstairs in the darkness?

The Parisian clock struck one. Delia came back into the room, raked the fire, picked up a shawl, and wrapped in it, returned to her vigil. Ah, how old she must have grown that she should feel the cold at such a moment! It reminded her of what the future held for her: neuralgia, rheumatism, stiffness, accumulating infirmities. And never had she kept a moonlight watch with a lover's arms to warm her . . .

The square still lay silent. Yet the ball must surely be ending: the gayest dances did not last long after one in the morning, and the drive from University Place to Gramercy Park was a short one. Delia leaned in the embrasure and listened.

Hoof-beats, muffled by the snow, sounded in Irving Place, and the Petrus Vandergraves' family coach drew up before the opposite house. The Vandergrave girls and their brother sprang out and mounted the steps; then the coach stopped again a few doors farther on, and the Parmly Ralstons, brought home by their cousins, descended at their own door. The next carriage that rounded the corner must therefore be the John Juniuses', bringing Tina.

The gilt clock struck half-past one. Delia wondered, knowing that young Delia, out of regard for John Junius's business hours, never stayed late at evening parties. Doubtless Tina had delayed her; Mrs. Ralston felt a little annoyed with Tina's thoughtlessness in keeping her cousin up. But the feeling was swept away by an immediate wave of sympathy. "We must go away somewhere, and lead plain lives among plain people." If Charlotte carried out her threat—and Delia knew she would hardly have spoken unless her resolve had been taken—it might be that at that very moment poor Tina was dancing her last *valse*.

Another quarter of an hour passed; then, just as the cold was finding a way through Delia's shawl, she saw two people turn into the deserted square from Irving Place. One was a young man in opera hat and ample cloak. To his arm clung a figure so closely wrapped and muffled that, until the corner light fell on it, Delia hesitated. After that, she wondered that she had not at once recognized Tina's dancing step, and her manner of tilting her head a little sideways to look up at the person she was talking to.

Tina—Tina and Lanning Halsey, walking home alone in the small hours from the Vandergrave ball! Delia's first thought was of an accident: the carriage might have broken down, or else her daughter been taken ill and obliged to return home. But no; in the latter case she would have sent the carriage on with Tina. And if there had been an accident of any sort the young people would have been hastening to apprise Mrs. Ralston; instead of which, through the bitter brilliant night, they sauntered like lovers in a midsummer glade, and Tina's thin slippers might have been falling on daisies instead of snow.

Delia began to tremble like a girl. In a flash she had the answer to a question which had long been the subject of her secret conjectures. How did lovers like Charlotte and Clement Spender contrive to meet? What Latmian solitude hid their clandestine joys? In the exposed compact little society to which they all belonged, how was it possible—literally—for such encounters to take place? Delia would never have dared to put the question to Charlotte; there were moments when she almost preferred not to know, not even to hazard a guess. But now, at a glance, she understood. How often Charlotte Lovell, staying alone in town with her infirm grandmother, must have walked home from evening parties with Clement Spender, how often have let herself and him into the darkened house in Mercer Street, where there was no one to spy upon their coming but a deaf old lady and her aged servants, all securely sleeping overhead! Delia, at the thought, saw the grim drawing-room which had been their moonlit forest, the drawing-room into which old Mrs. Lovell no longer descended, with its swathed chandelier and hard Empire sofas, and the eyeless marble caryatids of the mantel; she pictured the shaft of moonlight falling across the swans and garlands of the faded carpet, and in that icy light two young figures in each other's arms.

Yes: it must have been some such memory that had roused Charlotte's suspicions, excited her fears, sent her down in the darkness to confront the culprits. Delia shivered at the irony of the confrontation. If Tina had but known! But to Tina, of course, Charlotte was still what she had long since resolved to be: the image of prudish spinsterhood. And Delia could imagine how quietly and decently the scene below stairs would presently be enacted: no astonishment, no reproaches, no insinuations, but a smiling and resolute ignoring of excuses.

"What, Tina? You walked home with Lanning? You imprudent child—in this wet snow! Ah, I see: Delia was worried about the baby, and ran off early, promising to send back the carriage—and it never came? Well, my dear, I congratulate you on finding Lanning to see you home. . . Yes—I sat up because I couldn't for the life of me remember whether you'd taken the latch-key—was there ever such a flighty old aunt? But don't tell your Mamma, dear, or she'd scold me for being so forgetful, and for staying downstairs in the cold. . . You're quite sure you have the key? Ah, Lanning has it? Thank you, Lanning; so kind! Goodnight—or one really ought to say, good morning."

As Delia reached this point in her mute representation of Charlotte's monologue the front door slammed below, and young Lanning Halsey walked slowly away across the square. Delia saw him pause on the opposite pavement, look up at the house-front, and then turn lingeringly away. His dismissal had taken exactly as long as Delia had calculated it would. A moment later she saw a passing light under her door, heard the starched rustle of Charlotte's petticoats, and knew that mother and daughter had reached their rooms.

Slowly, with stiff motions, she began to undress, blew out her candles, and knelt by her bedside, her face hidden.

X

LYING awake till morning, Delia lived over every detail of the fateful day when she had assumed the charge of Charlotte's child. At the time she had been hardly more than a child herself, and there had been no one for her to turn to, no one to fortify her resolution, or to advise her how to put it into effect. Since then, the accumulated experiences of twenty years ought to have prepared her for emergencies, and taught her to advise others instead of seeking their guidance. But these years of experience weighed on her like chains binding her down to her narrow plot of life; independent action struck her as more dangerous, less conceivable, than when she had first ventured on it. There seemed to be so many more people to "consider" now ("consider" was the Ralston word): her children, their children, the families into which they had married. What would the Halseys say, and what the Ralstons? Had she then become a Ralston through and through?

A few hours later she sat in old Dr. Lanskell's library, her eyes on his sooty Smyrna rug. For some years now Dr. Lanskell had no longer practised: at most, he continued to go to a few old patients, and to give consultations in "difficult" cases. But he remained a power in his former kingdom, a sort of lay Pope or medical Elder to whom the patients he had once healed of physical ills often returned for moral medicine. People were agreed that Dr. Lanskell's judgments was sound; but what secretly drew them to him was the fact that, in the most totem-ridden of communities, he was known not to be afraid of anything.

Now, as Delia sat and watched his massive silver-headed figure moving ponderously about the room, between rows of medical books in calf bindings and the Dying Gladiators and Young Augustuses of grateful patients, she already felt the reassurance given by his mere bodily presence.

"You see, when I first took Tina I didn't perhaps consider sufficiently—"

The Doctor halted behind his desk and brought his fist down on it with a genial thump. "Thank goodness you didn't! There are considerers enough in this town without you, Delia Lovell."

She looked up quickly. "Why do you call me Delia Lovell?"

"Well, because today I rather suspect you *are*," he rejoined astutely; and she met this with a wistful laugh.

"Perhaps, if I hadn't been, once before—I mean, if I'd always been a prudent deliberate Ralston it would have been kinder to Tina in the end."

Dr. Lanskell sank his gouty bulk into the armchair behind his desk, and beamed at her through ironic spectacles. "I hate in-the-end kindnesses: they're about as nourishing as the third day of cold mutton."

She pondered. "Of course I realize that if I adopt Tina—"

"Yes?"

"Well, people will say. . ." A deep blush rose to her throat, covered her cheeks and brow, and ran like fire under her decently-parted hair.

He nodded: "Yes."

"Or else—" the blush darkened—"that she's Jim's—"

Again Dr. Lanskell nodded. "That's what they're more likely to think; and what's the harm if they do? I know Jim: he asked you no questions when you took the child —but he knew whose she was."

She raised astonished eyes. "He knew—?"

"Yes: he came to me. And—well—in the baby's interest I violated professional secrecy. That's how Tina got a home. You're not going to denounce me, are you?"

"Oh, Dr. Lanskell—" Her eyes filled with painful tears. "Jim knew? And didn't tell me?"

"No. People didn't tell each other things much in those days, did they? But he admired you enormously for what you did. And if you assume—as I suppose you do—that he's now in a world of completer enlightenment, why not take it for granted that he'll admire you still more for what you're going to do? Presumably," the Doctor concluded sardonically, "people realize in heaven that it's a devilish sight harder, on earth, to do a brave thing at forty-five than at twenty-five."

"Ah, that's what I was thinking this morning," she confessed.

"Well, you're going to prove the contrary this afternoon." He looked at his watch, stood up and laid a fatherly hand on her shoulder. "Let people think what they choose; and send young Delia to me if she gives you any trouble. Your boy won't, you know, nor John Junius either; it must have been a woman who invented that third-and-fourth generation idea . . ."

An elderly maid-servant looked in, and Delia rose; but on the threshold she halted.

"I have an idea it's Charlotte I may have to send to you."

"Charlotte?"

"She'll hate what I'm going to do, you know."

Dr. Lanskell lifted his silver eyebrows. "Yes: poor Charlotte? I suppose she's jealous? That's where the truth of the third-and-fourth generation business comes in, after all. Somebody always has to foot the bill."

"Ah—if only Tina doesn't!"

"Well—that's just what Charlotte will come to recognize in time. So your course is clear."

He guided her out through the dining-room, where some poor people and one or two old patients were already waiting.

Delia's course, in truth, seemed clear enough till, that afternoon, she summoned Charlotte alone to her bedroom. Tina was lying down with a headache: it was in those days the accepted state of young ladies in sentimental dilemmas, and greatly simplified the communion of their elders.

Delia and Charlotte had exchanged only conventional phrases over their midday meal; but Delia still had the sense that her cousin's decision was final. The events of the previous evening had no doubt confirmed Charlotte's view that the time had come for such a decision.

Miss Lovell, closing the bedroom door with her dry

deliberateness, advanced toward the chintz lounge between the windows.

"You wanted to see me, Delia?"

"Yes.—Oh, don't sit there," Mrs. Ralston exclaimed uncontrollably.

Charlotte stared: was it possible that she did not remember the sobs of anguish she had once smothered in those very cushions?

"Not—?"

"No; come nearer to me. Sometimes I think I'm a little deaf," Delia nervously explained, pushing a chair up to her own.

"Ah." Charlotte seated herself. "I hadn't remarked it. But if you are, it may have saved you from hearing at what hour of the morning Tina came back from the Vandergraves' last night. She would never forgive herself —inconsiderate as she is—if she thought she'd waked you."

"She didn't wake me," Delia answered. Inwardly she thought: "Charlotte's mind is made up; I shan't be able to move her."

"I suppose Tina enjoyed herself very much at the ball?" she continued.

"Well, she's paying for it with a headache. Such excitements are not meant for her, I've already told you—"

"Yes," Mrs. Ralston interrupted. "It's to continue our talk of last night that I've asked you to come up."

"To continue it?" The brick-red circles appeared on Charlotte's dried cheeks. "Is it worth while? I think I ought to tell you at once that my mind's made up. I suppose you'll admit that I know what's best for Tina."

"Yes; of course. But won't you at least allow me a share in your decision?"

"A share?"

Delia leaned forward, laying a warm hand on her cousin's interlocked fingers. "Charlotte, once in this room, years ago, you asked me to help you—you believed I could. Won't you believe it again?"

Charlotte's lips grew rigid. "I believe the time has come for me to help myself."

"At the cost of Tina's happiness?"

"No; but to spare her greater unhappiness."

"But, Charlotte, Tina's happiness is all I want."

"Oh, I know. You've done all you could do for my child."

"No; not all." Delia rose, and stood before her cousin with a kind of solemnity. "But now I'm going to." It was as if she had pronounced a vow.

Charlotte Lovell looked up at her with a glitter of apprehension in her hunted eyes.

"If you mean that you're going to use your influence with the Halseys—I'm very grateful to you; I shall always be grateful. But I don't want a compulsory marriage for my child."

Delia flushed at the other's incomprehension. It seemed to her that her tremendous purpose must be written on her face. "I'm going to adopt Tina—give her my name," she announced.

Charlotte Lovell stared at her stonily. "Adopt her—adopt her?"

"Don't you see dear, the difference it will make? There's my mother's money—the Lovell money; it's not much, to be sure; but Jim always wanted it to go back to the Lovells. And my Delia and her brother are so handsomely provided for. There's no reason why my little fortune shouldn't go to Tina. And why she shouldn't be known as Tina Ralston." Delia paused. "I believe—I think I know—that Jim would have approved of that too."

"*Approved?*"

"Yes. Can't you see that when he let me take the child he must have foreseen and accepted whatever—whatever might eventually come of it?"

Charlotte stood up also. "Thank you, Delia. But nothing more must come of it, except our leaving you; our leaving you now. I'm sure that's what Jim would have approved."

Mrs. Ralston drew back a step or two. Charlotte's cold resolution benumbed her courage, and she could find no immediate reply.

"Ah, then it's easier for you to sacrifice Tina's happiness than your pride?" she exclaimed.

"My pride? I've no right to any pride, except in my child. And that I'll never sacrifice."

"No one asks you to. You're not reasonable. You're cruel. All I want is to be allowed to help Tina, and you speak as if I were interfering with your rights."

"My rights?" Charlotte echoed the words with a desolate laugh. "What are they? I have no rights, either before the law or in the heart of my own child."

"How can you say such things? You know how Tina loves you."

"Yes; compassionately—as I used to love my old-maid aunts. There were two of them—you remember? Like withered babies! We children used to be warned never to say anything that might shock Aunt Josie or Aunt Nonie; exactly as I heard you telling Tina the other night—"

"Oh—" Delia murmured.

Charlotte Lovell continued to stand before her, haggard, rigid, unrelenting. "No, it's gone on long enough. I mean to tell her everything; and to take her away."

"To tell her about her birth?"

"I was never ashamed of it," Charlotte panted.

"You do sacrifice her, then—sacrifice her to your desire for mastery?"

The two women faced each other, both with weapons spent. Delia, through the tremor of her own indignation, saw her antagonist slowly waver, step backward, sink down with a broken murmur on the lounge. Charlotte hid her face in the cushions, clenching them with violent hands. The same fierce maternal passion that had once flung her down upon those same cushions was now bowing her still lower, in the throes of a bitterer renunciation. Delia seemed to hear the old cry: "But how can I give up my baby?" Her own momentary resentment melted, and she bent over the mother's labouring shoulders.

"Chatty—it won't be like giving her up this time. Can't we just go on loving her together?"

Charlotte did not answer. For a long time she lay silent, immovable, her face hidden: she seemed to fear to turn it to the face bent down to her. But presently Delia was aware of a gradual relaxing of the stretched muscles, and saw that one of her cousin's arms was faintly stirring and grouping. She lowered her hand to the seeking fingers, and it was caught and pressed to Charlotte's lips.

XI

Tina Lovell—now Miss Clementina Ralston—was to be married in July to Lanning Halsey. The engagement had been announced only in the previous April; and the female elders of the tribe had begun by crying out against the indelicacy of so brief a betrothal. It was unanimously agreed in the New York of those times that "young people should be given the chance to get to know each other"; though the greater number of the couples constituting New York society had played together as children, and been born of parents as long and as familiarly acquainted, yet some mysterious law of decorum required that the newly affianced should always be regarded as being also newly known to each other. In the southern states things were differently conducted: headlong engagements, even runaway marriages, were not uncommon in their annals; but such rashness was less consonant with the sluggish blood of New York, where the pace of life was still set with a Dutch deliberateness.

In a case as unusual as Tina Ralston's, however, it was no great surprise to any one that tradition should have been disregarded. In the first place, everybody knew that she was no more Tina Ralston than you or I; unless, indeed, one were to credit the rumours about poor Jim's unsuspected "past," and his widow's magnanimity. But the opinion of the majority was against this. People were reluctant to charge a dead man with an offense from which he could not clear himself; and the Ralstons unanimously declared that, thoroughly as they disapproved of Mrs. James Ralston's action, they were convinced that she would not have adopted Tina if her doing so could have been construed as "casting a slur" on her late husband.

No: the girl was perhaps a Lovell—though even that idea was not generally held—but she was certainly not a Ralston. Her brown eyes and flighty ways too obviously excluded her from the clan for any formal excommunication to be needful. In fact, most people believed that—as Dr. Lanskell had always affirmed—her origin was really undiscoverable, that she represented one of the unsolved mysteries which occasionally perplex and irritate well-regulated societies, and that her adoption by Delia Ralston was simply one more proof of the Lovell clannishness, since the child had been taken in by Mrs. Ralston only because her cousin Charlotte was so attached to it. To say that Mrs. Ralston's son and daughter were pleased with the idea of Tina's adoption would be an exaggeration; but they abstained from comment, minimizing the effect of their mother's whim by a dignified silence. It was the old New York way for families thus to screen the eccentricities of an individual member, and where there was "money enough to go round" the heirs would have been thought vulgarly grasping to protest at the alienation of a small sum from the general inheritance.

Nevertheless, Delia Ralston, from the moment of Tina's adoption, was perfectly aware of a different attitude on the part of both her children. They dealt with her patiently, almost parentally, as with a minor in whom one

juvenile lapse has been condoned, but who must be sub-
jected, in consequence, to a stricter vigilance; and society
treated her in the same indulgent but guarded manner.

She had (it was Sillerton Jackson who first phrased it)
an undoubted way of "carrying things off"; since that
dauntless woman, Mrs. Manson Mingott, had broken her
husband's will, nothing so like her attitude had been seen
in New York. But Mrs. Ralston's method was different,
and less easy to analyze. What Mrs. Manson Mingott had
accomplished by dint of epigram, invective, insistency and
runnings to and fro, the other achieved without raising
her voice or seeming to take a step from the beaten path.
When she had persuaded Jim Ralston to take in the
foundling baby, it had been done in the turn of a hand,
one didn't know when or how; and the next day he and
she were as untroubled and beaming as usual. And now,
this adoption—! Well, she had pursued the same method;
as Sillerton Jackson said, she behaved as if her adopting
Tina had always been an understood thing, as if she
wondered that people should wonder. And in face of her
wonder theirs seemed foolish, and they gradually desisted.

In reality, behind Delia's assurance there was a tumult
of doubts and uncertainties. But she had once learned
that one can do almost anything (perhaps even murder)
if one does not attempt to explain it; and the lesson had
never been forgotten. She had never explained the taking
over of the foundling baby; nor was she now going to
explain its adoption. She was just going about her business as if nothing had happened that needed to be accounted for; and a long inheritance of moral modesty
helped her to keep her questionings to herself.

These questionings were in fact less concerned with

public opinion than with Charlotte Lovell's private thoughts. Charlotte, after her first moment of tragic resistance, had shown herself pathetically, almost painfully, grateful. That she had reason to be, Tina's attitude abundantly revealed. Tina, during the first days after her return from the Vandergrave ball, had shown a closed and darkened face that terribly reminded Delia of the ghastliness of Charlotte Lovell's sudden reflection, years before, in Delia's own bedroom mirror. The first chapter of the mother's history was already written in the daughter's eyes; and the Spender blood in Tina might well precipitate the sequence. During those few days of silent observation Delia discovered, with terror and compassion, the justification of Charlotte's fears. The girl had nearly been lost to them both: at all costs such a risk must not be renewed.

The Halseys, on the whole, had behaved admirably. Lanning wished to marry dear Delia Ralston's protégée— who was shortly, it was understood, to take her adopted mother's name, and inherit her fortune. To what better could a Halsey aspire than one more alliance with a Ralston? The families had always intermarried. The Halsey parents gave their blessing with a precipitation which showed that they too had their anxieties, and that the relief of seeing Lanning "settled" would more than compensate for the conceivable drawbacks of the marriage; though, once it was decided on, they would not admit even to themselves that such drawbacks existed. Old New York always thought away whatever interfered with the perfect propriety of its arrangements.

Charlotte Lovell of course perceived and recognized all this. She accepted the situation—in her private hours with

Delia—as one more in the long list of mercies bestowed on an undeserving sinner. And one phrase of hers perhaps gave the clue to her acceptance: "Now at least she'll never suspect the truth." It had come to be the poor creature's ruling purpose that her child should never guess the tie between them . . .

But Delia's chief support was the sight of Tina. The older woman, whose whole life had been shaped and coloured by the faint reflection of a rejected happiness, hung dazzled in the light of bliss accepted. Sometimes, as she watched Tina's changing face, she felt as though her own blood were beating in it, as though she could read every thought and emotion feeding those tumultuous currents. Tina's love was a stormy affair, with continual ups and downs of rapture and depression, arrogance and self-abasement; Delia saw displayed before her, with an artless frankness, all the visions, cravings and imaginings of her own stifled youth.

What the girl really thought of her adoption it was not easy to discover. She had been given, at fourteen, the current version of her origin, and had accepted it as carelessly as a happy child accepts some remote and inconceivable fact which does not alter the familiar order of things. And she accepted her adoption in the same spirit. She knew that the name of Ralston had been given to her to facilitate her marriage with Lanning Halsey; and Delia had the impression that all irrelevant questionings were submerged in an overwhelming gratitude. "I've always thought of you as my Mamma; and now, you dearest, you really are," Tina had whispered, her cheek against Delia's; and Delia had laughed back: "Well, if the lawyers can make me so!" But there the matter dropped, swept away on the current of Tina's bliss. They were all, in those days, Delia, Charlotte, even the gallant Lanning, rather like straws whirling about on a sunlit torrent.

The golden flood bore them onward, nearer and nearer to the enchanted date; and Delia, deep in bridal preparations, wondered at the comparative indifference with which she had ordered and inspected her own daughter's twelve-dozen-of-everything. There had been nothing to quicken the pulse in young Delia's placid bridal; but as Tina's wedding approached imagination burgeoned like the year. The wedding was to be celebrated at Lovell Place, the old house on the Sound where Delia Lovell had herself been married, and where, since her mother's death, she spent her summers. Although the neighbourhood was already overspread with a net-work of mean streets, the old house, with its thin colonnaded verandah, still looked across an uncurtailed lawn and leafy shrubberies to the narrows of Hell Gate; and the drawing-rooms kept their frail slender settees, their Sheraton consoles and cabinets. It had been thought useless to discard them for more fashionable furniture, since the growth of the city made it certain that the place must eventually be sold.

Tina, like Mrs. Ralston, was to have a "house-wedding," though Episcopalian society was beginning to disapprove of such ceremonies, which were regarded as the despised *pis-aller* of Baptists, Methodists, Unitarians and the other altarless sects. In Tina's case, however, both Delia and Charlotte felt that the greater privacy of a marriage in the house made up for its more secular character; and the Halseys favoured their decision. The ladies accordingly settled themselves at Lovell Place before the end of June, and every morning young Lanning Halsey's catboat was seen beating across the bay, and furling its sail at the anchorage below the lawn.

There had never been a fairer June in any one's memory. The damask roses and mignonette below the verandah had never sent such a breath of summer through the tall French windows; the gnarled orange-trees brought out from the old arcaded orange-house had never been so thickly blossomed; the very haycocks on the lawn gave out whiffs of Araby.

The evening before the wedding Delia Ralston sat on the verandah watching the moon rise across the Sound. She was tired with the multitude of last preparations, and sad at the thought of Tina's going. On the following evening the house would be empty: till death came, she and Charlotte would sit alone together beside the evening lamp. Such repinings were foolish—they were, she reminded herself, "not like her." But too many memories stirred and murmured in her: her heart was haunted. As she closed the door on the silent drawing-room—already transformed into a chapel, with its lace-hung altar, the tall alabaster vases awaiting their white roses and June lilies, the strip of red carpet dividing the rows of chairs from door to chancel—she felt that it had perhaps been a mistake to come back to Lovell Place for the wedding. She saw herself again, in her high-waisted "India mull" embroidered with daisies, her flat satin sandals, her Brussels veil—saw again her reflection in the shallow pier-glass as she had left that same room on Jim Ralston's triumphant arm, and the one terrified glance she had exchanged with her own image before she took her stand under the bell of white roses in the hall, and smiled upon the congratulating company. Ah, what a different image the pier-glass would reflect tomorrow!

Charlotte Lovell's brisk step sounded indoors, and she came out and joined Mrs. Ralston.

"I've been to the kitchen to tell Melissa Grimes that she'd better count on at least two hundred plates of ice-cream."

"Two hundred? Yes—I suppose she had, with all the Philadelphia connection coming." Delia pondered. "How about the doylies?" she enquired.

"With your aunt Cecilia Vandergrave's we shall manage beautifully."

"Yes.—Thank you, Charlotte, for taking all this trouble."

"Oh—" Charlotte protested, with her flitting sneer; and Delia perceived the irony of thanking a mother for oc-cupying herself with the details of her own daughter's wedding.

"Do sit down, Chatty," she murmured, feeling herself redden at her blunder.

Charlotte, with a sigh of fatigue, sat down on the nearest chair.

"We shall have a beautiful day tomorrow," she said, pensively surveying the placid heaven.

"Yes. Where is Tina?"

"She was very tired. I've sent her upstairs to lie down."

This seemed so eminently suitable that Delia made no immediate answer. After an interval she said: "We shall miss her."

Charlotte's reply was an inarticulate murmur.

The two cousins remained silent, Charlotte as usual bolt upright, her thin hands clutched on the arms of her old-fashioned rush-bottomed seat, Delia somewhat heavily sunk into the depths of a high-backed armchair. The two had exchanged their last remarks on the preparations for the morrow; nothing more remained to be said as to the number of guests, the brewing of the punch, the arrangements for the robing of the clergy, and the disposal of the presents in the best spare-room.

Only one subject had not yet been touched upon, and Delia, as she watched her cousin's profile grimly cut upon the melting twilight, waited for Charlotte to speak. But Charlotte remained silent.

"I have been thinking," Delia at length began, a slight tremor in her voice, "that I ought presently—"

She fancied she saw Charlotte's hands tighten on the knobs of the chair-arms.

"You ought presently—?"

"Well, before Tina goes to bed, perhaps go up for a few minutes—"

Charlotte remained silent, visibly resolved on making no effort to assist her.

"Tomorrow," Delia continued, "we shall be in such a rush from the earliest moment that I don't see how, in the midst of all the interruptions and excitement, I can possibly—"

"Possibly?" Charlotte monotonously echoed.

Delia felt her blush deepening through the dusk. "Well, I suppose you agree with me, don't you, that a word ought to be said to the child as to the new duties and responsibilities that—well—what is usual, in fact, at such a time?" she falteringly ended.

"Yes, I have thought of that," Charlotte answered. She said no more, but Delia divined in her tone the stirring of that obscure opposition which, at the crucial moments of Tina's life, seemed automatically to declare itself. She could not understand why Charlotte should, at such times, grow so enigmatic and inaccessible, and in the present case she saw no reason why this change of mood should interfere with what she deemed to be her own duty. Tina must long for her guiding hand into the new life as much as she herself yearned for the exchange of half-confidences which would be her real farewell to her adopted daughter. Her heart beating a little more quickly than usual, she rose and walked through the open window into the shadowy drawing-room. The moon, between the columns of the verandah, sent a broad band of light across the rows of chairs, irradiated the lace-decked altar with its empty candlesticks and vases, and outlined with silver Delia's heavy reflection in the pier-glass.

She crossed the room toward the hall.

"Delia!" Charlotte's voice sounded behind her. Delia turned, and the two women scrutinized each other in the revealing light. Charlotte's face looked as it had looked on the dreadful day when Delia had suddenly seen it in the looking-glass above her shoulder.

"You were going up now to speak to Tina?" Charlotte asked.

"I—yes. It's nearly nine. I thought . . ."

"Yes; I understand." Miss Lovell made a visible effort at self-control. "Please understand me too, Delia, if I ask you—not to."

Delia looked at her cousin with a vague sense of apprehension. What new mystery did this strange request conceal? But no—such a doubt as flitted across her mind was inadmissible. She was too sure of her Tina!

"I confess I don't understand, Charlotte. You surely feel that, on the night before her wedding, a girl ought to have a mother's counsel, a mother's . . ."

"Yes; I feel that." Charlotte Lovell took a hurried breath. "But the question is: *which of us is her mother?*"

Delia drew back involuntarily. "Which of us—?" she stammered.

"Yes. Oh, don't imagine it's the first time I've asked myself the question! There—I mean to be calm; quite calm. I don't intend to go back to the past. I've accepted —accepted everything—gratefully. Only tonight—just tonight . . ."

Delia felt the rush of pity which always prevailed over every other sensation in her rare interchanges of truth with Charlotte Lovell. Her throat filled with tears, and she remained silent.

"Just tonight," Charlotte concluded, "*I'm* her mother."

"Charlotte! You're not going to tell her so—not now?" broke involuntarily from Delia.

Charlotte gave a faint laugh. "If I did, should you hate it as much as all that?"

"Hate it? What a word, between us!"

"Between us? But it's the word that's been between us since the beginning—the very beginning! Since the day when you discovered that Clement Spender hadn't quite broken his heart because he wasn't good enough for you; since you found your revenge and your triumph in keeping me at your mercy, and in taking his child from me!" Charlotte's words flamed up as if from the depth of the infernal fires; then the blaze dropped, her head sank forward, and she stood before Delia dumb and stricken.

Delia's first movement was one of an indignant recoil.

Where she had felt only tenderness, compassion, the impulse to help and befriend, these darknesses had been smouldering in the other's breast! It was as if a poisonous smoke had swept over some pure summer landscape. . .

Usually such feelings were quickly followed by a reaction of sympathy. But now she felt none. An utter weariness possessed her.

"Yes," she said slowly, "I sometimes believe you really have hated me from the very first; hated me for everything I've tried to do for you."

Charlotte raised her head sharply. "To do for me? But everything you've done has been done for Clement Spender!"

Delia stared at her with a kind of terror. "You are horrible, Charlotte. Upon my honour, I haven't thought of Clement Spender for years."

"Ah, but you have—you have! You've always thought of him in thinking of Tina—of him and nobody else! A woman never stops thinking of the man she loves. She thinks of him years afterward, in all sorts of unconscious ways, in thinking of all sorts of things—books, pictures, sunsets, a flower or a ribbon—or a clock on the mantelpiece," Charlotte broke off with her sneering laugh. "That was what I gambled on, you see—that's why I came to you that day. I knew I was giving Tina another mother."

Again the poisonous smoke seemed to envelop Delia: that she and Charlotte, two spent old women, should be standing before Tina's bridal altar and talking to each other of hatred, seemed unimaginably hideous and degrading.

"You wicked woman—you *are* wicked!" she exclaimed.

Then the evil mist cleared away, and through it she saw

the baffled pitiful figure of the mother who was not a mother, and who, for every benefit accepted, felt herself robbed of a privilege. She moved nearer to Charlotte and laid a hand on her arm.

"Not here! Don't let us talk like this here."

The other drew away from her. "Wherever you please, then. I'm not particular!"

"But tonight, Charlotte—the night before Tina's wedding? Isn't every place in this house full of her? How could we go on saying cruel things to each other anywhere?" Charlotte was silent, and Delia continued in a steadier voice: "Nothing you say can really hurt me—for long; and I don't want to hurt you—I never did."

"You tell me that—and you've left nothing undone to divide me from my daughter! Do you suppose it's been easy, all these years, to hear her call you 'mother'? Oh, I know, I know—it was agreed that she must never guess . . . but if you hadn't perpetually come between us she'd have had no one but me, she'd have felt about me as a child feels about its mother, she'd have *had* to love me better than any one else. With all your forbearances and your generosities you've ended by robbing me of my child. And I've put up with it all for her sake—because I knew I had to. But tonight—tonight she belongs to me. Tonight I can't bear that she should call you 'mother'."

Delia Ralston made no immediate reply. It seemed to her that for the first time she had sounded the deepest depths of maternal passion, and she stood awed of the echoes it gave back.

"How you must love her—to say such things to me," she murmured; then, with a final effort: "Yes, you're right. I won't go up to her. It's you who must go."

Charlotte started toward her impulsively; but with a hand lifted as if in defense, Delia moved across the room and out again to the verandah. As she sank down in her chair she heard the drawing-room door open and close, and the sound of Charlotte's feet on the stairs.

Delia sat alone in the night. The last drop of her magnanimity had been spent, and she tried to avert her shuddering mind from Charlotte. What was happening at this moment upstairs? With what dark revelations were Tina's bridal dreams to be defaced? Well, that was not matter for conjecture either. She, Delia Ralston, had played her part, done her utmost: there remained nothing now but to try to lift her spirit above the embittering sense of failure.

There was a strange element of truth in some of the things that Charlotte had said. With what divination her maternal passion had endowed her! Her jealousy seemed to have a million feelers. Yes; it was true that the sweetness and peace of Tina's bridal eve had been filled, for Delia, with visions of her own unrealized past. Softly, imperceptibly, it had reconciled her to the memory of what she had missed. All these last days she had been living the girl's life, she had been Tina, and Tina had been her own girlish self, the far-off Delia Lovell. Now for the first time, without shame, without self-reproach, without a pang or a scruple, Delia could yield to that vision of requited love from which her imagination had always turned away. She had made her choice in youth, and she had accepted it in maturity; and here in this bridal joy, so mysteriously her own, was the compensation for all she had missed and yet never renounced.

Delia understood now that Charlotte had guessed all this, and that the knowledge had filled her with a fierce resentment. Charlotte had said long ago that Clement Spender had never really belonged to her; now she had perceived that it was the same with Clement Spender's child. As the truth stole upon Delia her heart melted with the old compassion for Charlotte. She saw that it was a terrible, a sacrilegious thing to interfere with another's destiny, to lay the tenderest touch upon any human being's right to love and suffer after his own fashion. Delia had twice intervened in Charlotte Lovell's life: it was natural that Charlotte should be her enemy. If only she did not revenge herself by wounding Tina!

The adopted mother's thoughts reverted painfully to the little white room upstairs. She had meant her half-hour with Tina to leave the girl with thoughts as fragrant as the flowers she was to find beside her when she woke. And now—.

Delia started up from her musing. There was a step on the stair—Charlotte coming down through the silent house. Delia rose with a vague impulse of escape: she felt that she could not face her cousin's eyes. She turned the corner of the verandah, hoping to find the shutters of the dining-room unlatched, and to slip away unnoticed to her room; but in a moment Charlotte was beside her.

"Delia!"

"Ah, it's you? I was going up to bed." For the life of her Delia could not keep an edge of hardness from her voice.

"Yes: it's late. You must be very tired." Charlotte paused; her own voice was strained and painful.

"I *am* tired," Delia acknowledged.

In the moonlit hush the other went up to her, laying a timid touch on her arm.

"Not till you've seen Tina."

Delia stiffened. "Tina? But it's late! Isn't she sleeping? I thought you'd stay with her until—"

"I don't know if she's sleeping," Charlotte paused. "I haven't been in—but there's a light under her door."

"You haven't been in?"

"No: I just stood in the passage, and tried—"

"Tried—?"

"To think of something . . . something to say to her without . . . without her guessing. . ." A sob stopped her, but she pressed on with a final effort. "It's no use. You were right: there's nothing I can say. You're her real mother. Go to her. It's not your fault—or mine."

"Oh—" Delia cried.

Charlotte clung to her in inarticulate abasement. "You said I was wicked—I'm not wicked. After all, she was mine when she was little!"

Delia put an arm about her shoulder.

"Hush, dear! We'll go to her together."

The other yielded automatically to her touch, and side by side the two women mounted the stairs, Charlotte timing her impetuous step to Delia's stiffened movements. They walked down the passage to Tina's door; but there Charlotte Lovell paused and shook her head.

"No—you," she whispered, and turned away.

Tina lay in bed, her arms folded under her head, her happy eyes reflecting the silver space of sky which filled the window. She smiled at Delia through her dream.

"I knew you'd come."

Delia sat down beside her, and their clasped hands lay down upon the coverlet. They did not say much, after all; or else their communion had no need of words. Delia never knew how long she sat by the child's side: she abandoned herself to the spell of the moonlit hour.

But suddenly she though of Charlotte, alone behind the shut door of her own room, watching, struggling, listening. Delia must not, for her own pleasure, prolong that tragic vigil. She bent down to kiss Tina goodnight; then she paused on the threshold and turned back.

"Darling! Just one thing more."

"Yes?" Tina murmured through her dream.

"I want you to promise me—"

"Everything, everything, you darling mother!"

"Well, then, that when you go away tomorrow—at the very last moment, you understand—"

"Yes?"

"After you've said goodbye to me, and to everybody else—just as Lanning helps you into the carriage—"

"Yes?"

"That you'll give your last kiss to Aunt Charlotte. Don't forget—the very last."

THE SPARK

(The 'Sixties)

I

"You idiot!" said his wife, and threw down her cards.

I turned my head away quickly, to avoid seeing Hayley Delane's face; though why I wished to avoid it I could not have told you, much less why I should have imagined (if I did) that a man of his age and importance would notice what was happening to the wholly negligible features of a youth like myself.

I turned away so that he should not see how it hurt me to hear him called an idiot, even in joke—well, at least half in joke; yet I often thought him an idiot myself, and bad as my own poker was, I knew enough of the game to judge that his—when he wasn't attending—fully justified such an outburst from his wife. Why her sally disturbed me I couldn't have said; nor why, when it was greeted by a shrill guffaw from her "latest," young Bolton Byrne, I itched to cuff the little bounder; nor why, when Hayley Delane, on whom banter always dawned slowly but certainly, at length gave forth his low rich gurgle of appreciation—why then, most of all, I wanted to blot the whole scene from my memory. Why?

There they sat, as I had so often seen them, in Jack Alstrop's luxurious bookless library (I'm sure the rich rows behind the glass doors were hollow), while beyond the windows the pale twilight thickened to blue over Long Island lawns and woods and a moonlit streak of sea.

No one ever looked out at *that*, except to conjecture what sort of weather there would be the next day for polo, or hunting, or racing, or whatever use the season required the face of nature to be put to; no one was aware of the twilight, the moon or the blue shadows—and Hayley Delane least of all. Day after day, night after night, he sat anchored at somebody's poker-table, and fumbled absently with his cards. . .

Yes; that was the man. He didn't even (as it was once said of a great authority on heraldry) know his own silly business; which was to hang about in his wife's train, play poker with her friends, and giggle at her nonsense and theirs. No wonder Mrs. Delane was sometimes exasperated. As she said, *she* hadn't asked him to marry her! Rather not: all their contemporaries could remember what a thunderbolt it had been on his side. The first time he had seen her—at the theatre, I think: "Who's that? Over there—with the heaps of hair?"— "Oh, Leila Gracy? Why, she's not *really* pretty. . ." "Well, I'm going to marry her—" "Marry her? But her father's that old scoundrel Bill Gracy . . . the one. . ." "I'm going to marry her. . ." "The one who's had to resign from all his clubs. . ." "I'm going to marry her. . ." And he did; and it was she, if you please, who kept him dangling, and who would and who wouldn't, until some whipper-snapper of a youth, who was meanwhile making up his mind about *her*, had finally decided in the negative.

Such had been Hayley Delane's marriage; and such, I imagined, his way of conducting most of the transactions of his futile clumsy life. . . Big bursts of impulse—storms he couldn't control—then long periods of drowsing calm, during which, something made me feel, old regrets and remorses woke and stirred under the indolent surface of his nature. And yet, wasn't I simply romanticizing a commonplace case? I turned back from the window to look at the group. The bringing of candles to the card-tables had scattered pools of illumination throughout the shadowy room; in their radiance Delane's harsh head stood out like a cliff from a flowery plain. Perhaps it was only his bigness, his heaviness and swarthiness—perhaps his greater age, for he must have been at least fifteen years older than his wife and most of her friends; at any rate, I could never look at him without feeling that he belonged elsewhere, not so much in another society as in another age. For there was no doubt that the society he lived in suited him well enough. He shared cheerfully in all the amusements of his little set—rode, played polo, hunted and drove his four-in-hand with the best of them (you will see, by the last allusion, that we were still in the archaic 'nineties). Nor could I guess what other occupations he would have preferred, had he been given his choice. In spite of my admiration for him I could not bring myself to think it was Leila Gracy who had subdued him to what she worked in. What would he have chosen to do if he had not met her that night at the play? Why, I rather thought, to meet and marry somebody else just like her. No; the difference in him was not in his tastes—it was in something ever so much deeper. Yet what is deeper in a man than his tastes?

In another age, then, he would probably have been doing the equivalent of what he was doing now: idling, taking much violent exercise, eating more than was good for him, laughing at the same kind of nonsense, and worshipping, with the same kind of dull routine-worship,

the same kind of woman, whether dressed in a crinoline,
a farthingale, a peplum or the skins of beasts—it didn't
much matter under what sumptuary dispensation one
placed her. Only in that other age there might have been
outlets for other faculties, now dormant, perhaps even
atrophied, but which must—yes, really must—have had
something to do with the building of that big friendly
forehead, the monumental nose, and the rich dimple which
now and then furrowed his cheek with light. Did the
dimple even mean no more than Leila Gracy?

Well, perhaps it was *I* who was the idiot, if she'd only
known it; an idiot to believe in her husband, be obsessed
by him, oppressed by him, when, for thirty years now,
he'd been only the Hayley Delane whom everybody took
for granted, and was glad to see, and immediately forgot.
Turning from my contemplation of that great structural
head, I looked at his wife. Her head was still like something in the making, something just flowering, a girl's
head ringed with haze. Even the kindly candles betrayed
the lines in her face, the paint on her lips, the peroxide
on her hair; but they could not lessen her fluidity of outline, or the girlishness that lurked in her eyes, floating up
from their depths like a startled Naïad. There was an ir-
reducible innocence about her, as there so often is about
women who have spent their time in amassing sentimental
experiences. As I looked at the husband and wife, thus
confronted above the cards, I marvelled more and more
that it was she who ruled and he who bent the neck. You
will see by this how young I still was.

So young, indeed, that Hayley Delane had dawned on
me in my school-days as an accomplished fact, a finished
monument: like Trinity Church, the Reservoir or the

Knickerbocker Club. A New Yorker of my generation could no more imagine him altered or away than any of those venerable institutions. And so I had continued to take him for granted till, my Harvard days over, I had come back after an interval of world-wandering to settle down in New York, and he had broken on me afresh as something still not wholly accounted for, and more interesting than I had suspected.

I don't say the matter kept me awake. I had my own business (in a down-town office), and the pleasures of my age; I was hard at work discovering New York. But now and then the Hayley Delane riddle would thrust itself between me and my other interests, as it had done tonight just because his wife had sneered at him, and he had laughed and thought her funny. And at such times I found myself moved and excited out of all proportion to anything I knew about him, or had observed in him, to justify such emotions.

The game was over, the dressing-bell had rung. It rang again presently, with a discreet insistence: Alstrop, easy in all else, preferred that his guests should not be more than half an hour late for dinner.

"I say—*Leila!*" he finally remonstrated.

The golden coils drooped above her chips. "Yes—yes. Just a minute. Hayley, you'll have to pay for me.— There, I'm going!" She laughed and pushed back her chair.

Delane, laughing also, got up lazily. Byrne flew to open the door for Mrs. Delane; the other women trooped out with her. Delane, having settled her debts, picked up her gold-mesh bag and cigarette-case, and followed.

I turned toward a window opening on the lawn. There was just time to stretch my legs while curling-tongs and powder were being plied above stairs. Alstrop joined me, and we stood staring up at a soft dishevelled sky in which the first stars came and went.

"Curse it—looks rotten for our match tomorrow!"

"Yes—but what a good smell the coming rain does give to things!"

He laughed. "You're an optimist—like old Hayley."

We strolled across the lawn toward the woodland.

"Why like old Hayley?"

"Oh, he's a regular philosopher. I've never seen him put out, have you?"

"No. That must be what makes him look so sad," I exclaimed.

"Sad? Hayley? Why, I was just saying—"

"Yes, I know. But the only people who are never put out are the people who don't care; and not caring is about the saddest occupation there is. I'd like to see him in a rage just once."

My host gave a faint whistle, and remarked: "By Jove, I believe the wind's hauling round to the north. If it does—" He moistened his finger and held it up.

I knew there was no use in theorizing with Alstrop; but I tried another tack. "What on earth has Delane done with himself all these years?" I asked. Alstrop was forty, or thereabouts, and by a good many years better able than I to cast a backward glance over the problem.

But the effort seemed·beyond him "Why—what years?"

"Well—ever since he left college."

"Lord! How do I know? I wasn't there. Hayley must be well past fifty."

It sounded formidable to my youth; almost like a geological era. And that suited him, in a way—I could imagine him drifting, or silting, or something measurable by aeons, at the rate of about a millimetre a century.

"How long has he been married?" I asked.

"I don't know that either; nearly twenty years, I should say. The kids are growing up. The boys are both at Groton. Leila doesn't look it, I must say—not in some lights."

"Well, then, what's he been doing since he married?"

"Why, what should he have done? He's always had money enough to do what he likes. He's got his partnership in the bank, of course. They say that rascally old father-in-law, whom he refuses to see, gets a good deal of money out of him. You know he's awfully soft-hearted. But he can swing it all, I fancy. Then he sits on lots of boards —Blind Asylum, Children's Aid, S.P.C.A., and all the rest. And there isn't a better sport going."

"But that's not what I mean," I persisted.

Alstrop looked at me through the darkness. "You don't mean women? I never heard—but then one wouldn't, very likely. He's a shut-up fellow."

We turned back to dress for dinner. Yes, that was the word I wanted; he was a shut-up fellow. Even the rudimentary Alstrop felt it. But shut-up consciously, deliberately—or only instinctively, congenitally? There the mystery lay.

II

THE big polo match came off the next day. It was the first of the season, and, taking respectful note of the fact, the barometer, after a night of showers, jumped back to Fair.

All Fifth Avenue had poured down to see New York versus Hempstead. The beautifully rolled lawns and freshly painted club stand were sprinkled with spring dresses and abloom with sunshades, and coaches and other vehicles without number enclosed the farther side of the field.

Hayley Delane still played polo, though he had grown so heavy that the cost of providing himself with mounts must have been considerable. He was, of course, no longer regarded as in the first rank; indeed, in these later days, when the game has become an exact science, I hardly know to what use such a weighty body as his could be put. But in that far-off dawn of the sport his sureness and swiftness of stroke caused him to be still regarded as a useful back, besides being esteemed for the part he had taken in introducing and establishing the game.

I remember little of the beginning of the game, which resembled many others I had seen. I never played myself, and I had no money on: for me the principal interest of the scene lay in the May weather, the ripple of spring dresses over the turf, the sense of youth, fun, gaiety, of young manhood and womanhood weaving their eternal pattern under the conniving sky. Now and then they were interrupted for a moment by a quick "Oh" which turned all those tangled glances the same way, as two glittering streaks of men and horses dashed across the green, locked, swayed, rayed outward into starry figures, and rolled back. But it was for a moment only—then eyes wandered again, chatter began, and youth and sex had it their own way till the next charge shook them from their trance.

I was of the number of these divided watchers. Polo as a spectacle did not amuse me for long, and I saw about as little of it as the pretty girls perched beside their swains on coach-tops and club stand. But by chance my vague wanderings brought me to the white palings enclosing the field, and there, in a cluster of spectators, I caught sight of Leila Delane.

As I approached I was surprised to notice a familiar figure shouldering away from her. One still saw old Bill Gracy often enough in the outer purlieus of the big race-courses; but I wondered how he had got into the en-closure of a fashionable Polo Club. There he was, though, unmistakably; who could forget that swelling chest under the shabby-smart racing-coat, the gray top-hat always pushed back from his thin auburn curls, and the mixture of furtiveness and swagger which made his liquid glance so pitiful? Among the figures that rose here and there like warning ruins from the dead-level of old New York's re-spectability, none was more typical than Bill Gracy's; my gaze followed him curiously as he shuffled away from his daughter. "Trying to get more money out of her," I con-cluded; and remembered what Alstrop had said of De-lane's generosity.

"Well, if I were Delane," I thought, "I'd pay a good deal to keep that old ruffian out of sight."

Mrs. Delane, turning to watch her father's retreat, saw me and nodded. At the same moment Delane, on a tall deep-chested pony, ambled across the field, stick on shoulder. As he rode thus, heavily yet mightily, in his red-and-black shirt and white breeches, his head standing out like a bronze against the turf, I whimsically recalled the figure of Guidoriccio da Foligno, the famous mercenary, riding at a slow powerful pace across the fortressed fresco of the Town Hall of Siena. Why a New York banker of excessive weight and more than middle age, jogging on a pony across a Long Island polo field, should have reminded me of a martial figure on an armoured war-horse, I find it hard to explain. As far as I knew there were no turreted fortresses in Delane's background; and his too juvenile polo cap and gaudy shirt were a poor substitute for Guidoriccio's coat of mail. But it was the kind of trick the man was always playing: reminding me, in his lazy torpid way, of times and scenes and people greater than he could know. That was why he kept on interesting me.

It was this interest which caused me to pause by Mrs. Delane, whom I generally avoided. After a vague smile she had already turned her gaze on the field.

"You're admiring your husband?" I suggested, as Delane's trot carried him across our line of vision.

She glanced at me dubiously. "You think he's too fat to play, I suppose?" she retorted, a little snappishly.

"I think he's the finest figure in sight. He looks like a great general, a great soldier of fortune—in an old fresco, I mean."

She stared, perhaps suspecting irony, as she always did beneath the unintelligible.

"Ah, *he* can pay anything he likes for his mounts!" she murmured; and added, with a wandering laugh: "Do you mean it as a compliment? Shall I tell him what you say?"

"I wish you would."

But her eyes were off again, this time to the opposite end of the field. Of course—Bolton Byrne was playing on the other side! The fool of a woman was always like that —absorbed in her latest adventure. Yet there had been so many, and she must by this time have been so radiantly sure there would be more! But at every one the girl was born anew in her: she blushed, palpitated, "sat out" dances, plotted for tête-à-têtes, pressed flowers (I'll wager) in her copy of "Omar Khayyám," and was all white muslin and wild roses while it lasted. And the Byrne fever was then at its height.

It did not seem polite to leave her immediately, and I continued to watch the field at her side. "It's their last chance to score," she flung at me, leaving me to apply the ambiguous pronoun; and after that we remained silent.

The game had been a close one; the two sides were five each, and the crowd about the rails hung breathless on the last minutes. The struggle was short and swift, and dramatic enough to hold even the philanderers on the coachtops. Once I stole a glance at Mrs. Delane, and saw the colour rush to her cheek. Byrne was hurling himself across the field, crouched on the neck of his somewhat weedy mount, his stick swung like a lance—a pretty enough sight, for he was young and supple, and light in the saddle.

"They're going to win!" she gasped with a happy cry.

But just then Byrne's pony, unequal to the pace stumbled, faltered, and came down. His rider dropped from the saddle, hauled the animal to his feet, and stood for a minute half-dazed before he scrambled up again. That minute made the difference. It gave the other side their chance. The knot of men and horses tightened, wavered, grew loose, broke up in arrowing flights; and suddenly a ball—Delane's—sped through the enemy's goal, victorious. A roar of delight went up; "Good for old Hayley!" voices shouted. Mrs. Delane gave a little sour laugh. "That—that beastly pony; I warned him it was no good—and the ground still so slippery," she broke out.

"The pony? Why, he's a ripper. It's not every mount that will carry Delane's weight," I said. She stared at me unseeingly and turned away with twitching lips. I saw her speeding off toward the enclosure.

I followed hastily, wanting to see Delane in the moment of his triumph. I knew he took all these little sporting successes with an absurd seriousness, as if, mysteriously, they were the shadow of more substantial achievements, dreamed of, or accomplished, in some previous life. And perhaps the elderly man's vanity in holding his own with the youngsters was also an element of his satisfaction; how could one tell, in a mind of such monumental simplicity?

When I reached the saddling enclosure I did not at once discover him; an unpleasant sight met my eyes instead. Bolton Byrne, livid and withered—his face like an old woman's, I thought—rode across the empty field, angrily lashing his pony's flanks. He slipped to the ground, and as he did so, struck the shivering animal a last blow clean across the head. An unpleasant sight—

But retribution fell. It came like a black-and-red thunderbolt descending on the wretch out of the heaven. Delane had him by the collar, had struck him with his whip across the shoulders, and then flung him off like a thing too mean for human handling. It was over in the taking of a breath—then, while the crowd hummed and closed in, leaving Byrne to slink away as if he had become invisible, I saw my big Delane, grown calm and apathetic, turn to the pony and lay a soothing hand on its neck.

I was pushing forward, moved by the impulse to press that hand, when his wife went up to him. Though I was not far off I could not hear what she said; people did not speak loud in those days, or "make scenes," and the two or three words which issued from Mrs. Delane's lips must have been inaudible to everyone but her husband. On his dark face they raised a sudden redness; he made a motion of his free arm (the other hand still on the pony's neck), as if to wave aside an importunate child; then he felt in his pocket, drew out a cigarette, and lit it. Mrs. Delane, white as a ghost, was hurrying back to Alstrop's coach.

I was turning away too when I saw her husband hailed again. This time it was Bill Gracy, shoving and yet effacing himself, as his manner was, who came up, a facile tear on his lashes, his smile half tremulous, half defiant, a yellow-gloved hand held out.

"God bless you for it, Hayley—God bless you, my dear boy!"

Delane's hand reluctantly left the pony's neck. It wavered for an instant, just touched the other's palm, and was instantly engulfed in it. Then Delane, without speaking, turned toward the shed where his mounts were being rubbed down, while his father-in-law swaggered from the scene.

I had promised, on the way home, to stop for tea at a friend's house half-way between the Polo Club and Alstrop's. Another friend, who was also going there, offered me a lift, and carried me on to Alstrop's afterward.

During our drive, and about the tea-table, the talk of course dwelt mainly on the awkward incident of Bolton Byrne's thrashing. The women were horrified or admiring, as their humour moved them; but the men all agreed that it was natural enough. In such a case any pretext was permissible, they said; though it was stupid of Hayley to air his grievance on a public occasion. But then he *was* stupid—that was the consensus of opinion. If there was a blundering way of doing a thing that needed to be done, trust him to hit on it! For the rest, everyone spoke of him affectionately, and agreed that Leila was a fool . . . and nobody particularly liked Byrne, an "outsider" who had pushed himself into society by means of cheek and showy horsemanship. But Leila, it was agreed, had always had a weakness for "outsiders," perhaps because their admiration flattered her extreme desire to be thought "in."

"Wonder how many of the party you'll find left—this affair must have caused a good deal of a shake-up," my friend said, as I got down at Alstrop's door; and the same thought was in my own mind. Byrne would be gone, of course; and no doubt, in another direction, Delane and Leila. I wished I had a chance to shake that blundering hand of Hayley's. . .

Hall and drawing-room were empty; the dressing-bell must have sounded its discreet appeal more than once, and I was relieved to find it had been heeded. I didn't want to stumble on any of my fellow-guests till I had seen our host. As I was dashing upstairs I heard him call me from the library, and turned back.

"No hurry—dinner put off till nine," he said cheerfully; and added, on a note of inexpressible relief: "We've had a tough job of it—*ouf!*"

The room looked as if they had: the card tables stood untouched, and the deep armchair, gathered into confidential groups, seemed still deliberating on the knotty problem. I noticed that a good deal of whiskey and soda had gone toward its solution.

"What happened? Has Byrne left?"

"Byrne? No—thank goodness!" Alstrop looked at me almost reproachfully. "Why should he? That was just what we wanted to avoid."

"I don't understand. You don't mean that *he's* stayed and the Delanes have gone?"

"Lord forbid! Why should they, either? Hayley's apologized!"

My jaw fell, and I returned my host's stare.

"Apologized? To that hound? For what?"

Alstrop gave an impatient shrug. "Oh, for God's sake don't reopen the cursèd question," it seemed to say. Aloud he echoed: "For what? Why, after all, a man's got a right to thrash his own pony, hasn't he? It was beastly unsportsmanlike, of course—but it's nobody's business if Byrne chooses to be that kind of a cad. That's what Hayley saw—when he cooled down."

"Then I'm sorry he cooled down."

Alstrop looked distinctly annoyed. "I don't follow you. We had a hard enough job. You said you wanted to see him in a rage just once; but you don't want him to go on making an ass of himself, do you?"

"I don't call it making an ass of himself to thrash Byrne."

"And to advertise his conjugal difficulties all over Long Island, with twenty newspaper reporters at his heels?"

I stood silent, baffled but incredulous. "I don't believe he ever gave that a thought. I wonder who put it to him first in that way?"

Alstrop twisted his unlit cigarette about in his fingers. "We all did—as delicately as we could. But it was Leila who finally convinced him. I must say Leila was very game."

I still pondered: the scene in the paddock rose again before me, the quivering agonized animal, and the way Delane's big hand had been laid reassuringly on its neck.

"Nonsense! I don't believe a word of it!" I declared.

"A word of what I've been telling you?"

"Well, of the official version of the case."

To my surprise, Alstrop met my glance with an eye neither puzzled nor resentful. A shadow seemed to be lifted from his honest face.

"What *do* you believe?" he asked.

"Why, that Delane thrashed that cur for ill-treating the pony, and not in the least for being too attentive to Mrs. Delane. I was there, I tell you— I saw him."

Alstrop's brow cleared completely. "There's something to be said for that theory," he agreed, smiling over the match he was holding to his cigarette.

"Well, then—what was there to apologize for?"

"Why, for *that*—butting in between Byrne and his horse. Don't you see, you young idiot? If Hayley hadn't apologized, the mud was bound to stick to his wife. Everybody would have said the row was on her account. It's as plain as the knob on the door—there wasn't anything else for him to do. He saw it well enough after she'd said a dozen words to him—"

"I wonder what those words are," I muttered.

"Don't know. He and she came downstairs together. He looked a hundred years old, poor old chap. 'It's the cruelty, it's the cruelty,' he kept saying: 'I hate cruelty.' I rather think he knows we're all on his side. Anyhow, it's all patched up and well patched up; and I've ordered my last 'eighty-four Georges Goulet brought up for dinner. Meant to keep it for my own wedding-breakfast; but since this afternoon I've rather lost interest in that festivity," Alstrop concluded with a celibate grin.

"Well," I repeated, as though it were a relief to say, "I could swear he did it for the pony."

"Oh, so could I," my host acquiesced as we went upstairs together.

On my threshold, he took me by the arm and followed me in. I saw there was still something on his mind.

"Look here, old chap—you say you were in there when it happened?"

"Yes. Close by—"

"Well," he interrupted, "for the Lord's sake don't allude to the subject tonight, will you?"

"Of course not."

"Thanks a lot. Truth is, it was a narrow squeak, and I couldn't help admiring the way Leila played up. She was in a fury with Hayley; but she got herself in hand in no time, and behaved very decently. She told me privately he was often like that—flaring out all of a sudden like a madman. You wouldn't imagine it, would you, with that quiet way of his? She says she thinks it's his old wound."

"What old wound?"

"Didn't you know he was wounded—where was it? Bull Run, I believe. In the head—"

No, I hadn't known; hadn't even heard, or remembered, that Delane had been in the Civil War. I stood and stared in my astonishment.

"Hayley Delane? In the war?"

"Why, of course. All through it."

"But Bull Run—Bull Run was at the very beginning." I broke off to go through a rapid mental calculation. "Look here, Jack, it can't be; he's not over fifty-three. You told me so yourself. If he was in it from the beginning he must have gone into it as a schoolboy."

"Well, that's just what he did: ran away from school to volunteer. His family didn't know what had become of him till he was wounded. I remember hearing my people talk about it. Great old sport, Hayley. I'd have given a lot not to have this thing happen; not at my place anyhow; but it *has,* and there's no help for it. Look here, you swear you won't make a sign, will you? I've got all the others into line, and if you'll back us up we'll have a regular Happy Family Evening. Jump into your clothes—it's nearly nine."

III

THIS is not a story-teller's story; it is not even the kind of episode capable of being shaped into one. Had it been, I should have reached my climax, or at any rate its first stage, in the incident at the Polo Club, and what I have left to tell would be the effect of that incident on the lives of the three persons concerned.

It is not a story, or anything in the semblance of a story, but merely an attempt to depict for you—and in so doing, perhaps make clearer to myself—the aspect and character of a man whom I loved, perplexedly but faithfully, for many years. I make no apology, therefore, for the fact that Bolton Byrne, whose evil shadow ought to fall across all my remaining pages, never again appears in them; and that the last I saw of him (for my purpose) was when, after our exaggeratedly cheerful and even noisy dinner that evening at Jack Alstrop's, I observed him shaking hands with Hayley Delane, and declaring, with pinched lips and a tone of falsetto cordiality: "Bear malice? Well, rather not—why, what rot! All's fair in—in polo, ain't it? I should say so! Yes—off first thing tomorrow. S'pose of course you're staying on with Jack over Sunday? I wish I hadn't promised the Gildermeres—." And therewith he vanishes, having served his purpose as a passing lantern-flash across the twilight of Hayley Delane's character.

All the while, I continued to feel that it was not Bolton

Byrne who mattered. While clubs and drawing-rooms twittered with the episode, and friends grew portentous in trying to look unconscious, and said "I don't know what you mean," with eyes beseeching you to speak if you knew more than they did, I had already discarded the whole affair, as I was sure Delane had. "It *was* the pony, and nothing but the pony," I chuckled to myself, as pleased as if I had owed Mrs. Delane a grudge, and were exulting in her abasement; and still there ran through my mind the phrase which Alstrop said Delane had kept repeating: "It was the cruelty—it was the cruelty. I hate cruelty."

How it fitted in, now, with the other fact my host had let drop—the fact that Delane had fought all through the civil war! It seemed incredible that it should have come to me as a surprise; that I should have forgotten, or perhaps never even known, this phase of his history. Yet in young men like myself, just out of college in the 'nineties, such ignorance was more excusable than now seems possible.

That was the dark time of our national indifference, before the country's awakening; no doubt the war seemed much farther from us, much less a part of us, than it does to the young men of today. Such was the case, at any rate, in old New York, and more particularly, perhaps, in the little clan of well-to-do and indolent old New Yorkers among whom I had grown up. Some of these, indeed, had fought bravely through the four years: New York had borne her part, a memorable part, in the long struggle. But I remember with what perplexity I first wakened to the fact—it was in my school-days—that if certain of my father's kinsmen and contemporaries had been in the war, others—how many!—had stood aside. I recall especially the shock with which, at school, I had heard a boy explain his father's lameness: "He's never got over that shot in the leg he got at Chancellorsville."

I stared; for my friend's father was just my own father's age. At the moment (it was at a school foot-ball match) the two men were standing side by side, in full sight of us— *his* father stooping, halt and old, mine, even to filial eyes, straight and youthful. Only an hour before I had been bragging to my friend about the wonderful shot my father was (he had taken me down to his North Carolina shooting at Christmas); but now I stood abashed.

The next time I went home for the holidays I said to my mother, one day when we were alone: "Mother, why didn't father fight in the war?" My heart was beating so hard that I thought she must have seen my excitement and been shocked. But she raised an untroubled face from her embroidery.

"Your father, dear? Why, because he was a married man." She had a reminiscent smile. "Molly was born already—she was six months old when Fort Sumter fell. I remember I was nursing her when Papa came in with the news. We couldn't believe it." She paused to match a silk placidly. "Married men weren't called upon to fight," she explained.

"But they *did*, though, Mother! Payson Gray's father fought. He was so badly wounded at Chancellorsville that he's had to walk with a stick ever since."

"Well, my dear, I don't suppose you would want your Papa to be like that, would you?" She paused again, and finding I made no answer, probably thought it pained me to be thus convicted of heartlessness, for she added, as if softening the rebuke: "Two of your father's cousins *did* fight: his cousins Harold and James. They were young men, with no family obligations. And poor Jamie was killed, you remember."

I listened in silence, and never again spoke to my mother of the war. Nor indeed to anyone—even myself. I buried the whole business out of sight, out of hearing, as I thought. After all, the war had all happened long ago; it had been over ten years when I was born. And nobody ever talked about it nowadays. Still, one did, of course, as one grew up, meet older men of whom it was said: "Yes, so-and-so was in the war." Many of them even continued to be known by the military titles with which they had left the service: Colonel Ruscott, Major Detrancy, old General Scole. People smiled a little, but admitted that, if it pleased them to keep their army rank, it was a right they had earned. Hayley Delane, it appeared, thought differently. He had never allowed himself to be called "'Major" or "Colonel" (I think he had left the service a Colonel). And besides he was years younger than these veterans. To find that he had fought at their side was like discovering that the grandmother one could remember playing with had been lifted up by her nurse to see General Washington. I always thought of Hayley Delane as belonging to my own generation rather than to my father's; though I knew him to be so much older than myself, and occasionally called him "sir," I felt on an equality with him, the equality produced by sharing the same amusements and talking of them in the same slang. And indeed he must have been ten or fifteen years younger than the few men I knew who had been in the war, none of whom, I was sure, had had to run away from school to volunteer; so that my forgetfulness (or perhaps even ignorance) of his past was not inexcusable.

Broad and Delane had been, for two or three genera-
tions, one of the safe and conservative private banks of
New York. My friend Hayley had been made a partner
early in his career; the post was almost hereditary in his
family. It happened that, not long after the scene at Alstrop's, I was offered a position in the house. The offer
came, not through Delane, but through Mr. Frederick
Broad, the senior member, who was an old friend of my
father's. The chance was too advantageous to be rejected,
and I transferred to a desk at Broad and Delane's my
middling capacities and my earnest desire to do my best.
It was owing to this accidental change that there gradually
grew up between Hayley Delane and myself a sentiment
almost filial on my part, elder-brotherly on his—for paternal one could hardly call him, even with his children.

My job need not have thrown me in his way, for his
business duties sat lightly on him, and his hours at the
bank were neither long nor regular. But he appeared to
take a liking to me, and soon began to call on me for the
many small services which, in the world of affairs, a young
man can render his elders. His great perplexity was the
writing of business letters. He knew what he wanted to
say; his sense of the proper use of words was clear and
prompt; I never knew anyone more impatient of the hazy
verbiage with which American primary culture was already corrupting our speech. He would put his finger at
once on these laborious inaccuracies, growling: "For
God's sake, translate it into English—" but when he had
to write, or worse still dictate, a letter his friendly forehead and big hands grew damp, and he would mutter, half
to himself and half to me: "How the devil shall I say:
'Your letter of the blankth came yesterday, and after

thinking over what you propose I don't like the looks of it'?"—"Why, say just that," I would answer; but he would shake his head and object: "My dear fellow, you're as bad as I am. You don't know how *to write good English*." In his mind there was a gulf fixed between speaking and writing the language. I could never get his imagination to bridge this gulf, or to see that the phrases which fell from his lips were "better English" than the written version, produced after much toil and pen-biting, which consisted in translating the same statement into some such language as: "I am in receipt of your communication of the 30th ultimo, and regret to be compelled to inform you in reply that, after mature consideration of the proposals therein contained, I find myself unable to pronounce a favourable judgment upon the same"—usually sending a furious dash through "the same" as "counterjumper's lingo," and then groaning over his inability to find a more Johnsonian substitute.

"The trouble with me," he used to say, "is that both my parents were martinets on grammar, and never let any of us children use a vulgar expression without correcting us." (By "vulgar" he meant either familiar or inexact.) "We were brought up on the best books—Scott and Washington Irving, old what's-his-name who wrote the *Spectator*, and Gibbon and so forth; and though I'm not a literary man, and never set up to be, I can't forget my early training, and when I see the children reading a newspaper-fellow like Kipling I want to tear the rubbish out of their hands. Cheap journalism—that's what most modern books are. And you'll excuse my saying, dear boy, that even you are too young to know how English ought to be *written*."

It was quite true—though I had at first found it difficult to believe—that Delane must once have been a reader. He surprised me, one night, as we were walking home from a dinner where we had met, by apostrophizing the moon, as she rose, astonished, behind the steeple of the "Heavenly Rest," with "She walks in beauty like the night"; and he was fond of describing a victorious charge in a polo match by saying: "Tell you what, we came down on 'em like the Assyrian." Nor had Byron been his only fare. There had evidently been a time when he had known the whole of Gray's "Elegy" by heart, and I once heard him murmuring to himself, as we stood together one autumn evening on the terrace of his country-house:

Now fades the glimmering landscape on the sight,
And all the air a solemn stillness holds . . .

Little sympathy as I felt for Mrs. Delane, I could not believe it was his marriage which had checked Delane's interest in books. To judge from his very limited stock of allusions and quotations, his reading seemed to have ceased a good deal earlier than his first meeting with Leila Gracy. Exploring him like a geologist, I found, for several layers under the Leila stratum, no trace of any interest in letters; and I concluded that, like other men I knew, his mind had been receptive up to a certain age, and had then snapped shut on what it possessed, like a replete crustacean never reached by another high tide. People, I had by this time found, all stopped living at one time or another, however many years longer they continued to be alive; and I suspected that Delane had stopped at about nineteen. That date would roughly coincide with the end of the Civil War, and with his return to the common-place existence from which he had never since deviated. Those four years had apparently filled to the brim every crevice of his being. For I could not hold that he had gone through them unawares, as some famous figures, puppets of fate, have been tossed from heights to depths of human experience without once knowing what was happening to them—forfeiting a crown by the insistence on some pre-scribed ceremonial, or by carrying on their flight a certain monumental dressing-case.

No, Hayley Delane had felt the war, had been made different by it; how different I saw only when I compared him to the other "veterans" who, from being regarded by me as the dullest of my father's dinner-guests, were now become figures of absorbing interest. Time was when, at my mother's announcement that General Scole or Major Detrancy was coming to dine, I had invariably found a pretext for absenting myself; now, when I knew they were expected, my chief object was to persuade her to invite Delane.

"But he's so much younger—he cares only for the sport-ing set. He won't be flattered at being asked with old gentlemen." And my mother, with a slight smile, would add: "If Hayley has a weakness, it's the wish to be thought younger than he is—on his wife's account, I suppose."

Once, however, she did invite him, and he accepted; and we got over having to ask Mrs. Delane (who un-doubtedly *would* have been bored) by leaving out Mrs. Scole and Mrs. Ruscott, and making it a "man's dinner" of the old-fashioned sort, with canvas-backs, a bowl of punch, and my mother the only lady present—the kind of evening my father still liked best.

I remember, at that dinner, how attentively I studied the contrasts, and tried to detect the point of resemblance, between General Scole, old Detrancy and Delane. Allusions to the war—anecdotes of Bull Run and Andersonville, of Lincoln, Seward and MacClellan, were often on Major Detrancy's lips, especially after the punch had gone round. "When a fellow's been through the war," he used to say as a preface to almost everything, from expressing his opinion of last Sunday's sermon to praising the roasting of a canvas-back. Not so General Scole. No one knew exactly why he had been raised to the rank he bore, but he tacitly proclaimed his right to it by never alluding to the subject. He was a tall and silent old gentleman with a handsome shock of white hair, half-shut blue eyes, glinting between veined lids, and an impressively upright carriage. His manners were perfect—so perfect that they stood him in lieu of language, and people would say afterward how agreeable he had been when he had only bowed and smiled, and got up and sat down again, with an absolute mastery of those difficult arts. He was said to be a judge of horses and Madeira, but he never rode, and was reported to give very indifferent wines to the rare guests he received in his grim old house in Irving Place.

He and Major Detrancy had one trait in common— the extreme caution of the old New Yorker. They viewed with instinctive distrust anything likely to derange their habits, diminish their comfort, or lay on them any unwonted responsibilities, civic or social; and slow as their other mental processes were, they showed a supernatural quickness in divining when a seemingly harmless conversation might draw them into "signing a paper," backing up even the mildest attempt at municipal reform, or pledging them to support, on however small a scale, any new and unfamiliar cause.

According to their creed, gentlemen subscribed as handsomely as their means allowed to the Charity Organization Society, the Patriarchs' Balls, the Children's Aid, and their own parochial charities. Everything beyond savoured of "politics," revivalist meetings, or the attempts of vulgar persons to buy their way into the circle of the elect; even the Society for the Prevention of Cruelty to Animals, being of more recent creation, seemed open to doubt, and they thought it rash of certain members of the clergy to lend it their names. "But then," as Major Detrancy said, "in this noisy age some people will do anything to attract notice." And they breathed a joint sigh over the vanished "Old New York" of their youth, the exclusive and impenetrable New York to which Rubini and Jenny Lind had sung and Mr. Thackeray lectured, the New York which had declined to receive Charles Dickens, and which, out of revenge, he had so scandalously ridiculed.

Yet Major Detrancy and General Scole had fought all through the war, had participated in horrors and agonies untold, endured all manner of hardships and privations, suffered the extremes of heat and cold, hunger, sickness and wounds; and it had all faded like an indigestion comfortably slept off, leaving them perfectly commonplace and happy.

The same was true, with a difference, of Colonel Ruscott, who, though not by birth of the same group, had long since been received into it, partly because he was a companion in arms, partly because of having married a

Hayley connection. I can see Colonel Ruscott still: a dapper handsome little fellow, rather too much of both, with a lustrous wave to his hair (or was it a wig?), and a dash too much of Cologne on too-fine cambric. He had been in the New York militia in his youth, had "gone out" with the great Seventh; and the Seventh, ever since, had been the source and centre of his being, as still, to some octogenarians, their University dinner is.

Colonel Ruscott specialized in chivalry. For him the war was "the blue and the grey," the rescue of lovely Southern girls, anecdotes about Old Glory, and the carrying of vital despatches through the enemy lines. Enchantments seemed to have abounded in his path during the four years which had been so drab and desolate to many; and the punch (to the amusement of us youngsters, who were not above drawing him) always evoked from his memory countless situations in which by prompt, respectful yet insinuating action, he had stamped his image indelibly on some proud Southern heart, while at the same time discovering where Jackson's guerillas lay, or at what point the river was fordable.

And there sat Hayley Delane, so much younger than the others, yet seeming at such times so much their elder that I thought to myself: "But if *he* stopped growing up at nineteen, they're still in long-clothes!" But it was only morally that he had gone on growing. Intellectually they were all on a par. When the last new play at Wallack's was discussed, or my mother tentatively alluded to the last new novel by the author of *Robert Elsmere* (it was her theory that, as long as the hostess was present at a man's dinner, she should keep the talk at the highest level), Delane's remarks were no more penetrating than his neighbours'—and he was almost sure not to have read the novel.

It was when any social question was raised: any of the problems concerning club administration, charity, or the relation between "gentlemen" and the community, that he suddenly stood out from them, not so much opposed as aloof.

He would sit listening, stroking my sister's long skye-terrier (who, defying all rules, had jumped up to his knees at dessert), with a grave half-absent look on his heavy face; and just as my mother (I knew) was thinking how bored he was, that big smile of his would reach out and light up his dimple, and he would say, with enough diffidence to mark his respect for his elders, yet a complete independence of their views: "After all, what does it matter who makes the first move? The thing is to get the business done."

That was always the gist of it. To everyone else, my father included, what mattered in everything, from Diocesan Meetings to Patriarchs' Balls, was just what Delane seemed so heedless of: the standing of the people who make up the committee or headed the movement. To Delane, only the movement itself counted; if the thing was worth doing, he pronounced in his slow lazy way, get it done somehow, even if its backers *were* Methodists or Congregationalists, or people who dined in the middle of the day.

"If they were convicts from Sing Sing I shouldn't care," he affirmed, his hand lazily flattering the dog's neck as I had seen it caress Byrne's terrified pony.

"Or lunatics out of Bloomingdale—as these 'reformers'

usually are," my father added, softening the remark with his indulgent smile.

"Oh, well," Delane murmured, his attention flagging, "I daresay we're well enough off as we are."

"Especially," added Major Detrancy with a playful sniff, "with the punch in the offing, as I perceive it to be."

The punch struck the note for my mother's withdrawal. She rose with her shy circular smile, while the gentlemen, all on their feet, protested gallantly at her desertion.

"Abandoning us to go back to Mr. Elsmere—we shall be jealous of the gentleman!" Colonel Ruscott declared, chivalrously reaching the door first; and as he opened it my father said, again with his indulgent smile: "Ah, my wife—she's a great reader."

Then the punch was brought.

IV

"You'll admit," Mrs. Delane challenged me, "that Hayley's perfect."

Don't imagine you have yet done with Mrs. Delane, any more than Delane had, or I. Hitherto I have shown you only one side, or rather one phase, of her; that during which, for obvious reasons, Hayley became an obstacle or a burden. In the intervals between her great passions, when somebody had to occupy the vacant throne in her bosom, her husband was always reinstated there; and during these interlunar periods he and the children were her staple subjects of conversation. If you had met her then for the first time you would have taken her for the perfect wife and mother, and wondered if Hayley ever got a day off; and you would have not been far wrong in conjecturing that he seldom did.

Only these intervals were rather widely spaced, and usually of short duration; and at other times, his wife being elsewhere engaged, it was Delane who elder-brothered his big boys and their little sister. Sometimes, on these occasions—when Mrs. Delane was abroad or at Newport—Delane used to carry me off for a week to the quiet old house in the New Jersey hills, full of Hayley and Delane portraits, of heavy mahogany furniture and the mingled smell of lavender bags and leather—leather boots, leather gloves, leather luggage, all the aromas that emanate from the cupboards and passages of a house inhabited by hard riders.

When his wife was at home he never seemed to notice

the family portraits or the old furniture. Leila carried off her own regrettable origin by professing a democratic scorn of ancestors in general. "I know enough bores in the flesh without bothering to remember all the dead ones," she said one day, when I had asked her the name of a stern-visaged old forbear in breast-plate and buff jerkin who hung on the library wall: and Delane, so practised in sentimental duplicities, winked jovially at the children, as who should say: "There's the proper American spirit for you, my dears! That's the way we all ought to feel."

Perhaps, however, he detected a tinge of irritation in my own look, for that evening, as we sat over the fire after Leila had yawned herself off to bed, he glanced up at the armoured image, and said. "That's old Durward Hayley—the friend of Sir Harry Vane the Younger and all that lot. I have some curious letters somewhere. . . But Leila's right, you know," he added loyally.

"In not being interested?"

"In regarding all that old past as dead. It *is* dead. We've got no use for it over here. That's what that queer fellow in Washington always used to say to me. . ."

"What queer fellow in Washington?"

"Oh, a sort of big backwoodsman who was awfully good to me when I was in hospital . . . after Bull Run. . ."

I sat up abruptly. It was the first time that Delane had mentioned his life during the war. I thought my hand was on the clue; but it wasn't.

"You were in hospital in Washington?"

"Yes; for a longish time. They didn't know much about disinfecting wounds in those days. . . But Leila," he resumed with his smiling obstinacy, "Leila's dead

right, you know. It's a better world now. Think of what
has been done to relieve suffering since then!" When he
pronounced the word "suffering" the vertical furrows in
his forehead deepened as though he felt the actual pang
of his old wound. "Oh, I believe in progress every bit as
much as *she* does—I believe we're working out toward
something better. If we weren't. . ." He shrugged his
mighty shoulders, reached lazily for the adjoining tray,
and mixed my glass of whiskey-and-soda.

"But the war—you were wounded at Bull Run?"

"Yes." He looked at his watch. "But I'm off to bed now.
I promised the children to take them for an early canter
tomorrow, before lessons, and I have to have my seven
or eight hours of sleep to feel fit. I'm getting on, you see.
Put out the lights when you come up."

No; he wouldn't talk about the war.

It was not long afterward that Mrs. Delane appealed
to me to testify to Hayley's perfection. She had come
back from her last absence—a six weeks' flutter at Newport
—rather painfully subdued and pinched-looking. For the
first time I saw in the corners of her mouth that middle-
aged droop which has nothing to do with the loss of
teeth. "How common-looking she'll be in a few years!" I
thought uncharitably.

"Perfect—perfect," she insisted; and then, plaintively:
"And yet—"

I echoed coldly: "And yet?"

"With the children, for instance. He's everything to
them. He's cut me out with my own children." She was
half joking, half whimpering.

Presently she stole an eye-lashed look at me, and added: "And at times he's so *hard*."

"Delane?"

"Oh, I know you won't believe it. But in business matters——have you never noticed? You wouldn't admit it, I suppose. But there are times when one simply can't move him." We were in the library, and she glanced up at the breast-plated forebear. "He's as hard to the touch as *that*." She pointed to the steel convexity.

"Not the Delane I know," I murmured, embarrassed by these confidences.

"Ah, you think you know him?" she half-sneered; then, with a dutiful accent: "I've always said he was a perfect father—and he's made the children think so. And yet—"

He came in, and dropping a pale smile on him she drifted away, calling to her children.

I thought to myself: "She's getting on, and something has told her so at Newport. Poor thing!"

Delane looked as preoccupied as she did; but he said nothing till after she had left us that evening. Then he suddenly turned to me.

"Look here. You're a good friend of ours. Will you help me to think out a rather bothersome question?"

"Me, sir?" I said, surprised by the "ours," and overcome by so solemn an appeal from my elder.

He made a wan grimace. "Oh, don't call me 'sir'; not during this talk." He paused, and then added: "You're remembering the difference in our ages. Well, that's just why I'm asking you. I want the opinion of somebody who hasn't had time to freeze into his rut—as most of my contemporaries have. The fact is, I'm trying to make my wife see that we've got to let her father come and live with us."

My open-mouthed amazement must have been marked enough to pierce his gloom, for he gave a slight laugh. "Well, yes—"

I sat dumbfounded. All New York knew what Delane thought of his suave father-in-law. He had married Leila in spite of her antecedents; but Bill Gracy, at the outset, had been given to understand that he would not be received under the Delane roof. Mollified by the regular payment of a handsome allowance, the old gentleman, with tears in his eyes, was wont to tell his familiars that personally he didn't blame his son-in-law. "Our tastes differ: that's all. Hayley's not a bad chap at heart; give you my word he isn't." And the familiars, touched by such magnanimity, would pledge Hayley in the champagne provided by his last remittance.

Delane, as I still remained silent, began to explain. "You see, somebody's got to look after him—who else is there?"

"But—" I stammered.

"You'll say he's always needed looking after? Well, I've done my best; short of having him here. For a long time that seemed impossible; I quite agreed with Leila—" (So it was Leila who had banished her father!) "But now," Delane continued, "it's different. The poor old chap's getting on: he's been breaking up very fast this last year. And some bloodsucker of a woman has got hold of him, and threatened to rake up old race-course rows, and I don't know what. If we don't take him in he's bound to go under. It's his last chance—he feels it is. He's scared; he wants to come."

I was still silent, and Delane went on: "You think, I suppose, what's the use? Why not let him stew in his own juice? With a decent allowance, of course. Well, I can't say . . . I can't tell you . . . only I feel it mustn't be. . ."

"And Mrs. Delane?"

"Oh, I see her point. The children are growing up; they've hardly known their grandfather. And having him in the house isn't going to be like having a nice old lady in a cap knitting by the fire. He takes up room, Gracy does; it's not going to be pleasant. She thinks we ought to consider the children first. But I don't agree. The world's too ugly a place; why should anyone grow up thinking it's a flower-garden? Let 'em take their chance. . . . And then"—he hesitated, as if embarrassed—"well, you know her; she's fond of society. Why shouldn't she be? She's made for it. And of course it'll cut us off, prevent our inviting people. She won't like that, though she doesn't admit that it has anything to do with her objecting."

So, after all, he judged the wife he still worshipped! I was beginning to see why he had that great structural head, those large quiet movements. There *was* something—

"What alternative does Mrs. Delane propose?"

He coloured. "Oh, more money. I sometimes fancy," he brought out, hardly above a whisper, "that she thinks I've suggested having him here because I don't want to give more money. She won't understand, you see, that more money would just precipitate things."

I coloured too, ashamed of my own thought. Had she not, perhaps, understood; was it not her perspicacity which made her hold out? If her father was doomed to go under, why prolong the process? I could not be sure, now, that Delane did not suspect this also, and allow for it. There was apparently no limit to what he allowed for.

"*You'll* never be frozen into a rut," I ventured, smiling.

"Perhaps not frozen; but sunk down deep. I'm that already. Give me a hand up, do!" He answered my smile.

I was still in the season of cocksureness, and at a distance could no doubt have dealt glibly with the problem. But at such short range, and under those melancholy eyes, I had a chastening sense of inexperience.

"You don't care to tell what you think?" He spoke almost reproachfully.

"Oh, it's not that . . . I'm trying to. But it's so—so awfully evangelical," I brought out—for some of us were already beginning to read the Russians.

"Is it? Funny, that, too. For I have an idea I got it, with other things, from an old heathen; that chap I told you about, who used to come and talk to me by the hour in Washington."

My interest revived. "That chap in Washington—was he a heathen?"

"Well, he didn't go to church." Delane did, regularly taking the children, while Leila slept off the previous night's poker, and joining in the hymns in a robust baritone, always half a tone flat.

He seemed to guess that I found his reply inadequate, and added helplessly: "You know I'm no scholar: I don't know what you'd call him." He lowered his voice to add: "I don't think he believed in our Lord. Yet he taught me Christian charity."

"He must have been an unusual sort of man, to have made such an impression on you. What was his name?"

"There's the pity! I must have heard it, but I was all foggy with fever most of the time, and can't remember. Nor what became of him either. One day he didn't turn up—that's all I recall. And soon afterward I was off again, and didn't think of him for years. Then, one day, I had to settle something with myself, and, by George, there he was, telling me the right and wrong of it! Queer— he comes like that, at long intervals; turning-points, I suppose." He frowned, his heavy head sunk forward, his eyes distant, pursuing the vision.

"Well—hasn't he come this time?"

"Rather! That's my trouble—I can't see things in any way but his. And I want another eye to help me."

My heart was beating rather excitedly. I felt small, trivial and inadequate, like an intruder on some grave exchange of confidences.

I tried to postpone my reply, and at the same time to satisfy another curiosity. "Have you ever told Mrs. Delane about—about him?"

Delane roused himself and turned to look at me. He lifted his shaggy eyebrows slightly, protruded his lower lip, and sank once more into abstraction.

"Well, sir," I said, answering the look, "*I* believe in him."

The blood rose in his dark cheek. He turned to me again, and for a second the dimple twinkled through his gloom. "That's your answer?"

I nodded breathlessly.

He got up, walked the length of the room, and came back, pausing in front of me. "He just vanished. I never even knew his name. . ."

V

DELANE was right; having Bill Gracy under one's roof was not like harbouring a nice old lady. I looked on at the sequence of our talk and marvelled.

New York—the Delanes' New York—sided unhesitatingly with Leila. Society's attitude toward drink and dishonesty was still inflexible: a man who had had to resign from his clubs went down into a pit presumably bottomless. The two or three people who thought Delane's action "rather fine" made haste to add: "But he ought to have taken a house for the old man in some quiet place in the country." Bill Gracy cabined in a quiet place in the country! Within a week he would have set the neighbourhood on fire. He was simply not to be managed by proxy; Delane had understood that, and faced it.

Nothing in the whole unprecedented situation was more odd, more unexpected and interesting, than Mr. Gracy's own perception of it. He too had become aware that his case was without alternative.

"They *had* to have me here, by gad; I see that myself. Old firebrand like me . . . couldn't be trusted! Hayley saw it from the first—fine fellow, my son-in-law. He made no bones about telling me so. Said: 'I can't trust you, father' . . . said it right out to me. By gad, if he'd talked to me like that a few years sooner I don't answer for the consequences! But I ain't my own man any longer. . .

I've got to put up with being treated like a baby. . . . I forgave him on the spot, sir—on the spot." His fine eye filled, and he stretched a soft old hand, netted with veins and freckles, across the table to me.

In the virtual seclusion imposed by his presence I was one of the few friends the Delanes still saw. I knew Leila was grateful to me for coming; but I did not need that incentive. It was enough that I could give even a negative support to Delane. The first months were horrible; but he was evidently saying to himself: "Things will settle down gradually," and just squaring his great shoulders to the storm.

Things didn't settle down; as embodied in Bill Gracy they continued in a state of effervescence. Filial care, good food and early hours restored the culprit to comparative health; he became exuberant, arrogant and sly. Happily his first imprudence caused a relapse alarming even to himself. He saw that his powers of resistance were gone, and, tremulously tender over his own plight, he relapsed into a plaintive burden. But he was never a passive one. Some part or other he had to play, usually to somebody's detriment.

One day a strikingly dressed lady forced her way in to see him, and the house echoed with her recriminations. Leila objected to the children's assisting at such scenes, and when Christmas brought the boys home she sent them to Canada with a tutor, and herself went with the little girl to Florida. Delane, Gracy and I sat down alone to our Christmas turkey, and I wondered what Delane's queer friend of the Washington hospital would have thought of that festivity. Mr. Gracy was in a melting mood, and reviewed his past with an edifying prolixity. "After all, women and children have always loved me," he summed up, a tear on his lashes. "But I've been a curse to you and Leila, and I know it, Hayley. That's my only merit, I suppose—that I *do* know it! Well, here's to turning over a new leaf . . ." and so forth.

One day, a few months later, Mr. Broad, the head of the firm, sent for me, I was surprised, and somewhat agitated at the summons, for I was not often called into his august presence.

"Mr. Delane has a high regard for your ability," he began affably.

I bowed, thrilled at what I supposed to be a hint of promotion; but Mr. Broad went on: "I know you are at his house a great deal. In spite of the difference in age he always speaks of you as an old friend." Hopes of promotion faded, yet left me unregretful. Somehow, this was even better. I bowed again.

Mr. Broad was becoming embarrassed. "You see Mr. William Gracy rather frequently at his son-in-law's?"

"He's living there," I answered bluntly.

Mr. Broad heaved a sigh. "Yes. It's a fine thing of Mr. Delane . . . but does he quite realize the consequences? His own family side with his wife. You'll wonder at my speaking with such frankness . . . but I've been asked . . . it has been suggested . . ."

"If he weren't there he'd be in the gutter."

Mr. Broad sighed more deeply. "Ah, it's a problem. . . You may ask why I don't speak directly to Mr. Delane . . . but it's so delicate, and he's so uncommunicative. Still, there are Institutions. . . You don't feel there's anything to be done?

I was silent, and he shook hands, murmured: "This is

confidential," and made a motion of dismissal. I withdrew to my desk, feeling that the situation must indeed be grave if Mr. Broad could so emphasize it by consulting me.

New York, to ease its mind of the matter, had finally decided that Hayley Delane was "queer." There were the two of them, madmen both, hobnobbing together under his roof; no wonder poor Leila found the place untenable! That view, bruited about, as things are, with a mysterious underground rapidity, prepared me for what was to follow.

One day during the Easter holidays I went to dine with the Delanes, and finding my host alone with old Gracy I concluded that Leila had again gone off with the children. She had: she had been gone a week, and had just sent a letter to her husband saying that she was sailing from Montreal with the little girl. The boys would be sent back to Groton with a trusted servant. She would add nothing more, as she did not wish to reflect unkindly on what his own family agreed with her in thinking an act of ill-advised generosity. He knew that she was worn out by the strain he had imposed on her, and would understand her wishing to get away for a while. . .

She had left him.

Such events were not, in those days, the matters of course they have since become; and I doubt if, on a man like Delane, the blow would ever have fallen lightly. Certainly that evening was the grimmest I ever passed in his company. I had the same impression as on the day of Bolton Byrne's chastisement: the sense that Delane did not care a fig for public opinion. His knowing that it sided with his wife did not, I believe, affect him in the least; nor did her own view of his conduct—and for that I was unprepared. What really ailed him, I discovered, was his loneliness. He missed her, he wanted her back—her trivial irritating presence was the thing in the world he could least dispense with. But when he told me what she had done he simply added: "I see no help for it; we've both of us got a right to our own opinion."

Again I looked at him with astonishment. Another voice seemed to be speaking through his lips, and I had it on mine to say: "Was that what your old friend in Washington would have told you?" But at the door of the dining-room, where we had lingered, Mr. Gracy's flushed countenance and unreverend auburn locks appeared between us.

"Look here, Hayley; what about our little game? If I'm to be packed off to bed at ten like a naughty boy you might at least give me my hand of poker first." He winked faintly at me as we passed into the library, and added, in a hoarse aside: "If he thinks he's going to boss me like Leila he's mistaken. Flesh and blood's one thing; now she's gone I'll be damned if I take any bullying."

That threat was the last flare of Mr. Gracy's indomitable spirit. The act of defiance which confirmed it brought on a severe attack of pleurisy. Delane nursed the old man with dogged patience, and he emerged from the illness diminished, wizened, the last trace of auburn gone from his scant curls, and nothing left of his old self but a harmless dribble of talk.

Delane taught him to play patience, and he used to sit for hours by the library fire, puzzling over the cards, or talking to the children's parrot, which he fed and tended

with a touching regularity. He also devoted a good deal
of time to collecting stamps for his youngest grandson,
and his increasing gentleness and playful humour so en-
deared him to the servants that a trusted housemaid had
to be dismissed for smuggling cocktails into his room. On
fine days Delane, coming home earlier from the bank,
would take him for a short stroll; and one day, happening
to walk up Fifth Avenue behind them, I noticed that the
younger man's broad shoulders were beginning to stoop
like the other's, and that there was less lightness in his
gait than in Bill Gracy's jaunty shamble. They looked
like two old men doing their daily mile on the sunny side
of the street. Bill Gracy was no longer a danger to the
community, and Leila might have come home. But I understood from Delane that she was still abroad with her
daughter.

Society soon grows used to any state of things which is
imposed upon it without explanation. I had noticed that
Delane never explained; his chief strength lay in that
negative quality. He was probably hardly aware that
people were beginning to say: "Poor old Gracy—after all,
he's making a decent end. It was the proper thing for
Hayley to do—but his wife ought to come back and share
the burden with him." In important matters he was so
careless of public opinion that he was not likely to notice
its veering. He wanted Leila to come home; he missed her
and the little girl more and more; but for him there was
no "ought" about the matter.

And one day she came. Absence had rejuvenated her,
she had some dazzling new clothes, she had made the
acquaintance of a charming Italian nobleman who was

coming to New York on the next steamer . . . she was ready to forgive her husband, to be tolerant, resigned and even fond. Delane, with his amazing simplicity, took all this for granted; the effect of her return was to make him feel he had somehow been in the wrong, and he was ready to bask in her forgiveness. Luckily for her own popularity she arrived in time to soothe her parent's declining moments. Mr. Gracy was now a mere mild old pensioner and Leila used to drive out with him regularly, and refuse dull invitations "because she had to be with Papa." After all, people said, she had a heart. Her husband thought so too, and triumphed in the conviction. At that time life under the Delane roof, though melancholy, was idyllic; it was a pity old Gracy could not have been kept alive longer, so miraculously did his presence unite the household it had once divided. But he was beyond being aware of this, and from a cheerful senility sank into coma and death. The funeral was attended by the whole of New York, and Leila's crape veil was of exactly the right length—a matter of great importance in those days.

Life has a way of overgrowing its achievements as well as its ruins. In less time than seemed possible in so slow-moving a society, the Delanes' family crisis had been smothered and forgotten. Nothing seemed changed in the mutual attitude of husband and wife, or in that of their little group toward the couple. If anything, Leila had gained in popular esteem by her assiduity at her father's bedside; though as a truthful chronicler I am bound to add that she partly forfeited this advantage by plunging into a flirtation with the Italian nobleman before her crape trimmings had been replaced by *passementerie*. On such fundamental observances old New York still took its stand.

As for Hayley Delane, he emerged older, heavier, more stooping, but otherwise unchanged, from the ordeal. I am not sure that anyone except myself was aware that there had been an ordeal. But my conviction remained. His wife's return had changed him back into a card-playing, ball-going, race-frequenting elderly gentleman; but I had seen the waters part, and a granite rock thrust up from them. Twice the upheaval had taken place; and each time in obedience to motives unintelligible to the people he lived among. Almost any man can take a stand on a principle his fellow-citizens are already occupying; but Hayley Delane held out for things his friends could not comprehend, and did it for reasons he could not explain. The central puzzle subsisted.

Does it subsist for me to this day? Sometimes, walking up town from the bank where in my turn I have become an institution, I glance through the rails of Trinity churchyard and wonder. He has lain there ten years or more now; his wife has married the President of a rising Western University, and grown intellectual and censorious; his children are scattered and established. Does the old Delane vault hold his secret, or did I surprise it one day; did he and I surprise it together?

It was one Sunday afternoon, I remember, not long after Bill Gracy's edifying end. I had not gone out of town that week-end, and after a long walk in the frosty blue twilight of Central Park I let myself into my little flat. To my surprise I saw Hayley Delane's big overcoat and tall hat in the hall. He used to drop in on me now and then, but mostly on the way home from a dinner where we happened to have met; and I was rather startled at his appearance at that hour and on a Sunday. But he lifted an untroubled face from the morning paper.

"You didn't expect a call on a Sunday? Fact is, I'm out of a job. I wanted to go down to the country, as usual, but there's some grand concert or other that Leila was booked for this afternoon; and a dinner tonight at Alstrop's. So I dropped in to pass the time of day. What *is* there to do on a Sunday afternoon, anyhow?"

There he was, the same old usual Hayley, as much put to it as the merest fribble of his set to employ an hour un-filled by poker! I was glad he viewed me as a possible alternative, and laughingly told him so. He laughed too—we were on terms of brotherly equality—and told me to go ahead and read two or three notes which had arrived in my absence. "Gad—how they shower down on a fellow at your age!" he chuckled.

I broke the seals and was glancing through the letters when I heard an exclamation at my back.

"By Jove—there he is!" Hayley Delane shouted. I turned to see what he meant.

He had taken up a book—an unusual gesture, but it lay at his elbow, and I suppose he had squeezed the news-papers dry. He held the volume out to me without speak-ing, his forefinger resting on the open page; his swarthy face was in a glow, his hand shook a little. The page to which his finger pointed bore the steel engraving of a man's portrait.

"It's him to the life—I'd know those old clothes of his again anywhere," Delane exulted, jumping up from his seat.

I took the book and stared first at the portrait and then at my friend.

"Your pal in Washington?"

He nodded excitedly. "That chap I've often told you about—yes!" I shall never forget the way his smile flew out and reached the dimple. There seemed a network of them spangling his happy face. His eyes had grown absent, as if gazing down invisible vistas. At length they travelled back to me.

"How on earth did the old boy get his portrait in a book? Has somebody been writing something about him?" His sluggish curiosity awakened, he stretched his hand for the volume. But I held it back.

"Lots of people have written about him; but this book is his own."

"You mean he wrote it?" He smiled incredulously. "Why, the poor chap hadn't any education!"

"Perhaps he had more than you think. Let me keep the book a moment longer, and read you something from it."

He signed an assent, though I could see the apprehension of the printed page already clouding his interest.

"What sort of things did he write?"

"Things for *you*. Now listen."

He settled back into his armchair, composing a painfully attentive countenance, and I sat down and began:

A sight in camp in the day-break grey and dim.
As from my tent I emerge so early, sleepless,
As slow I walk in the cool fresh air, the path near by the
  hospital tent,
Three forms I see on stretchers lying, brought out there,
  untended lying,

Over each the blanket spread, ample brownish woollen
     blanket,
Grey and heavy blanket, folding, covering all.

Curious, I halt, and silent stand:
Then with light fingers I from the face of the nearest, the
     first, just lift the blanket:
Who are you, elderly man so gaunt and grim, with well-
     grey'd hair, and flesh all sunken about the eyes?
Who are you, my dear comrade?
Then to the second I step—And who are you, my child
     and darling?
Who are you, sweet boy, with cheeks yet blooming?

Then to the third—a face nor child, nor old, very calm, as
     of beautiful yellow-white ivory;
Young man, I think I know you—I think this face of yours
     is the face of the Christ himself;
Dead and divine, and brother of all, and here again he
     lies.

I laid the open book on my knee, and stole a glance at
Delane. His face was a blank, still composed in the heavy
folds of enforced attention. No spark had been struck
from him. Evidently the distance was too great between
the far-off point at which he and English poetry had
parted company, and this new strange form it had put on.
I must find something which would bring the matter
closely enough home to surmount the unfamiliar me-
dium.

Vigil strange I kept on the field one night,
When you, my son and my comrade, dropt at my side. . .

The starlit murmur of the verse flowed on, muffled,
insistent; my throat filled with it, my eyes grew dim. I
said to myself, as my voice sank on the last line: "He's
reliving it all now, seeing it again—knowing for the first
time that someone else saw it as he did."

Delane stirred uneasily in his seat, and shifted his
crossed legs one over the other. One hand absently stroked
the fold of his carefully ironed trousers. His face was still
a blank. The distance had not yet been bridged between
Gray's "Elegy" and this unintelligible harmony. But I was
not discouraged. I ought not to have expected any of it to
reach him—not just at first—except by way of the closest
personal appeal. I turned from the "Lovely and Soothing
Death," at which I had reopened the book, and looked
for another page. My listener leaned back resignedly.

Bearing the bandages, water and sponge,
Straight and swift to my wounded I go. . .

I read on to the end. Then I shut the book and looked
up again. Delane sat silent, his great hands clasping the
arms of his chair, his head slightly sunk on his breast.
His lids were dropped, as I imagined reverentially. My
own heart was beating with a religious emotion; I had
never felt the oft-read lines as I felt them then.

A little timidly, he spoke at length "Did *he* write that?"

"Yes; just about the time you were seeing him, probably."

Delane still brooded; his expression grew more and more timid. "What do you . . . er . . . call it . . . exactly?" he ventured.

I was puzzled for a moment; then: "Why, poetry . . . rather a free form, of course. . . You see, he was an originator of new verse-forms . . ."

"New verse-forms?" Delane echoed forlornly. He stood up in his heavy way, but did not offer to take the book from me again. I saw in his face the symptoms of approaching departure.

"Well, I'm glad to have seen his picture after all these years," he said; and on the threshold he paused to ask: "What was his name, by the way?"

When I told him he repeated it with a smile of slow relish. "Yes; that's it. Old Walt—that was what all the fellows used to call him. He was a great chap: I'll never forget him.—I rather wish, though," he added, in his mildest tone of reproach, "you hadn't told me that he wrote all that rubbish."

NEW YEAR'S DAY

(The 'Seventies)

I

"She was *bad* . . . always. They used to meet at the Fifth Avenue Hotel," said my mother, as if the scene of the offence added to the guilt of the couple whose past she was revealing. Her spectacles slanted on her knitting, she dropped the words in a hiss that might have singed the snowy baby-blanket which engaged her indefatigable fingers. (It was typical of my mother to be always employed in benevolent actions while she uttered uncharitable words.)

"They used to meet at the Fifth Avenue Hotel"; how the precision of the phrase characterized my old New York! A generation later, people would have said, in reporting an affair such as Lizzie Hazeldean's with Henry Prest: "They met in hotels"—and today who but a few superannuated spinsters, still feeding on the venom secreted in their youth, would take any interest in the tracing of such topographies?

Life has become too telegraphic for curiosity to linger on any given point in a sentimental relation; as old Sillerton Jackson, in response to my mother, grumbled through his perfect "china set": "Fifth Avenue Hotel? They might meet in the middle of Fifth Avenue nowadays, for all that anybody cares."

But what a flood of light my mother's tart phrase had

suddenly focussed on an unremarked incident of my boyhood!

The Fifth Avenue Hotel . . . Mrs. Hazeldean and
Henry Prest . . . the conjunction of these names had arrested her darting talk on a single point of my memory,
as a search-light, suddenly checked in its gyrations, is held
motionless while one notes each of the unnaturally sharp
and lustrous images it picks out.

At the time I was a boy of twelve, at home from school
for the holidays. My mother's mother, Grandmamma
Parrett, still lived in the house in West Twenty-third
Street which Grandpapa had built in his pioneering
youth, in days when people shuddered at the perils of
living north of Union Square—days that Grandmamma
and my parents looked back to with a joking incredulity
as the years passed and the new houses advanced steadily
Park-ward, outstripping the Thirtieth Streets, taking the
Reservoir at a bound, and leaving us in what, in my
school-days, was already a dullish back-water between
Aristocracy to the south and Money to the north.

Even then fashion moved quickly in New York, and my
infantile memory barely reached back to the time when
Grandmamma, in lace lappets and creaking "moiré," used
to receive on New Year's Day, supported by her handsome
married daughters. As for old Sillerton Jackson, who, once
a social custom had dropped into disuse, always affected
never to have observed it, he stoutly maintained that the
New Year's Day ceremonial had never been taken seriously
except among families of Dutch descent, and that that was
why Mrs. Henry van der Luyden had clung to it, in a reluctant half-apologetic way, long after her friends had
closed their doors on the first of January, and the date

had been chosen for those out-of-town parties which are so often used as a pretext for absence when the unfashionable are celebrating their rites.

Grandmamma of course, no longer received. But it would have seemed to her an exceedingly odd thing to go out of town in winter, especially now that the New York houses were luxuriously warmed by the new hot-air furnaces, and searchingly illuminated by gas chandeliers. No, thank you—no country winters for the chilblained generation of prunella sandals and low-necked sarcenet, the generation brought up in unwarmed and unlit houses, and shipped off to die in Italy when they proved unequal to the struggle of living in New York! Therefore Grandmamma, like most of her contemporaries, remained in town on the first of January, and marked the day by a family reunion, a kind of supplementary Christmas—though to us juniors the absence of presents and plumpudding made it but a pale and moonlike reflection of the Feast.

Still, the day was welcome as a lawful pretext for overeating, dawdling, and looking out of the window: a Dutch habit still extensively practised in the best New York circles. On the day in question, however, we had not yet placed ourselves behind the plate-glass whence it would presently be so amusing to observe the funny gentlemen who trotted about, their evening ties hardly concealed behind their overcoat collars, darting in and out of chocolate-coloured house-fronts on their sacramental round of calls. We were still engaged in placidly digesting around the ravaged luncheon table when a servant dashed in to say that the Fifth Avenue Hotel was on fire.

Oh, then the fun began—and what fun it was! For

Grandmamma's house was just opposite the noble edifice of white marble which I associated with such deep-piled carpets, and such a rich sultry smell of anthracite and coffee, whenever I was bidden to "step across" for a messenger-boy, or to buy the evening paper for my elders.

The hotel, for all its sober state, was no longer fashionable. No one, in my memory, had ever known any one who went there; it was frequented by "politicians" and "Westerners," two classes of citizens whom my mother's intonation always seemed to deprive of their vote by ranking them with illiterates and criminals.

But for that very reason there was all the more fun to be expected from the calamity in question; for had we not, with infinite amusement, watched the arrival, that morning, of monumental "floral pieces" and towering frosted cakes for the New Year's Day reception across the way? The event was a communal one. All the ladies who were the hotel's "guests" were to receive together in the densely lace-curtained and heavily chandeliered public parlours, and gentlemen with long hair, imperials and white gloves had been hastening since two o'clock to the scene of revelry. And now, thanks to the opportune conflagration, we were going to have the excitement not only of seeing the Fire Brigade in action (supreme joy of the New York youngster), but of witnessing the flight of the ladies and their visitors, staggering out through the smoke in gala array. The idea that the fire might be dangerous did not mar these pleasing expectations. The house was solidly built; New York's invincible Brigade was already at the door, in a glare of polished brass, coruscating helmets and horses shining like table-silver; and my tall cousin Hubert Wesson, dashing across at the first alarm, had promptly returned to say that all risk was over, though the two lower floors were so full of smoke and water that the lodgers, in some confusion, were being transported to other hotels. How then could a small boy see in the event anything but an unlimited lark?

Our elders, once reassured, were of the same mind. As they stood behind us in the windows, looking over our heads, we heard chuckles of amusement mingled with ironic comment.

"Oh, my dear, look—here they all come! The New Year ladies! Low neck and short sleeves in broad daylight, every one of them! Oh, and the fat one with the paper roses in her hair . . . they *are* paper, my dear . . . off the frosted cake, probably! Oh! Oh! Oh! *Oh!*"

Aunt Sabina Wesson was obliged to stuff her lace handkerchief between her lips, while her firm poplin-cased figure rocked with delight.

"Well, my dear," Grandmamma gently reminded her, "in my youth we wore low-necked dresses all day long and all the year around."

No one listened. My cousin Kate, who always imitated Aunt Sabina, was pinching my arm in an agony of mirth. "Look at them scuttling! The parlours must be full of smoke. Oh, but this one is still funnier; the one with the tall feather in her hair! Granny, did you wear feathers in your hair in the daytime? Oh, don't ask me to believe it! And the one with the diamond necklace! And all the gentlemen in white ties! Did Grandpapa wear a white tie at two o'clock in the afternoon?" Nothing was sacred to Kate, and she feigned not to notice Grandmamma's mild frown of reproval.

"Well, they do in Paris, to this day, at weddings—wear

evening clothes and white ties," said Sillerton Jackson with authority. "When Minnie Transome of Charleston was married at the Madeleine to the Duc de . . ."

But no one listened even to Sillerton Jackson. One of the party had abruptly exclaimed: "Oh, there's a lady running out of the hotel who's not in evening dress!"

The exclamation caused all our eyes to turn toward the person indicated, who had just reached the threshold; and someone added, in an odd voice: "Why, her figure looks like Lizzie Hazeldean's—"

A dead silence followed. The lady who was not in evening dress paused. Standing on the door-step with lifted veil, she faced our window. Her dress was dark and plain—almost conspicuously plain—and in less time than it takes to tell she had put her hand to her closely-patterned veil and pulled it down over her face. But my young eyes were keen and far-sighted; and in that hardly perceptible interval I had seen a vision. Was she beautiful—or was she only someone apart? I felt the shock of a small pale oval, dark eyebrows curved with one sure stroke, lips made for warmth, and now drawn up in a grimace of terror; and it seemed as if the mysterious something, rich, secret and insistent, that broods and murmurs behind a boy's conscious thoughts, had suddenly peered out at me. . . As the dart reached me her veil dropped.

"But it *is* Lizzie Hazeldean!" Aunt Sabina gasped. She had stopped laughing, and her crumpled handkerchief fell to the carpet.

"Lizzie—*Lizzie?*" The name was echoed over my head with varying intonations of reprobation, dismay and half-veiled malice.

Lizzie Hazeldean? Running out of the Fifth Avenue

Hotel on New Year's Day with all those dressed-up women? But what on earth could she have been doing there? No; nonsense! It was impossible. . .

"There's Henry Prest with her," continued Aunt Sabina in a precipitate whisper.

"With her?" someone gasped; and "Oh—" my mother cried with a shudder.

The men of the family said nothing, but I saw Hubert Wesson's face crimson with surprise. Henry Prest! Hubert was forever boring us youngsters with his Henry Prest! That was the kind of chap Hubert meant to be at thirty: in his eyes Henry Prest embodied all the manly graces. Married? No, thank you! That kind of man wasn't made for the domestic yoke. Too fond of ladies' society, Hubert hinted with his undergraduate smirk; and handsome, rich, independent—an all-round sportsman, good horseman, good shot, crack yachtsman (had his pilot's certificate, and always sailed his own sloop, whose cabin was full of racing trophies); gave the most delightful little dinners, never more than six, with cigars that beat old Beaufort's; was awfully decent to the younger men, chaps of Hubert's age included—all combined, in short, all the qualities, mental and physical, which make up, in such eyes as Hubert's, that oracular and irresistible figure, the man of the world. "Just the fellow," Hubert always solemnly concluded, "that I should go straight to if ever I got into any kind of row that I didn't want the family to know about"; and our blood ran pleasantly cold at the idea of our old Hubert's ever being in such an unthinkable predicament.

I felt sorry to have missed a glimpse of this legendary figure; but my gaze had been enthralled by the lady, and now the couple had vanished in the crowd.

The group in our window continued to keep an embarrassed silence. They looked almost frightened; but what struck me even more deeply was that not one of them looked surprised. Even to my boyish sense it was clear that what they had just seen was only the confirmation of something they had long been prepared for. At length one of my uncles emitted a whistle, was checked by a severe glance from his wife, and muttered: "I'll be damned"; another uncle began an unheeded narrative of a fire at which he had been present in his youth, and my mother said to me severely: "You ought to be at home preparing your lessons—a big boy like you!" a remark so obviously unfair that it served only to give the measure of her agitation.

"I don't believe it," said Grandmamma, in a low voice of warning, protest and appeal. I saw Hubert steal a grateful look at her.

But nobody else listened: every eye still strained through the window. Livery-stable "hacks," of the old blue-curtained variety, were driving up to carry off the fair fugitives; for the day was bitterly cold, and lit by one of those harsh New York suns of which every ray seems an icicle. Into these ancient vehicles the ladies, now regaining their composure, were being piled with their removable possessions, while their kid-gloved callers ("So like the White Rabbit!" Kate exulted) appeared and reappeared in the doorway, gallantly staggering after them under bags, reticules, bird-cages, pet dogs and heaped-up finery. But to all this—as even I, a little boy, was aware—nobody in Grandmamma's window paid the slightest attention. The thoughts of one and all, with a mute and guarded eagerness, were still following the movements of those two who were so obviously unrelated to the rest. The whole business—discovery, comment, silent visual pursuit—could hardly, all told, have filled a minute, perhaps not as much; before the sixty seconds were over, Mrs. Hazeldean and Henry Prest had been lost in the crowd, and, while the hotel continued to empty itself into the street, had gone their joint or separate ways. But in my grandmother's window the silence continued unbroken.

"Well, it's over: here are the firemen coming out again," someone said at length.

We youngsters were all alert at that; yet I felt that the grown-ups lent but a half-hearted attention to the splendid sight which was New York's only pageant: the piling of scarlet ladders on scarlet carts, the leaping up on the engine of the helmeted flame-fighters, and the disciplined plunge forward of each pair of broad-chested black steeds, as one after another the chariots of fire rattled off.

Silently, almost morosely, we withdrew to the drawing-room hearth; where, after an interval of languid monosyllables, my mother, rising first, slipped her knitting into its bag, and turning on me with renewed severity, said: "This racing after fire-engines is what makes you too sleepy to prepare your lessons"—a comment so wide of the mark that once again I perceived, without understanding, the extent of the havoc wrought in her mind by the sight of Mrs. Hazeldean and Henry Prest coming out of the Fifth Avenue Hotel together.

It was not until many years later that chance enabled me to relate this fugitive impression to what had preceded and what came after it.

II

MRS. HAZELDEAN paused at the corner of Fifth Avenue and Madison Square. The crowd attracted by the fire still enveloped her; it was safe to halt and take breath.

Her companion, she knew, had gone in the opposite direction. Their movements, on such occasions, were as well-ordered and as promptly executed as those of the New York Fire Brigade; and after their precipitate descent to the hall, the discovery that the police had barred their usual exit, and the quick: "You're all right?" to which her imperceptible nod had responded, she was sure he had turned down Twenty-third Street toward Sixth Avenue.

"The Parretts' windows were full of people," was her first thought.

She dwelt on it a moment, and then reflected: "Yes, but in all that crowd and excitement nobody would have been thinking of *me!*"

Instinctively she put her hand to her veil, as though recalling that her features had been exposed when she ran out, and unable to remember whether she had covered them in time or not.

"What a fool I am! It can't have been off my face for more than a second—" but immediately afterward another disquieting possibility assailed her. "I'm almost sure

I saw Sillerton Jackson's head in one of the windows, just behind Sabina Wesson's. No one else has that particularly silvery gray hair." She shivered, for everyone in New York knew that Sillerton Jackson saw everything, and could piece together seemingly unrelated fragments of fact with the art of a skilled china-mender.

Meanwhile, after sending through her veil the circular glance which she always shot about her at that particular corner, she had begun to walk up Broadway. She walked well—fast, but not too fast; easily, assuredly, with the air of a woman who knows that she has a good figure, and expects rather than fears to be identified by it. But under this external appearance of ease she was covered with cold beads of sweat.

Broadway, as usual at that hour, and on a holiday, was nearly deserted; the promenading public still slowly poured up and down Fifth Avenue.

"Luckily there was such a crowd when we came out of the hotel that no one could possibly have noticed me," she murmured over again, reassured by the sense of having the long thoroughfare to herself. Composure and presence of mind were so necessary to a woman in her situation that they had become almost a second nature to her, and in a few minutes her thick uneven heart-beats began to subside and to grow steadier. As if to test their regularity, she paused before a florist's window, and looked appreciatively at the jars of roses and forced lilac, the compact bunches of lilies-of-the-valley and violets, the first pots of close-budded azaleas. Finally she opened the shop-door, and after examining the Jacqueminots and Marshal Niels, selected with care two perfect specimens of a new silvery-pink rose, waited for the florist to wrap them in cotton-wool, and slipped their long stems into her muff for more complete protection.

"It's so simple, after all," she said to herself as she walked on. "I'll tell him that as I was coming up Fifth Avenue from Cousin Cecilia's I heard the fire-engines turning into Twenty-third Street, and ran after them. Just what *he* would have done . . . once . . ." she ended on a sigh.

At Thirty-first Street she turned the corner with a quicker step. The house she was approaching was low and narrow; but the Christmas holly glistening between frilled curtains, the well-scrubbed steps, the shining bell and door-knob, gave it a welcoming look. From garret to basement it beamed like the abode of a happy couple.

As Lizzie Hazeldean reached the door a curious change came over her. She was conscious of it at once—she had so often said to herself, when her little house rose before her: "It makes me feel younger as soon as I turn the corner." And it was true even today. In spite of her agitation she was aware that the lines between her eyebrows were smoothing themselves out, and that a kind of inner lightness was replacing the heavy tumult of her breast. The lightness revealed itself in her movements, which grew as quick as a girl's as she ran up the steps. She rang twice—it was her signal—and turned an unclouded smile on her elderly parlourmaid.

"Is Mr. Hazeldean in the library, Susan? I hope you've kept up the fire for him."

"Oh, yes, ma'am. But Mr. Hazeldean's not in," said Susan returning the smile respectfully.

"*Not in?* With his cold—and in this weather?"

"That's what I told him, ma'am. But he just laughed—"

"Just laughed? What do you mean, Susan?" Lizzie Hazeldean felt herself turning pale. She rested her hand quickly on the hall table.

"Well, ma'am, the minute he heard the fire-engine, off he rushed like a boy. It seems the Fifth Avenue Hotel's on fire: there's where he's gone."

The blood left Mrs. Hazeldean's lips; she felt it shuddering back to her heart. But a second later she spoke in a tone of natural and good-humoured impatience.

"What madness! How long ago—can you remember?" Instantly, she felt the possible imprudence of the question, and added: "The doctor said he ought not to be out more than a quarter of an hour, and only at the sunniest time of the day."

"I know, that, ma'am, and so I reminded him. But he's been gone nearly an hour, I should say."

A sense of deep fatigue overwhelmed Mrs. Hazeldean. She felt as if she had walked for miles against an icy gale: her breath came laboriously.

"How could you let him go?" she wailed; then, as the parlourmaid again smiled respectfully, she added: "Oh, I know—sometimes one can't stop him. He gets so restless, being shut up with these long colds."

"That's what I *do* feel, ma'am."

Mistress and maid exchanged a glance of sympathy, and Susan felt herself emboldened to suggest: "Perhaps the outing will do him good," with the tendency of her class to encourage favoured invalids in disobedience.

Mrs. Hazeldean's look grew severe. "Susan! I've often warned you against talking to him in that way—"

Susan reddened, and assumed a pained expression.

"How can you think it, ma'am?—me that never say anything to anybody, as all in the house will bear witness."

Her mistress made an impatient movement. "Oh, well, I daresay he won't be long. The fire's over."

"Ah—you knew of it too, then, ma'am?"

"Of the fire? Why, of course, I *saw* it, even—" Mrs. Hazeldean smiled. "I was walking home from Washington Square—from Miss Cecilia Winter's—and at the corner of Twenty-third Street there was a huge crowd, and clouds of smoke. . . It's very odd that I shouldn't have run across Mr. Hazeldean." She looked limpidly at the parlourmaid. "But, then, of course, in all that crowd and confusion . . ."

Half-way up the stairs she turned to call back: "Make up a good fire in the library, please, and bring the tea up. It's too cold in the drawing-room."

The library was on the upper landing. She went in, drew the two roses from her muff, tenderly unswathed them, and put them in a slim glass on her husband's writing-table. In the doorway she paused to smile at this touch of summer in the firelit wintry room; but a moment later her frown of anxiety reappeared. She stood listening intently for the sound of a latch-key; then, hearing nothing, passed on to her bedroom.

It was a rosy room, hung with one of the new English chintzes, which also covered the deep sofa, and the bed with its rose-lined pillow-covers. The carpet was cherry red, the toilet-table ruffled and looped like a ball-dress. Ah, how she and Susan had ripped and sewn and hammered, and pieced together old scraps of lace and ribbon and muslin, in the making of that airy monument! For weeks after she had done over the room her husband never came into it without saying: "I can't think how you managed to squeeze all this loveliness out of that last cheque of your stepmother's."

On the dressing-table Lizzie Hazeldean noticed a long florist's box, one end of which had been cut open to give space to the still longer stems of a bunch of roses. She snipped the string, and extracted from the box an envelope which she flung into the fire without so much as a glance at its contents. Then she pushed the flowers aside, and after rearranging her dark hair before the mirror, carefully dressed herself in a loose garment of velvet and lace which lay awaiting her on the sofa, beside her high-heeled slippers and stockings of open-work silk.

She had been one of the first women in New York to have tea every afternoon at five, and to put off her walking-dress for a tea-gown.

III

She returned to the library, where the fire was beginning to send a bright blaze through the twilight. It flashed on the bindings of Hazeldean's many books, and she smiled absently at the welcome it held out. A latch-key rattled, and she heard her husband's step, and the sound of his cough below in the hall.

"What madness—what madness!" she murmured.

Slowly—how slowly for a young man!—he mounted the stairs, and still coughing came into the library. She ran to him and took him in her arms.

"Charlie! How could you! In this weather? It's nearly dark!"

His long thin face lit up with a deprecating smile. "I suppose Susan's betrayed me, eh? Don't be cross. You've missed such a show! The Fifth Avenue Hotel's been on fire."

"Yes; I know." She paused, just perceptibly. "I *didn't* miss it, though—I rushed across Madison Square for a look at it myself."

"You did? You were there too? What fun!" The idea appeared to him with boyish amusement.

"Naturally I was! On my way home from Cousin Cecilia's . . ."

"Ah, of course. I'd forgotten you were going there. But how odd, then, that we didn't meet!"

"If we *had* I should have dragged you home long ago. I've been in at least half an hour, and the fire was already over when I got there. What a baby you are to have stayed out so long, staring at smoke and a fire-engine!"

He smiled, still holding her, and passing his gaunt hand softly and wistfully over her head. "Oh, don't worry, I've been indoors, safely sheltered, and drinking old Mrs. Parrett's punch. The old lady saw me from her window, and sent one of the Wesson boys across the street to fetch me in. They had just finished a family luncheon. And Sillerton Jackson, who was there, drove me home. So you see,—"

He released her, and moved toward the fire, and she stood motionless, staring blindly ahead, while the thoughts spun through her mind like a mill-race.

"Sillerton Jackson—" she echoed, without in the least knowing what she said.

"Yes; he has the gout again—luckily for me!—and his sister's brougham came to the Parretts' to fetch him."

She collected herself. "You're coughing more than you did yesterday," she accused him.

"Oh, well—the air's sharpish. But I shall be all right presently. . . Oh, those roses!" He paused in admiration before his writing-table

Her face glowed with a reflected pleasure, though all the while the names he had pronounced—"The Parretts, the Wessons, Sillerton Jackson"—were clanging through her brain like a death-knell.

"They *are* lovely, aren't they?" she beamed.

"Much too lovely for me. You must take them down to the drawing-room."

"No; we're going to have tea up here."

"That's jolly—it means there'll be no visitors, I hope?"
She nodded, smiling.

"Good! But the roses—no, they mustn't be wasted on this desert air. You'll wear them in your dress this evening?"

She started perceptibly, and moved slowly back toward the hearth.

"This evening? . . . Oh, I'm going to Mrs. Struthers's," she said, remembering.

"Yes, you are. Dearest—I want you to!"

"But what shall you do alone all the evening? With that cough, you won't go to sleep till late."

"Well, if I don't, I've a lot of new books to keep me busy."

"Oh, your books—!" She made a little gesture, half teasing, half impatient, in the direction of the freshly cut volumes stacked up beside his student lamp. It was an old joke between them that she had never been able to believe anyone could really "care for reading." Long as she and her husband had lived together, this passion of his remained for her as much of a mystery as on the day when she had first suprised him, mute and absorbed, over what the people she had always lived with would have called "a deep book." It was her first encounter with a born reader; or at least, the few she had known had been, like her step-mother, the retired opera-singer, feverish devourers of circulating library fiction: she had never before lived in a house with books in it. Gradually she had learned to take a pride in Hazeldean's reading, as if it had been some rare accomplishment; she had perceived that it reflected credit on him, and was even conscious of its adding to the charm of his talk, a charm she had always felt without being able to define it. But still, in her heart of hearts she regarded books as a mere expedient, and felt sure that they were only an aid to patience, like jackstraws or a game of patience, with the disadvantage of requiring a greater mental effort.

"Shan't you be too tired to read tonight?" she questioned wistfully.

"Too tired? Why, you goose, reading is the greatest rest in the world!—I want you to go to Mrs. Struthers's, dear; I want to see you again in the black velvet dress," he added with his coaxing smile.

The parlourmaid brought in the tray, and Mrs. Hazeldean busied herself with the tea-caddy. Her husband had stretched himself out in the deep armchair which was his habitual seat. He crossed his arms behind his neck, leaning his head back wearily against them, so that, as she glanced at him across the hearth, she saw the salient muscles in his long neck, and the premature wrinkles about his ears and chin. The lower part of his face was singularly ravaged; only the eyes, those quiet ironic grey eyes, and the white forehead above them, reminded her of what he had been seven years before. Only seven years!

She felt a rush of tears: no, there were times when fate was too cruel, the future too horrible to contemplate, and the past—the past, oh, how much worse! And there he sat, coughing, coughing—and thinking God knows what, behind those quiet half-closed lids. At such times he grew so mysteriously remote that she felt lonelier than when he was not in the room.

"Charlie!"

He roused himself. "Yes?"

"Here's your tea."

He took it from her in silence, and she began, nervously, to wonder why he was not talking. Was it because he was afraid it might make him cough again, afraid she would be worried, and scold him? Or was it because he was thinking—thinking of things he had heard at old Mrs. Parrett's, or on the drive home with Sillerton Jackson . . . hints they might have dropped . . . insinuations . . . she didn't know what . . . or of something he had *seen,* perhaps, from old Mrs. Parrett's window? She looked across at his white forehead, so smooth and impenetrable in the lamplight, and thought: "Oh, God, it's like a locked door. I shall dash my brains out against it some day!"

For, after all, it was not impossible that he had actually seen her, seen her from Mrs. Parrett's window, or even from the crowd around the door of the hotel. For all she knew, he might have been near enough, in that crowd, to put out his hand and touch her. And he might have held back, benumbed, aghast, not believing his own eyes. . . She couldn't tell. She had never yet made up her mind how he would look, how he would behave, what he would say, if ever he *did* see or hear anything. . .

No! That was the worst of it. They had lived together for nearly nine years—and how closely!—and nothing that she knew of him, or had observed in him, enabled her to forecast exactly what, in that particular case, his state of mind and his attitude would be. In his profession, she knew, he was celebrated for his shrewdness and insight; in personal matters he often seemed, to her alert mind, oddly absent-minded and indifferent. Yet that might be merely his instinctive way of saving his strength for things he considered more important. There were times when she was sure he was quite deliberate and self-controlled enough to feel in one way and behave in another: perhaps even to have thought out a course in advance—just as, at the first bad symptoms of illness, he had calmly made his will, and planned everything about her future, the house and the servants. . . No, she couldn't tell; there always hung over her the thin glittering menace of a danger she could neither define nor localize—like that avenging lightning which groped for the lovers in the horrible poem he had once read aloud to her (what a choice!) on a lazy afternoon of their wedding journey, as they lay stretched under Italian stone-pines.

The maid came in to draw the curtains and light the lamps. The fire glowed, the scent of the roses drifted on the warm air, and the clock ticked out the minutes, and softly struck a half hour, while Mrs. Hazeldean continued to ask herself, as she so often had before: "Now, what would be the *natural* thing for me to say?"

And suddenly the words escaped from her, she didn't know how: "I wonder you didn't see me coming out of the hotel—for I actually squeezed my way in."

Her husband made no answer. Her heart jumped convulsively; then she lifted her eyes and saw that he was asleep. How placid his face looked—years younger than when he was awake! The immensity of her relief rushed over her in a warm glow, the counterpart of the icy sweat which had sent her chattering homeward from the fire. After all, if he could fall asleep, fall into such a peaceful sleep as that—tired, no doubt, by his imprudent walk, and the exposure to the cold—it meant, beyond all doubt, beyond all conceivable dread, that he knew nothing, had seen nothing, suspected nothing: that she was safe, safe, safe!

The violence of the reaction made her long to spring to her feet and move about the room. She saw a crooked picture that she wanted to straighten, she would have liked to give the roses another tilt in their glass. But there he sat, quietly sleeping, and the long habit of vigilance made her respect his rest, watching over it as patiently as if it had been a sick child's.

She drew a contented breath. Now she could afford to think of his outing only as it might affect his health; and she knew that this sudden drowsiness, even if it were a sign of extreme fatigue, was also the natural restorative for that fatigue. She continued to sit behind the tea-tray, her hands folded, her eyes on his face, while the peace of the scene entered into her, and held her under brooding wings.

IV

At Mrs. Struthers's, at eleven o'clock that evening, the long over-lit drawing-rooms were already thronged with people.

Lizzie Hazeldean paused on the threshold and looked about her. The habit of pausing to get her bearings, of sending a circular glance around any assemblage of people, any drawing-room, concert-hall or theatre that she entered, had become so instinctive that she would have been surprised had anyone pointed out to her the unobservant expression and careless movements of the young women of her acquaintance, who also looked about them, it is true, but with the vague unseeing stare of youth, and of beauty conscious only of itself.

Lizzie Hazeldean had long since come to regard most women of her age as children in the art of life. Some savage instinct of self-defence, fostered by experience, had always made her more alert and perceiving than the charming creatures who passed from the nursery to marriage as if lifted from one rose-lined cradle into another. "Rocked to sleep—that's what they've always been," she used to think sometimes, listening to their innocuous talk during the long after-dinners in hot drawing-rooms, while their husbands, in the smoking-rooms below, exchanged ideas which, if no more striking, were at least based on more direct experiences.

But then, as all the old ladies said, Lizzie Hazeldean had always preferred the society of men.

The man she now sought was not visible, and she gave a little sigh of ease. "If only he has had the sense to stay away!" she thought.

She would have preferred to stay away herself; but it had been her husband's whim that she should come. "You know you always enjoy yourself at Mrs. Struthers's—everybody does. The old girl somehow manages to have the most amusing house in New York. Who is it who's going to sing tonight? . . . If you don't go, I shall know it's because I've coughed two or three times oftener than usual, and you're worrying about me. My dear girl, it will take more than the Fifth Avenue Hotel fire to kill *me*. . . My heart's feeling unusually steady. . . Put on your black velvet, will you?—with these two roses. . ."

So she had gone. And here she was, in her black velvet, under the glitter of Mrs. Struthers's chandeliers, amid all the youth and good looks and gaiety of New York; for, as Hazeldean said, Mrs. Struthers's house was more amusing than anybody else's, and whenever she opened her doors the world flocked through them.

As Mrs. Hazeldean reached the inner drawing-room the last notes of a rich tenor were falling on the attentive silence. She saw Campanini's low-necked throat subside into silence above the piano, and the clapping of many tightly-fitting gloves was succeeded by a general movement, and the usual irrepressible outburst of talk.

In the breaking-up of groups she caught a glimpse of Sillerton Jackson's silvery crown. Their eyes met across bare shoulders, he bowed profoundly, and she fancied that a dry smile lifted his moustache. "He doesn't usually bow to me as low as that," she thought apprehensively.

But as she advanced into the room her self-possession returned. Among all these stupid pretty women she had such a sense of power, of knowing almost everything better than they did, from the way of doing her hair to the art of keeping a secret! She felt a thrill of pride in the slope of her white shoulders above the black velvet, in the one curl escaping from her thick chignon, and the slant of the gold arrow tipped with diamonds which she had thrust in to retain it. And she had done it all without a maid, with no one cleverer than Susan to help her! Ah, as a woman she knew her business. . .

Mrs. Struthers, plumed and ponderous, with diamond stars studding her black wig like a pin-cushion, had worked her resolute way back to the outer room. More people were coming in; and with her customary rough skill she was receiving, distributing, introducing them. Suddenly her smile deepened; she was evidently greeting an old friend. The group about her scattered, and Mrs. Hazeldean saw that, in her cordial absent-minded way, and while her wandering hostess-eye swept the rooms, she was saying a confidential word to a tall man whose hand she detained. They smiled at each other; then Mrs. Struthers's glance turned toward the inner room, and her smile seemed to say: "You'll find her there."

The tall man nodded. He looked about him composedly, and began to move toward the centre of the throng, speaking to everyone, appearing to have no object beyond that of greeting the next person in his path, yet quietly, steadily pursuing that path, which led straight to the inner room.

Mrs. Hazeldean had found a seat near the piano. A good-looking youth, seated beside her, was telling her at considerable length what he was going to wear at the Beauforts' fancy-ball. She listened, approved, suggested; but her glance never left the advancing figure of the tall man.

Handsome? Yes, she said to herself; she had to admit that he was handsome. A trifle too broad and florid, perhaps; though his air and his attitude so plainly denied it that, on second thoughts, one agreed that a man of his height had, after all, to carry some ballast. Yes; his assurance made him, as a rule, appear to people exactly as he chose to appear; that is, as a man over forty, but carrying his years carelessly, an active muscular man, whose blue eyes were still clear, whose fair hair waved ever so little less thickly than it used to on a low sunburnt forehead, over eyebrows almost silvery in their blondness, and blue eyes the bluer for their thatch. Stupid-looking? By no means. His smile denied that. Just self-sufficient enough to escape fatuity, yet so cool that one felt the fundamental coldness, he steered his way through life as easily and resolutely as he was now working his way through Mrs. Struthers's drawing-rooms.

Half-way, he was detained by a tap of Mrs. Wesson's red fan. Mrs. Wesson—surely, Mrs. Hazeldean reflected, Charles had spoken of Mrs. Sabina Wesson's being with her mother, old Mrs. Parrett, while they watched the fire? Sabina Wesson was a redoubtable woman, one of the few of her generation and her clan who had broken with tradition, and gone to Mrs. Struthers's almost as soon as the Shoe-Polish Queen had bought her house in Fifth Avenue, and issued her first challenge to society. Lizzie Hazeldean shut her eyes for an instant; then, rising from her seat, she joined the group about the singer. From there she wandered on to another knot of acquaintances.

"Look here: the fellow's going to sing again. Let's get into that corner over there."

She felt ever so slight a touch on her arm, and met Henry Prest's composed glance.

A red-lit and palm-shaded recess divided the drawing-rooms from the dining-room, which ran across the width of the house at the back. Mrs. Hazeldean hesitated; then she caught Mrs. Wesson's watchful glance, lifted her head with a smile and followed her companion.

They sat down on a small sofa under the palms, and a couple, who had been in search of the same retreat, paused on the threshold, and with an interchange of glances passed on. Mrs. Hazeldean smiled more vividly.

"Where are my roses? Didn't you get them?" Prest asked. He had a way of looking her over from beneath lowered lids, while he affected to be examining a glove-button or contemplating the tip of his shining boot.

"Yes, I got them," she answered.

"You're not wearing them. I didn't order those."

"No."

"Whose are they, then?"

She unfolded her mother-of-pearl fan, and bent above its complicated traceries.

"Mine," she pronounced.

"Yours? Well, obviously. But I suppose someone sent them to you?"

"*I* did." She hesitated a second. "I sent them to myself."

He raised his eyebrows a little. "Well, they don't suit you—that washy pink! May I ask why you didn't wear mine?"

"I've already told you. . . I've often asked you never to send flowers . . . on the day. . ."

"Nonsense. That's the very day. . . What's the matter? Are you still nervous?"

She was silent for a moment; then she lowered her voice to say: "You ought not to have come here tonight."

"My dear girl, how unlike you! You *are* nervous."

"Didn't you see all those people in the Parretts' window?"

"What, opposite? Lord, no; I just took to my heels! It was the deuce, the back way being barred. But what of it? In all that crowd, do you suppose for a moment—"

"My husband was in the window with them," she said, still lower.

His confident face fell for a moment, and then almost at once regained its look of easy arrogance.

"Well—?"

"Oh, nothing—as yet. Only I ask you . . . to go away now."

"Just as you asked me not to come! Yet *you* came, because you had the sense to see that if you didn't . . . and I came for the same reason. Look here, my dear, for God's sake don't lose your head!"

The challenge seemed to rouse her. She lifted her chin, glanced about the thronged room which they commanded from their corner, and nodded and smiled invitingly at several acquaintances, with the hope that some one of them might come up to her. But though they all returned her greetings with a somewhat elaborate cordiality, not one advanced toward her secluded seat.

She turned her head slightly toward her companion. "I ask you again to go," she repeated.

"Well, I will then, after the fellow's sung. But I'm bound to say you're a good deal pleasanter—"

The first bars of *"Salve, Dimora"* silenced him, and they sat side by side in the meditative rigidity of fashionable persons listening to expensive music. She had thrown herself into a corner of the sofa, and Henry Prest, about whom everything was discreet but his eyes, sat apart from her, one leg crossed over the other, one hand holding his folded opera-hat on his knee, while the other hand rested beside him on the sofa. But an end of her tulle scarf lay in the space between them; and without looking in his direction, without turning her glance from the singer, she was conscious that Prest's hand had reached and drawn the scarf toward him. She shivered a little, made an involuntary motion as though to gather it about her—and then desisted. As the song ended, he bent toward her slightly, said: "Darling" so low that it seemed no more than a breath on her cheek, and then, rising, bowed, and strolled into the other room.

She sighed faintly, and, settling herself once more in her corner, lifted her brilliant eyes to Sillerton Jackson. who was approaching. "It *was* good of you to bring Charlie home from the Parretts' this afternoon." She held out her hand, making way for him at her side.

"Good of me?" he laughed. "Why, I was glad of the chance of getting him safely home; it was rather naughty of *him* to be where he was, I suspect." She fancied a slight pause, as if he waited to see the effect of this, and her lashes beat her cheeks. But already he was going on: "Do you encourage him, with that cough, to run about town after fire-engines?"

She gave back the laugh.

"I don't discourage him—ever—if I can help it. But it *was* foolish of him to go out today," she agreed; and all the while she kept on asking herself, as she had that afternoon, in her talk with her husband: "Now, what would be the *natural* thing for me to say?"

Should she speak of having been at the fire herself—or should she not? The question dinned in her brain so loudly that she could hardly hear what her companion was saying; yet she had, at the same time, a queer feeling of his never having been so close to her, or rather so closely intent on her, as now. In her strange state of nervous lucidity, her eyes seemed to absorb with a new precision every facial detail of whoever approached her; and old Sillerton Jackson's narrow mask, his withered pink cheeks, the veins in the hollow of his temples, under the carefully-tended silvery hair, and the tiny blood-specks in the white of his eyes as he turned their cautious blue gaze on her, appeared as if presented under some powerful lens. With his eye-glasses dangling over one white-gloved hand, the other supporting his opera-hat on his knee, he suggested, behind that assumed carelessness of pose, the patient fixity of a naturalist holding his breath near the crack from which some tiny animal might suddenly issue —if one watched long enough, or gave it, completely enough, the impression of not looking for it, or dreaming it was anywhere near. The sense of that tireless attention made Mrs. Hazeldean's temples ache as if she sat under a

glare of light ever brighter than that of the Struthers'
chandeliers—a glare in which each quiver of a half-formed
thought might be as visible behind her forehead as the
faint lines wrinkling its surface into an uncontrollable
frown of anxiety. Yes, Prest was right; she was losing her
head—losing it for the first time in the dangerous year
during which she had had such continual need to keep it
steady.

"What is it? What has happened to me?" she wondered.

There had been alarms before—how could it be otherwise? But they had only stimulated her, made her more
alert and prompt; whereas tonight she felt herself quivering away into she knew not what abyss of weakness. What
was different, then? Oh, she knew well enough! It was
Charles . . . that haggard look in his eyes, and the lines
of his throat as he had leaned back sleeping. She had
never before admitted to herself how ill she thought him;
and now, to have to admit it, and at the same time not to
have the complete certainty that the look in his eyes was
caused by illness only, made the strain unbearable.

She glanced about her with a sudden sense of despair.
Of all the people in those brilliant animated groups—of
all the women who called her Lizzie, and the men who
were familiars at her house—she knew that not one, at that
moment, guessed, or could have understood, what she was
feeling. . . Her eyes fell on Henry Prest, who had come
to the surface a little way off, bending over the chair of
the handsome Mrs. Lyman. "And *you* least of all!" she
thought. "Yet God knows," she added with a shiver, "they
all have their theories about me!"

"My dear Mrs. Hazeldean, you look a little pale. Are

you cold? Shall I get you some champagne?" Sillerton Jackson was officiously suggesting.

"If you think the other women look blooming! My dear man, it's this hideous vulgar overhead lighting. . ." She rose impatiently. It had occurred to her that the thing to do—the "natural" thing—would be to stroll up to Jinny Lyman, over whom Prest was still attentively bending. *Then* people would see if she was nervous, or ill—or afraid!

But half-way she stopped and thought: "Suppose the Parretts and Wessons *did* see me? Then my joining Jinny while he's talking to her will look—how will it look?" She began to regret not having had it out on the spot with Sillerton Jackson, who could be trusted to hold his tongue on occasion, especially if a pretty woman threw herself on his mercy. She glanced over her shoulder as if to call him back; but he had turned away, been absorbed into another group, and she found herself, instead, abruptly face to face with Sabina Wesson. Well, perhaps that was better still. After all, it all depended on how much Mrs. Wesson had seen, and what line she meant to take, supposing she *had* seen anything. She was not likely to be as inscrutable as old Sillerton. Lizzie wished now that she had not forgotten to go to Mrs. Wesson's last party.

"Dear Mrs. Wesson, it was so kind of you—"

But Mrs. Wesson was not there. By the exercise of that mysterious protective power which enables a woman desirous of not being waylaid to make herself invisible, or to transport herself, by means imperceptible, to another part of the earth's surface, Mrs. Wesson, who, two seconds earlier, appeared in all her hard handsomeness to be bearing straight down on Mrs. Hazeldean, with a scant yard of clear *parquet* between them—Mrs. Wesson, as her animated back and her active red fan now called on all the company to notice, had never been there at all, had never seen Mrs. Hazeldean (*Was* she at Mrs. Struthers's last Sunday? How odd! I must have left before she got there—"), but was busily engaged, on the farther side of the piano, in examining a picture to which her attention appeared to have been called by the persons nearest her.

"Ah, how *life-like!* That's what I always feel when I see a Meissonier," she was heard to exclaim, with her well-known instinct for the fitting epithet.

Lizzie Hazeldean stood motionless. Her eyes dazzled as if she had received a blow on the forehead. "So *that's* what it feels like!" she thought. She lifted her head very high, looked about her again, tried to signal to Henry Prest, but saw him still engaged with the lovely Mrs. Lyman, and at the same moment caught the glance of young Hubert Wesson, Sabina's eldest, who was standing in disengaged expectancy near the supper-room door.

Hubert Wesson, as his eyes met Mrs. Hazeldean's, crimsoned to the forehead, hung back a moment, and then came forward, bowing low—again that too low bow! "So *he* saw me too," she thought. She put her hand on his arm with a laugh. "Dear me, how ceremonious you are! Really, I'm not as old as that bow of yours implies. My dear boy, I hope you want to take me in to supper at once. I was out in the cold all the afternoon, gazing at the Fifth Avenue Hotel fire, and I'm simply dying of hunger and fatigue."

There, the die was cast—she had said it loud enough

for all the people nearest her to hear! And she was sure now that it was the right, the "natural" thing to do.

Her spirits rose, and she sailed into the supper-room like a goddess, steering Hubert to an unoccupied table in a flowery corner.

"No—I think we're very well by ourselves, don't you? Do you want that fat old bore of a Lucy Vanderlow to join us? If you *do*, of course . . . I can see she's dying to . . . but then, I warn you, I shall ask a young man! Let me see—shall I ask Henry Prest? You see he's hovering! No, it *is* jollier with just you and me, isn't it?" She leaned forward a little, resting her chin on her clasped hands, her elbows on the table, in an attitude which the older women thought shockingly free, but the younger ones were beginning to imitate.

"And now, some champagne, please—and *hot* terrapin! . . . But I suppose you were at the fire yourself, weren't you?" she leaned still a little nearer to say.

The blush again swept over young Wesson's face, rose to his forehead, and turned the lobes of his large ears to balls of fire ("It looks," she thought, "as if he had on huge coral earrings."). But she forced him to look at her, laughed straight into his eyes, and went on: "Did you ever see a funnier sight than all those dressed-up absurdities rushing out into the cold? It looked like the end of an Inauguration Ball! I was so fascinated that I actually pushed my way into the hall. The firemen were furious, but they couldn't stop me—nobody can stop me at a fire! You should have seen the ladies scuttling downstairs—the fat ones! Oh, but I beg your pardon; I'd forgotten that you admire . . . avoirdupois. No? But . . . Mrs. Van . . . so stupid of me! Why, you're actually blushing! I assure you, you're as red as your mother's fan—and visible from as great a distance! Yes, please; a little more champagne. . ."

And then the inevitable began. She forgot the fire, forgot her anxieties, forgot Mrs. Wesson's affront, forgot everything but the amusement, the passing childish amusement, of twirling around her little finger this shy clumsy boy, as she had twirled so many others, old and young, not caring afterward if she ever saw them again, but so absorbed in the sport, and in her sense of knowing how to do it better than the other women—more quietly, more insidiously, without ogling, bridling or grimacing— that sometimes she used to ask herself with a shiver: "What was the gift given to me for?" Yes; it always amused her at first: the gradual dawn of attraction in eyes that had regarded her with indifference, the blood rising to the face, the way she could turn and twist the talk as though she had her victim on a leash, spinning him after her down winding paths of sentimentality, irony, caprice . . . and leaving him, with beating heart and dazzled eyes, to visions of an all-promising morrow. . . "My only accomplishment!" she murmured to herself as she rose from the table followed by young Wesson's fascinated gaze, while already, on her own lips, she felt the taste of cinders.

"But at any rate," she thought, "he'll hold his tongue about having seen me at the fire."

V

She let herself in with her latch-key, glanced at the notes and letters on the hall-table (the old habit of allowing nothing to escape her), and stole up through the darkness to her room.

A fire still glowed in the chimney, and its light fell on two vases of crimson roses. The room was full of their scent.

Mrs. Hazeldean frowned, and then shrugged her shoulders. It had been a mistake, after all, to let it appear that she was indifferent to the flowers; she must remember to thank Susan for rescuing them. She began to undress, hastily yet clumsily, as if her deft fingers were all thumbs; but first, detaching the two faded pink roses from her bosom, she put them with a reverent touch into a glass on the toilet-table. Then, slipping on her dressing-gown, she stole to her husband's door. It was shut, and she leaned her ear to the keyhole. After a moment she caught his breathing, heavy, as it always was when he had a cold, but regular, untroubled. . . With a sigh of relief she tiptoed back. Her uncovered bed, with its fresh pillows and satin coverlet, sent her a rosy invitation; but she cowered down by the fire, hugging her knees and staring into the coals.

"So *that's* what it feels like!" she repeated.

It was the first time in her life that she had ever been

deliberately "cut"; and the cut was a deadly injury in old New York. For Sabina Wesson to have used it, consciously, deliberately—for there was no doubt that she had purposely advanced toward her victim—she must have done so with intent to kill. And to risk that, she must have been sure of her facts, sure of corroborating witnesses, sure of being backed up by all her clan.

Lizzie Hazeldean had her clan too—but it was a small and weak one, and she hung on its outer fringe by a thread of little-regarded cousinship. As for the Hazeldean tribe, which was large and stronger (though nothing like the great organized Wesson-Parrett *gens*, with half New York and all Albany at its back)—well, the Hazeldeans were not much to be counted on, and would even, perhaps, in a furtive negative way, be not too sorry ("if it were not for poor Charlie") that poor Charlie's wife should at last be made to pay for her good looks, her popularity, above all for being, in spite of her origin, treated by poor Charlie as if she were one of them!

Her origin was, of course, respectable enough. Everybody knew all about the Winters—she had been Lizzie Winter. But the Winters were very small people, and her father, the Reverend Arcadius Winter, the sentimental over-popular Rector of a fashionable New York church, after a few seasons of too great success as preacher and director of female consciences, had suddenly had to resign and go to Bermuda for his health—or was it France? —to some obscure watering-place, it was rumoured. At any rate, Lizzie, who went with him (with a crushed bedridden mother), was ultimately, after the mother's death, fished out of a girls' school in Brussels—they seemed to have been in so many countries at once!—and brought back to New York by a former parishioner of poor Arcadius's, who had always "believed in him," in spite of the Bishop and who took pity on his lonely daughter.

The parishioner, Mrs. Mant, was "one of the Hazeldeans." She was a rich widow, given to generous gestures which she was often at a loss how to complete; and when she had brought Lizzie Winter home, and sufficiently celebrated her own courage in doing so, she did not quite know what step to take next. She had fancied it would be pleasant to have a clever handsome girl about the house; but her housekeeper was not of the same mind. The spare-room sheets had not been out of lavender for twenty years—and Miss Winter always left the blinds up in her room, and the carpet and curtains, unused to such exposure, suffered accordingly. Then young men began to call—they called in numbers. Mrs. Mant had not supposed that the daughter of a clergyman—and a clergyman "under a cloud"—would expect visitors. She had imagined herself taking Lizzie Winter to Church Fairs, and having the stitches of her knitting picked up by the young girl, whose "eyes were better" than her benefactress's. But Lizzie did not know how to knit—she possessed no useful accomplishments—and she was visibly bored by Church Fairs, where her presence was of little use, since she had no money to spend. Mrs. Mant began to see her mistake; and the discovery made her dislike her protégée, whom she secretly regarded as having intentionally misled her.

In Mrs. Mant's life, the transition from one enthusiasm to another was always marked by an interval of disillusionment, during which, Providence having failed to fulfill her requirements, its existence was openly called into question. But in this flux of moods there was one fixed point: Mrs. Mant was a woman whose life revolved about a bunch of keys. What treasures they gave access to, what disasters would have ensued had they been forever lost, was not quite clear; but whenever they were missed the household was in an uproar, and as Mrs. Mant would trust them to no one but herself, these occasions were frequent. One of them arose at the very moment when Mrs. Mant was recovering from her enthusiasm for Miss Winter. A minute before, the keys had been there, in a pocket of her work-table; she had actually touched them in hunting for her buttonhole-scissors. She had been called away to speak to the plumber about the bath-room leak, and when she left the room there was no one in it but Miss Winter. When she returned, the keys were gone. The house had been turned inside out; everyone had been, if not accused, at least suspected; and in a rash moment Mrs. Mant had spoken of the police. The housemaid had thereupon given warning, and her own maid threatened to follow; when suddenly the Bishops's hints recurred to Mrs. Mant. The Bishop had always implied that there had been something irregular in Dr. Winter's accounts, besides the other unfortunate business.

Very mildly, she had asked Miss Winter if she might not have seen the keys, and "picked them up without thinking." Miss Winter permitted herself to smile in denying the suggestion; the smile irritated Mrs. Mant; and in a moment the floodgates were opened. She saw nothing to smile at in her question—unless it was of a kind that Miss Winter was already used to, prepared for . . . with that sort of background . . . her unfortunate father. . .

"Stop!" Lizzie Winter cried. She remembered now, as

if it had happened yesterday, the abyss suddenly opening at her feet. It was her first direct contact with human cruelty. Suffering, weakness, frailties other than Mrs. Mant's restricted fancy could have pictured, the girl had known, or at least suspected; but she had found as much kindness as folly in her path, and no one had ever before attempted to visit upon her the dimly-guessed shortcomings of her poor old father. She shook with horror as much as with indignation, and her "Stop!" blazed out so violently that Mrs. Mant, turning white, feebly groped for the bell.

And it was then, at that very moment, that Charles Hazeldean came in—Charles Hazeldean, the favourite nephew, the pride of the tribe. Lizzie had seen him only once or twice, for he had been absent since her return to New York. She had thought him distinguished-looking, but rather serious and sarcastic; and he had apparently taken little notice of her—which perhaps accounted for her opinion.

"Oh, Charles, dearest Charles—that you should be here to hear such things said to me!" his aunt gasped, her hand on her outraged heart.

"What things? Said by whom? I see no one here to say them but Miss Winter," Charles had laughed, taking the girl's icy hand.

"Don't shake hands with her! She has insulted me! She has ordered me to keep silence—in my own house. 'Stop!' she said, when I was trying, in the kindness of my heart, to get her to admit privately . . . Well, if she prefers to have the police. . ."

"I do! I ask you to send for them!" Lizzie cried.

How vividly she remembered all that followed: the finding of the keys, Mrs. Mant's reluctant apologies, her own cold acceptance of them, and the sense on both sides of the impossibility of continuing their life together! She had been wounded to the soul, and her own plight first revealed to her in all its destitution. Before that, despite the ups and downs of a wandering life, her youth, her good looks, the sense of a certain bright power over people and events, had hurried her along on a spring tide of confidence; she had never thought of herself as the dependent, the beneficiary, of the persons who were kind to her. Now she saw herself, at twenty, a penniless girl, with a feeble discredited father carrying his snowy head, his unctuous voice, his edifying manner from one cheap watering-place to another, through an endless succession of sentimental and pecuniary entanglements. To him she could be of no more help than he to her; and save for him she was alone. The Winter cousins, as much humiliated by his disgrace as they had been puffed-up by his triumphs, let it be understood, when the breach with Mrs. Mant became known, that they were not in a position to interfere; and among Dr. Winter's former parishioners none was left to champion him. Almost at the same time, Lizzie heard that he was about to marry a Portuguese opera-singer and be received into the Church of Rome; and this crowning scandal too promptly justified his family.

The situation was a grave one, and called for energetic measures. Lizzie understood it—and a week later she was engaged to Charles Hazeldean.

She always said afterward that but for the keys he would

never have thought of marrying her; while he laughingly affirmed that, on the contrary, but for the keys she would never have looked at *him*.

But what did it all matter, in the complete and blessed understanding which was to follow on their hasty union? If all the advantages on both sides had been weighed and found equal by judicious advisers, harmony more complete could hardly have been predicted. As a matter of fact, the advisers, had they been judicious, would probably have found only elements of discord in the characters concerned. Charles Hazeldean was by nature an observer and a student, brooding and curious of mind: Lizzie Winter (as she looked back at herself)—what was she, what would she ever be, but a quick, ephemeral creature, in whom a perpetual and adaptable activity simulated mind, as her grace, her swiftness, her expressiveness simulated beauty? So others would have judged her; so, now, she judged herself. And she knew that in fundamental things she was still the same. And yet she had satisfied him: satisfied him, to all appearances, as completely in the quiet later years as in the first flushed hours. As completely, or perhaps even more so. In the early months, dazzled gratitude made her the humbler, fonder worshipper; but as her powers expanded in the warm air of comprehension, as she felt herself grow handsomer, cleverer, more competent and more companionable than he had hoped, or she had dreamed herself capable of becoming, the balance was imperceptibly reversed, and the triumph in his eyes when they rested on her.

The Hazeldeans were conquered; they had to admit it. Such a brilliant recruit to the clan was not to be disowned. Mrs. Mant was left to nurse her grievance in solitude, till she too fell into line, carelessly but handsomely forgiven.

Ah, those first years of triumph! They frightened Lizzie now as she looked back. One day, the friendless defenceless daughter of a discredited man; the next, almost, the wife of Charlie Hazeldean, the popular successful young lawyer, with a good practice already assured, and the best of professional and private prospects. His own parents were dead, and had died poor; but two or three childless relatives were understood to be letting their capital accumulate for his benefit, and meanwhile in Lizzie's thrifty hands his earnings were largely sufficient.

Ah, those first years! There had been barely six; but even now there were moments when their sweetness drenched her to the soul. . . Barely six; and then the sharp re-awakening of an inherited weakness of the heart that Hazeldean and his doctors had imagined to be completely cured. Once before, for the same cause, he had been sent off, suddenly, for a year of travel in mild climate and distant scenes; and his first return had coincided with the close of Lizzie's sojourn at Mrs. Mant's. The young man felt sure enough of the future to marry and take up his professional duties again, and for the following six years he had led, without interruption, the busy life of a successful lawyer; then had come a second breakdown, more unexpectedly, and with more alarming symptoms. The "Hazeldean heart" was a proverbial boast in the family; the Hazeldeans privately considered it more distinguished than the Sillerton gout, and far more refined than the Wesson liver; and it had permitted most of them to survive, in valetudinarian ease, to a ripe old age, when they died of some quite other disorder. But

Charles Hazeldean had defied it, and it took its revenge, and took it savagely.

One by one, hopes and plans faded. The Hazeldeans went south for a winter; he lay on a deck-chair in a Florida garden, and read and dreamed, and was happy with Lizzie beside him. So the months passed; and by the following autumn he was better, returned to New York, and took up his profession. Intermittently but obstinately, he had continued the struggle for two more years; but before they were over husband and wife understood that the good days were done.

He could be at his office only at lengthening intervals; he sank gradually into invalidism without submitting to it. His income dwindled; and, indifferent for himself, he fretted ceaselessly at the thought of depriving Lizzie of the least of her luxuries.

At heart she was indifferent to them too; but she could not convince him of it. He had been brought up in the old New York tradition, which decreed that a man, at whatever cost, must provide his wife with what she had always "been accustomed to"; and he had gloried too much in her prettiness, her elegance, her easy way of wearing her expensive dresses, and his friends' enjoyment of the good dinners she knew how to order, not to accustom her to everything which could enhance such graces. Mrs. Mant's secret satisfaction rankled in him. She sent him Baltimore terrapin, and her famous clam broth, and a dozen of the old Hazeldean port, and said "I told you so" to her confidants when Lizzie was mentioned; and Charles Hazeldean knew it, and swore at it.

"I won't be pauperized by her!" he declared; but Lizzie

smiled away his anger, and persuaded him to taste the terrapin and sip the port.

She was smiling faintly at the memory of the last passage between him and Mrs. Mant when the turning of the bedroom door-handle startled her. She jumped up, and he stood there. The blood rushed to her forehead; his expression frightened her; for an instant she stared at him as if he had been an enemy. Then she saw that the look in his face was only the remote lost look of excessive physical pain.

She was at his side at once, supporting him, guiding him to the nearest armchair. He sank into it, and she flung a shawl over him, and knelt at his side while his inscrutable eyes continued to repel her.

"Charles . . . Charles," she pleaded.

For a while he could not speak; and she said to herself that she would perhaps never know whether he had sought her because he was ill, or whether illness had seized him as he entered her room to question, accuse, or reveal what he had seen or heard that afternoon.

Suddenly he lifted his hand and pressed back her forehead, so that her face lay bare under his eyes.

"Love, love, you've been happy?"

"*Happy?*" The word choked her. She clung to him, burying her anguish against his knees. His hand stirred weakly in her hair, and gathering her whole strength into the gesture, she raised her head again, looked into his eyes, and breathed back: "And you?"

He gave her one full look; all their life together was in it, from the first day to the last. His hand brushed her once more, like a blessing, and then dropped. The moment of their communion was over; the next she was preparing remedies, ringing for the servants, ordering the doctor to be called. Her husband was once more the harmless helpless captive that sickness makes of the most dreaded and the most loved.

VI

It was in Mrs. Mant's drawing-room that, some half-year later, Mrs. Charles Hazeldean, after a moment's hesitation, said to the servant that, yes, he might show in Mr. Prest.

Mrs. Mant was away. She had been leaving for Washington to visit a new protégée when Mrs. Hazeldean arrived from Europe, and after a rapid consultation with the clan had decided that it would not be "decent" to let poor Charles's widow go to an hotel. Lizzie had therefore the strange sensation of returning, after nearly nine years, to the house from which her husband had triumphantly rescued her; of returning there, to be sure, in comparative independence, and without danger of falling into her former bondage, yet with every nerve shrinking from all that the scene revived.

Mrs. Mant, the next day, had left for Washington; but before starting she had tossed a note across the breakfast-table to her visitor.

"Very proper—he was one of Charlie's oldest friends, I believe?" she said, with her mild frosty smile. Mrs. Hazeldean glanced at the note, turned it over as if to examine the signature, and restored it to her hostess.

"Yes. But I don't think I care to see anyone just yet."

There was a pause, during which the butler brought in fresh griddle-cakes, replenished the hot milk, and withdrew. As the door closed on him, Mrs. Mant said, with a dangerous cordiality: "No one would misunderstand your receiving an old friend of your husband's . . . like Mr. Prest."

Lizzie Hazeldean cast a sharp glance at the large empty mysterious face across the table. They *wanted* her to receive Henry Prest, then? Ah, well . . . perhaps she understood. . .

"Shall I answer this for you, my dear? Or will you?" Mrs. Mant pursued.

"Oh, as you like. But don't fix a day, please. Later—"

Mrs. Mant's face again became vacuous. She murmured: "You must not shut yourself up too much. It will not do to be morbid. I'm sorry to have to leave you here alone—"

Lizzie's eyes filled: Mrs. Mant's sympathy seemed more cruel than her cruelty. Every word that she used had a veiled taunt for its counterpart.

"Oh, you mustn't think of giving up your visit—"

"My dear, how can I? It's a *duty*. I'll send a line to Henry Prest, then. . . If you would sip a little port at luncheon and dinner we should have you looking less like a ghost. . ."

Mrs. Mant departed; and two days later—the interval was "decent"—Mr. Henry Prest was announced. Mrs. Hazeldean had not seen him since the previous New Year's Day. Their last words had been exchanged in Mrs. Struthers's crimson boudoir, and since then half a year had elapsed. Charles Hazeldean had lingered for a fortnight; but though there had been ups and downs, and intervals of hope when none could have criticised his wife for seeing her friends, her door had been barred against everyone. She had not excluded Henry Prest more rigorously than the others; he had simply been one of the many who received, day by day, the same answer: "Mrs. Hazeldean sees no one but the family."

Almost immediately after her husband's death she had sailed for Europe on a long-deferred visit to her father, who was now settled at Nice; but from this expedition she had presumably brought back little comfort, for when she arrived in New York her relations were struck by her air of ill-health and depression. It spoke in her favour, however; they were agreed that she was behaving with propriety.

She looked at Henry Prest as if he were a stranger: so difficult was it, at the first moment, to fit his robust and splendid person into the region of twilight shades which, for the last months, she had inhabited. She was beginning to find that everyone had an air of remoteness; she seemed to see people and life through the confusing blur of the long crape veil in which it was a widow's duty to shroud her affliction. But she gave him her hand without perceptible reluctance.

He lifted it toward his lips, in an obvious attempt to combine gallantry with condolence, and then, half-way up, seemed to feel that the occasion required him to release it.

"Well—you'll admit that I've been patient!" he exclaimed.

"Patient? Yes. What else was there to be?" she rejoined with a faint smile, as he seated himself beside her, a little too near.

"Oh, well . . . of course! I understood all that, I hope

you'll believe. But mightn't you at least have answered my letters—one or two of them?"

She shook her head. "I couldn't write."

"Not to anyone? Or not to me?" he queried, with ironic emphasis.

"I wrote only the letters I had to—no others."

"Ah, I see." He laughed slightly. "And you didn't consider that letters to *me* were among them?"

She was silent, and he stood up and took a turn across the room. His face was redder than usual, and now and then a twitch passed over it. She saw that he felt the barrier of her crape, and that it left him baffled and resentful. A struggle was still perceptibly going on in him between his traditional standard of behaviour at such a meeting, and primitive impulses renewed by the memory of their last hours together. When he turned back and paused before her his ruddy flush had paled, and he stood there, frowning, uncertain, and visibly resenting the fact that she made him so.

"You sit there like a stone!" he said.

"I feel like a stone."

"Oh, come—!"

She knew well enough what he was thinking: that the only way to bridge over such a bad beginning was to get the woman into your arms—and talk afterward. It was the classic move. He had done it dozens of times, no doubt, and was evidently asking himself why the deuce he couldn't do it now. . . But something in her look must have benumbed him. He sat down again beside her.

"What you must have been through, dearest!" He waited and coughed. "I can understand your being—all broken up. But I know nothing; remember, I know nothing as to what actually happened. . ."

"Nothing happened."

"As to—what we feared? No hint—?"

She shook her head.

He cleared his throat before the next question. "And you don't think that in your absence he may have spoken —to anyone?"

"Never!"

"Then, my dear, we seem to have had the most unbelievable good luck; and I can't see—"

He had edged slowly nearer, and now laid a large ringed hand on her sleeve. How well she knew those rings—the two dull gold snakes with malevolent jewelled eyes! She sat as motionless as if their coils were about her, till slowly his tentative grasp relaxed.

"Lizzie, you know"—his tone was discouraged—"this is morbid. . ."

"Morbid?"

"When you're safe out of the worst scrape . . . and free, my darling, *free!* Don't you realize it? I suppose the strain's been too much for you; but I want you to feel that now—"

She stood up suddenly, and put half the length of the room between them.

"Stop! Stop! Stop!" she almost screamed, as she had screamed long ago at Mrs. Mant.

He stood up also, darkly red under his rich sunburn, and forced a smile.

"Really," he protested, "all things considered—and after a separation of six months!" She was silent. "My dear," he continued mildly, "will you tell me what you expect me to think?"

"Oh, don't take that tone," she murmured.

"What tone?"

"As if—as if—you still imagined we could go back—"

She saw his face fall. Had he ever before, she wondered, stumbled upon an obstacle in that smooth walk of his? It flashed over her that this was the danger besetting men who had a "way with women"—the day came when they might follow it too blindly.

The reflection evidently occurred to him almost as soon as it did to her. He summoned another propitiatory smile, and drawing near, took her hand gently. "But I don't want to go back. . . I want to go forward, dearest. . . Now that at last you're free."

She seized on the word as if she had been waiting for her cue. "Free! Oh, that's it—*free!* Can't you see, can't you understand, that I mean to stay free?"

Again a shadow of distrust crossed his face, and the smile he had begun for her reassurance seemed to remain on his lips for his own.

"But of course! Can you imagine that I want to put you in chains? I want you be as free as you please—free to love me as much as you choose!" He was visibly pleased with the last phrase.

She drew away her hand, but not unkindly. "I'm sorry —I *am* sorry, Henry. But you don't understand."

"What don't I understand?"

"That what you ask is quite impossible—ever. I can't go on . . . in the old way. . ."

She saw his face working nervously. "In the old way? You mean—?" Before she could explain he hurried on

with an increasing majesty of manner: "Don't answer! I
see—I understand. When you spoke of freedom just now I
was misled for a moment—I frankly own I was—into thinking that, after your wretched marriage, you might prefer discreeter ties . . . an apparent independence which
would leave us both. . . I say *apparent,* for on my side
there has never been the least wish to conceal. . . But if
I was mistaken, if on the contrary what you wish is . . . is
to take advantage of your freedom to regularize our . . .
our attachment. . ."

She said nothing, not because she had any desire to have
him complete the phrase, but because she found nothing
to say. To all that concerned their common past she was
aware of offering a numbed soul. But her silence evidently
perplexed him, and in his perplexity he began to lose his
footing, and to flounder in a sea of words.

"Lizzie! Do you hear me? If I was mistaken, I say—and
I hope I'm not above owning that at times I *may* be mistaken; if I was—why, by God, my dear, no woman ever
heard me speak the words before; but here I am to have
and to hold, as the Book says! Why, hadn't you realized
it? Lizzie, look up—! *I'm asking you to marry me.*"

Still, for a moment, she made no reply, but stood gazing
about her as if she had the sudden sense of unseen
presences between them. At length she gave a faint laugh.
It visibly ruffled her visitor.

"I'm not conscious," he began again, "of having said
anything particularly laughable—" He stopped and scrutinized her narrowly, as though checked by the thought
that there might be some thing not quite normal. . .
Then, apparently reassured, he half-murmured his only
French phrase: *"La joie fait peur . . .* eh?"

She did not seem to hear. "I wasn't laughing at you," she said, "but only at the coincidences of life. It was in this room that my husband asked me to marry him."

"Ah?" Her suitor appeared politely doubtful of the good taste, or the opportunity, of producing this reminiscence. But he made another call on his magnanimity. "Really? But, I say, my dear, I couldn't be expected to know it, could I? If I'd guessed that such a painful association—"

"Painful?" She turned upon him. "A painful association? Do you think that was what I meant?" Her voice sank. "This room is sacred to me."

She had her eyes on his face, which, perhaps because of its architectural completeness, seemed to lack the mobility necessary to follow such a leap of thought. It was so ostensibly a solid building, and not a nomad's tent. He struggled with a ruffled pride, rose again to playful magnanimity, and murmured: "Compassionate angel!"

"Oh, compassionate? To whom? Do you imagine—did I ever say anything to make you doubt the truth of what I'm telling you?"

His brows fretted: his temper was up. "*Say* anything? No," he insinuated ironically; then, in a hasty plunge after his lost forbearance, added with exquisite mildness: "Your tact was perfect . . . always. I've invariably done you that justice. No one could have been more thoroughly the . . . the lady. I never failed to admire your good-breeding in avoiding any reference to your . . . your other life."

She faced him steadily: "Well, that other life *was* my life—my only life! Now you know."

There was a silence. Henry Prest drew out a monogrammed handkerchief and passed it over his dry lips. As he did so, a whiff of his eau de Cologne reached her, and she winced a little. It was evident that he was seeking what to say next; wondering, rather helplessly, how to get back his lost command of the situation. He finally induced his features to break again into a persuasive smile.

"Not your *only* life, dearest," he reproached her.

She met it instantly. "Yes; so you thought—because I chose you should."

"You chose—?" The smile became incredulous.

"Oh, deliberately. But I suppose I've no excuse that you would not dislike to hear. . . Why shouldn't we break off now?"

"Break off . . . this conversation?" His tone was aggrieved. "Of course I've no wish to force myself—"

She interrupted him with a raised hand. "Break off for good, Henry."

"For good?" He stared, and gave a quick swallow, as though the dose were choking him. "For good? Are you really—? You and I? Is this serious, Lizzie?"

"Perfectly. But if you prefer to hear . . . what can only be painful. . ."

He straightened himself, threw back his shoulders, and said in an uncertain voice: "I hope you don't take me for a coward."

She made no direct reply, but continued: "Well, then, you thought I loved you, I suppose—"

He smiled again, revived his moustache with a slight twist, and gave a hardly perceptible shrug. "You . . . ah . . . managed to produce the illusion. . ."

"Oh, well, yes: a woman *can*—so easily! That's what men often forget. You thought I was a lovelorn mistress; and I was only an expensive prostitute."

"Elizabeth!" he gasped, pale now to the ruddy eyelids. She saw that the word had wounded more than his pride, and that, before realizing the insult to his love, he was shuddering at the offence to his taste. Mistress! Prostitute! Such words were banned. No one reproved coarseness of language in women more than Henry Prest; one of Mrs. Hazeldean's greatest charms (as he had just told her) had been her way of remaining, "through it all," so ineffably "the lady." He looked at her as if a fresh doubt of her sanity had assailed him.

"Shall I go on?" she smiled.

He bent his head stiffly. "I am still at a loss to imagine for what purpose you made a fool of me."

"Well, then, it was as I say. I wanted money—money for my husband."

He moistened his lips. "For your husband?"

"Yes; when he began to be so ill; when he needed comforts, luxury, the opportunity to get away. He saved me, when I was a girl, from untold humiliation and wretchedness. No one else lifted a finger to help me—not one of my own family. I hadn't a penny or a friend. Mrs. Mant had grown sick of me, and was trying to find an excuse to throw me over. Oh, you don't know what a girl has to put up with—a girl alone in the world—who depends for her clothes, and her food, and the roof over her head, on the whims of a vain capricious old woman! It was because *he* knew, because he understood, that he married me. . . He took me out of misery into blessedness. He put me up above them all . . . he put me beside himself. I didn't

care for anything but that; I didn't care for the money or
the freedom; I cared only for him. I would have followed
him into the desert—I would have gone barefoot to be
with him. I would have starved, begged, done anything
for him—*anything*." She broke off, her voice lost in a sob.
She was no longer aware of Prest's presence—all her consciousness was absorbed in the vision she had evoked. "It
was *he* who cared—who wanted me to be rich and independent and admired! He wanted to heap everything
on me—during the first years I could hardly persuade him
to keep enough money for himself. . . And then he was
taken ill; and as he got worse, and gradually dropped out
of affairs, his income grew smaller, and then stopped altogether; and all the while there were new expenses piling
up—nurses, doctors, travel; and he grew frightened; frightened not for himself but for me. . . And what was I to
do? I had to pay for things somehow. For the first year I
managed to put off paying—then I borrowed small sums
here and there. But that couldn't last. And all the while
I had to keep on looking pretty and prosperous, or else he
began to worry, and think we were ruined, and wonder
what would become of me if he didn't get well. By the
time you came I was desperate—I would have done anything, anything! He thought the money came from my
Portuguese stepmother. She really was rich, as it happens.
Unluckily my poor father tried to invest her money, and
lost it all; but when they were first married she sent a
thousand dollars—and all the rest, all you gave me, I built
on that."

She paused pantingly, as if her tale were at an end.
Gradually her consciousness of present things returned,
and she saw Henry Prest, as if far off, a small indistinct

figure looming through the mist of her blurred eyes. She thought to herself: "He doesn't believe me," and the thought exasperated her.

"You wonder, I suppose," she began again, "that a woman should dare confess such things about herself—"

He cleared his throat. "About herself? No; perhaps not. But about her husband."

The blood rushed to her forehead. "About her husband? But you don't dare to imagine—?"

"You leave me," he rejoined icily, "no other inference that I can see." She stood dumbfounded, and he added: "At any rate, it certainly explains your extraordinary coolness—pluck, I used to think it. I perceived that I needn't have taken such precautions."

She considered this. "You think, then, that he knew? You think, perhaps, that I knew he did?" She pondered again painfully, and then her face lit up. "He never knew —never! That's enough for me—and for you it doesn't matter. Think what you please. He was happy to the end —that's all I care for."

"There can be no doubt about your frankness," he said with pinched lips.

"There's no longer any reason for not being frank."

He picked up his hat, and studiously considered its lining; then he took the gloves he had laid in it, and drew them thoughtfully through his hands. She thought: "Thank God, he's going!"

But he set the hat and gloves down on a table, and moved a little nearer to her. His face looked as ravaged as a reveller's at daybreak.

"You—leave positively nothing to the imagination!" he murmured.

"I told you it was useless—" she began; but he interrupted her: "Nothing, that is—if I believed you." He moistened his lips again, and tapped them with his handkerchief. Again she had a whiff of the eau de Cologne. "But I don't!" he proclaimed. "Too many memories . . . too many . . . proofs, my dearest. . ." He stopped, smiling somewhat convulsively. She saw that he imagined the smile would soothe her.

She remained silent, and he began once more, as if appealing to her against her own verdict: "I know better, Lizzie. In spite of everything, *I know you're not that kind of woman.*"

"I took your money—"

"As a favour. I knew the difficulties of your position. . . I understood completely. I beg of you never again to allude to—all that." It dawned on her that anything would be more endurable to him than to think he had been a dupe—and one of two dupes! The part was not one that he could conceive of having played. His pride was up in arms to defend her, not so much for her sake as for his own. The discovery gave her a baffling sense of helplessness; against that impenetrable self-sufficiency all her affirmations might spend themselves in vain.

"No man who has had the privilege of being loved by you could ever for a moment. . ."

She raised her head and looked at him. "You have never had that privilege," she interrupted.

His jaw fell. She saw his eyes from uneasy supplication to a cold anger. He gave a little inarticulate grunt before his voice came back to him.

"You spare no pains in degrading yourself in my eyes."

"I am not degrading myself. I am telling you the truth.

I needed money. I knew no way of earning it. You were willing to give it . . . for what you call the privilege. . ."

"Lizzie," he interrupted solemnly, "don't go on! I believe I enter into all your feelings—I believe I always have. In so sensitive, so hypersensitive a nature, there are moments when every other feeling is swept away by scruples. . . For those scruples I only honour you the more. But I won't hear another word now. If I allowed you to go on in your present state of . . . nervous exaltation . . . you might be the first to deplore. . . I wish to forget everything you have said. . . I wish to look forward, not back. . ." He squared his shoulders, took a deep breath, and fixed her with a glance of recovered confidence. "How little you know me if you believe that I could fail you *now!*"

She returned his look with a weary steadiness. "You are kind—you mean to be generous, I'm sure. But don't you see that I *can't* marry you?"

"I only see that, in the natural rush of your remorse—"

"Remorse? Remorse?" She broke in with a laugh. "Do you imagine I feel any remorse? I'd do it all over again tomorrow—for the same object! I got what I wanted—I gave him that last year, that last good year. It was the relief from anxiety that kept him alive, that kept him happy. Oh, he *was* happy—I know that!" She turned to Prest with a strange smile. "I do thank you for that—I'm not ungrateful."

"You . . . you . . . *ungrateful?* This . . . is really . . . indecent. . ." He took up his hat again, and stood in the middle of the room as if waiting to be waked from a bad dream.

"You are—rejecting an opportunity—" he began.

She made a faint motion of assent.

"You do realize it? I'm still prepared to—to help you, if you should. . ." She made no answer, and he continued: "How do you expect to live—since you have chosen to drag in such considerations?"

"I don't care how I live. I never wanted the money for myself."

He raised a deprecating hand. "Oh, don't—*again!* The woman I had meant to. . ." Suddenly, to her surprise, she saw a glitter of moisture on his lower lids. He applied his handkerchief to them, and the waft of scent checked her momentary impulse of compunction. That Cologne water! It called up picture after picture with a hideous precision. "Well, it was worth it," she murmured doggedly.

Henry Prest restored his handkerchief to his pocket. He waited, glanced about the room, turned back to her.

"If your decision is final—"

"Oh, final!"

He bowed. "There is one thing more—which I should have mentioned if you had ever given me the opportunity of seeing you after—after last New Year's Day. Something I preferred not to commit to writing—"

"Yes?" she questioned indifferently.

"Your husband, you are positively convinced, had no idea . . . that day . . . ?"

"None."

"Well, others, it appears, had." He paused. "Mrs. Wesson saw us."

"So I suppose. I remember now that she went out of her way to cut me that evening at Mrs. Struthers's."

"Exactly. And she was not the only person who saw us. If people had not been disarmed by your husband's falling

ill that very day you would have found yourself—os-
tracized."

She made no comment, and he pursued, with a last
effort: "In your grief, your solitude, you haven't yet realized what your future will be—how difficult. It is what I
wished to guard you against—it was my purpose in asking
you to marry me." He drew himself up and smiled as if
he were looking at his own reflection in a mirror, and
thought favourably of it. "A man who has had the misfortune to compromise a woman is bound in honour—
Even if my own inclination were not what it is, I should
consider. . ."

She turned to him with a softened smile. Yes, he had
really brought himself to think that he was proposing to
marry her to save her reputation. At this glimpse of the
old hackneyed axioms on which he actually believed that
his conduct was based, she felt anew her remoteness from
the life he would have drawn her back to.

"My poor Henry, don't you see how far I've got beyond
the Mrs. Wessons? If all New York wants to ostracize me,
let it! I've had my day . . . no woman has more than
one. Why shouldn't I have to pay for it? I'm ready."

"Good heavens!" he murmured.

She was aware that he had put forth his last effort. The
wound she had inflicted had gone to the most vital spot;
she had prevented his being magnanimous, and the injury
was unforgivable. He was glad, yes, actually glad now, to
have her know that New York meant to cut her; but,
strive as she might, she could not bring herself to care
either for the fact, or for his secret pleasure in it. Her own
secret pleasures were beyond New York's reach and his.

"I'm sorry," she reiterated gently. He bowed, without trying to take her hand, and left the room.

As the door closed she looked after him with a dazed stare. "He's right, I suppose; I don't realize yet—" She heard the shutting of the outer door, and dropped to the sofa, pressing her hands against her aching eyes. At that moment, for the first time, she asked herself what the next day, and the next, would be like. . .

"If only I cared more about reading," she moaned, remembering how vainly she had tried to acquire her husband's tastes, and how gently and humorously he had smiled at her efforts. "Well—there are always cards; and when I get older, knitting and patience, I suppose. And if everybody cuts me I shan't need any evening dresses. That will be an economy, at any rate," she concluded with a little shiver.

VII

.   .   .   .   .   .

"SHE was *bad* . . . always. They used to meet at the Fifth Avenue Hotel."

I must go back now to this phrase of my mother's—the phrase from which, at the opening of my narrative, I broke away for a time in order to project more vividly on the scene that anxious moving vision of Lizzie Hazeldean: a vision in which memories of my one boyish glimpse of her were pieced together with hints collected afterward.

When my mother uttered her condemnatory judgment I was a young man of twenty-one, newly graduated from Harvard, and at home again under the family roof in New York. It was long since I had heard Mrs. Hazeldean spoken of. I had been away, at school and at Harvard, for the greater part of the interval, and in the holidays she was probably not considered a fitting subject of conversation, especially now that my sisters came to the table.

At any rate, I had forgotten everything I might ever have picked up about her when, on the evening after my return, my cousin Hubert Wesson—now towering above me as a pillar of the Knickerbocker Club, and a final authority on the ways of the world—suggested our joining her at the opera.

"Mrs. Hazeldean? But I don't know her. What will she think?

"That it's all right. Come along. She's the jolliest woman I know. We'll go back afterward and have supper with her—jolliest house I know." Hubert twirled a self-conscious moustache.

We were dining at the Knickerbocker, to which I had just been elected, and the bottle of Pommery we were finishing disposed me to think that nothing could be more fitting for two men of the world than to end their evening in the box of the jolliest woman Hubert knew. I groped for my own moustache, gave a twirl in the void, and followed him, after meticulously sliding my overcoat sleeve around my silk hat as I had seen him do.

But once in Mrs. Hazeldean's box I was only an overgrown boy again, bathed in such blushes as used, at the same age, to visit Hubert, forgetting that I had a moustache to twirl, and knocking my hat from the peg on which I had just hung it, in my zeal to pick up a programme she had not dropped.

For she was really too lovely—too formidably lovely. I was used by now to mere unadjectived loveliness, the kind that youth and spirits hang like a rosy veil over commonplace features, an average outline and a pointless merriment. But this was something calculated, accomplished, finished—and just a little worn. It frightened me with my first glimpse of the infinity of beauty and the multiplicity of her pit-falls. What! There were women who need not fear crow's-feet, were more beautiful for being pale, could let a silver hair or two show among the dark, and their eyes brood inwardly while they smiled and chatted? But then no young man was safe for a moment! But then the world I had hitherto known had been only a warm pink nursery, while this new one was a place of darkness, perils and enchantments. . .

It was the next day that one of my sisters asked me where I had been the evening before, and that I puffed out my chest to answer: "With Mrs. Hazeldean—at the opera." My mother looked up, but did not speak till the governess had swept the girls off; then she said with pinched lips: "Hubert Wesson took you to Mrs. Hazeldean's box?"

"Yes."

"Well, a young man may go where he pleases. I hear Hubert is still infatuated; it serves Sabina right for not letting him marry the youngest Lyman girl. But don't mention Mrs. Hazeldean again before your sisters. . . They say her husband never knew—I suppose if he *had* she would never have got old Miss Cecilia Winter's money." And it was then that my mother pronounced the name of Henry Prest, and added that phrase about the Fifth Avenue Hotel which suddenly woke my boyish memories. . .

In a flash I saw again, under its quickly-lowered veil, the face with the exposed eyes and the frozen smile, and felt through my grown-up waistcoat the stab to my boy's heart and the loosened murmur of my soul; felt all this, and at the same moment tried to relate that former face, so fresh and clear despite its anguish, to the smiling guarded countenance of Hubert's "jolliest woman I know."

I was familiar with Hubert's indiscriminate use of his one adjective, and had not expected to find Mrs. Hazeldean "jolly" in the literal sense: in the case of the lady he happened to be in love with the epithet simply meant that she justified his choice. Nevertheless, as I compared Mrs. Hazeldean's earlier face to this one, I had my first sense of what may befall in the long years between youth and maturity, and of how short a distance I had travelled on that mysterious journey. If only she would take me by the hand!

I was not wholly unprepared for my mother's comment. There was no other lady in Mrs. Hazeldean's box when we entered; none joined her during the evening, and our hostess offered no apology for her isolation. In the New York of my youth every one knew what to think of a woman who was seen "alone at the opera"; if Mrs. Hazeldean was not openly classed with Fanny Ring, our one conspicuous "professional," it was because, out of respect for her social origin, New York preferred to avoid such juxtapositions. Young as I was, I knew this social law, and had guessed, before the evening was over, that Mrs. Hazeldean was not a lady on whom other ladies called, though she was not, on the other hand, a lady whom it was forbidden to mention to other ladies. So I did mention her, with bravado.

No ladies showed themselves at the opera with Mrs. Hazeldean; but one or two dropped in to the jolly supper announced by Hubert, an entertainment whose jollity consisted in a good deal of harmless banter over broiled canvas-backs and celery, with the best of champagne. These same ladies I sometimes met at her house afterward. They were mostly younger than their hostess, and still, though precariously, within the social pale: pretty trivial creatures, bored with a monotonous prosperity, and yearning for such unlawful joys as cigarettes, plain speaking, and a drive home in the small hours with the young man of the moment. But such daring spirits were few in old New York, their appearances infrequent and somewhat furtive. Mrs. Hazeldean's society consisted mainly of men, men of all ages, from her bald or grey-headed contemporaries to youths of Hubert's accomplished years and raw novices of mine.

A great dignity and decency prevailed in her little circle. It was not the oppressive respectability which weighs on the reformed *déclassée,* but the air of ease imparted by a woman of distinction who has wearied of society and closed her doors to all save her intimates. One always felt, at Lizzie Hazeldean's, that the next moment one's grandmother and aunts might be announced; and yet so pleasantly certain that they wouldn't be.

What is there in the atmosphere of such houses that makes them so enchanting to a fastidious and imaginative youth? Why is it that "those women" (as the others call them) alone know how to put the awkward at ease, check the familiar, smile a little at the over-knowing, and yet encourage naturalness in all? The difference of atmosphere is felt on the very threshold. The flowers grow differently in their vases, the lamps and easy-chairs have found a cleverer way of coming together, the books on the table are the very ones that one is longing to get hold of. The most perilous coquetry may not be in a woman's way of arranging her dress but in her way of arranging her drawing-room; and in this art Mrs. Hazeldean excelled.

I have spoken of books; even then they were usually the first objects to attract me in a room, whatever else of beauty it contained; and I remember, on the evening of that first "jolly supper," coming to an astonished pause before the crowded shelves that took up one wall of the drawing-room. What! The goddess read, then? She could accompany one on those flights too? Lead one, no doubt? My heart beat high. . .

But I soon learned that Lizzie Hazeldean did not read. She turned but languidly even the pages of the last Ouida novel; and I remember seeing Mallock's *New Republic* uncut on her table for weeks. It took me no long time to make the discovery: at my very next visit she caught my glance of surprise in the direction of the rich shelves, smiled, coloured a little, and met it with the confession: "No, I can't read them. I've tried—I *have* tried—but print makes me sleepy. Even novels do. . ." "They" were the accumulated treasures of English poetry, and a rich and varied selection of history, criticism, letters, in English, French and Italian—she spoke these languages, I knew—books evidently assembled by a sensitive and widely-ranging reader. We were alone at the time, and Mrs. Hazeldean went on in a lower tone: "I kept just the few he liked best—my husband, you know." It was the first time that Charles Hazeldean's name had been spoken between us, and my surprise was so great that my candid cheek must have reflected the blush on hers. I had fancied that women in her situation avoided alluding to their husbands. But she continued to look at me, wistfully, humbly almost, as if there were something more that she wanted to say, and was inwardly entreating me to understand.

"He was a great reader: a student. And he tried so hard to make me read too—he wanted to share everything with me. And I *did* like poetry—some poetry—when he read it aloud to me. After his death I thought: 'There'll be his books. I can go back to them—I shall find him there.' And

I tried—oh, so hard—but it's no use. They've lost their meaning . . . as most things have." She stood up, lit a cigarette, pushed back a log on the hearth. I felt that she was waiting for me to speak. If life had but taught me how to answer her, what was there of her story I might not have learned? But I was too inexperienced; I could not shake off my bewilderment. What! This woman whom I had been pitying for matrimonial miseries which seemed to justify her seeking solace elsewhere—this woman could speak of her husband in such a tone! I had instantly perceived that the tone was not feigned; and a confused sense of the complexity—or the chaos—of human relations held me as tongue-tied as a schoolboy to whom a problem beyond his grasp is suddenly propounded.

Before the thought took shape she had read it, and with the smile which drew such sad lines about her mouth, had continued gaily: "What are you up to this evening, by the way? What do you say to going to the "Black Crook" with your cousin Hubert and one or two others? I have a box."

It was inevitable that, not long after this candid confession, I should have persuaded myself that a taste for reading was boring in a woman, and that one of Mrs. Hazeldean's chief charms lay in her freedom from literary pretensions. The truth was, of course, that it lay in her sincerity; in her humble yet fearless estimate of her own qualities and short-comings. I had never met its like in a woman of any age, and coming to me in such early days, and clothed in such looks and intonations, it saved me, in after years, from all peril of meaner beauties.

But before I had come to understand that, or to guess what falling in love with Lizzie Hazeldean was to do for me, I had quite unwittingly and fatuously done the falling. The affair turned out, in the perspective of the years, to be but an incident of our long friendship; and if I touch on it here it is only to illustrate another of my poor friend's gifts. If she could not read books she could read hearts; and she bent a playful yet compassionate gaze on mine while it still floundered in unawareness.

I remember it all as if it were yesterday. We were sitting alone in her drawing-room, in the winter twilight, over the fire. We had reached—in her company it was not difficult—the degree of fellowship when friendly talk lapses naturally into a friendlier silence, and she had taken up the evening paper while I glowered dumbly at the embers. One little foot, just emerging below her dress, swung, I remember, between me and the fire, and seemed to hold her all in the spring of its instep. . .

"Oh," she exclaimed, "poor Henry Prest—." She dropped the paper. "His wife is dead—poor fellow," she said simply.

The blood rushed to my forehead: my heart was in my throat. She had named him—named him at last, the recreant lover, the man who had "dishonoured" her! My hands were clenched: if he had entered the room they would have been at his throat. . .

And then, after a quick interval, I had again the humiliating disheartening sense of not understanding: of being too young, too inexperienced, to know. This woman, who spoke of her deceived husband with tenderness, spoke compassionately of her faithless lover! And she did the one as naturally as the other, not as if this impartial charity were an attitude she had determined to assume, but as if it were part of the lesson life had taught her.

"I didn't know he was married," I growled between my teeth.

She meditated absently. "Married? Oh, yes, when was it? The year after . . ." her voice dropped again . . . "after my husband died. He married a quiet cousin, who had always been in love with him, I believe. They had two boys.—You knew him?" she abruptly questioned.

I nodded grimly.

"People always thought he would never marry—he used to say so himself," she went on, still absently.

I burst out: "The—hound!"

"*Oh!*" she exclaimed. I started up, our eyes met, and hers filled with tears of reproach and understanding. We sat looking at each other in silence. Two of the tears overflowed, hung on her lashes, melted down her cheeks. I continued to stare at her shamefacedly; then I got to my feet, drew out my handkerchief, and tremblingly, reverently, as if I had touched a sacred image, I wiped them away.

My love-making went no farther. In another moment she had contrived to put a safe distance between us. She did not want to turn a boy's head; long since (she told me afterward) such amusements had ceased to excite her. But she did want my sympathy, wanted it overwhelmingly: amid the various feelings she was aware of arousing, she let me see that sympathy, in the sense of a moved understanding, had always been lacking. "But then," she added ingenuously, "I've never really been sure, because I've never told anyone my story. Only I take it for granted that, if I haven't, it's *their* fault rather than mine. . ." She smiled half-deprecatingly, and my bosom swelled, acknowledging the distinction. "And now I want to tell *you*—" she began.

I have said that my love for Mrs. Hazeldean was a brief episode in our long relation. At my age, it was inevitable that it should be so. The "fresher face" soon came, and in its light I saw my old friend as a middle-aged woman, turning grey, with a mechanical smile and haunted eyes. But it was in the first glow of my feeling that she had told me her story; and when the glow subsided, and in the afternoon light of a long intimacy I judged and tested her statements, I found that each detail fitted into the earlier picture.

My opportunities were many; for once she had told the tale she always wanted to be retelling it. A perpetual longing to relive the past, a perpetual need to explain and justify herself—the satisfaction of these two cravings, once she had permitted herself to indulge them, became the luxury of her empty life. She had kept it empty—emotionally, sentimentally empty—from the day of her husband's death, as the guardian of an abandoned temple might go on forever sweeping and tending what had once been the god's abode. But this duty performed, she had no other. She had done one great—or abominable—thing; rank it as you please, it had been done heroically. But there was nothing in her to keep her at that height. Her tastes, her interests, her conceivable occupations, were all on the level of a middling domesticity; she did not know how to create for herself any inner life in keeping with that one unprecedented impulse.

Soon after her husband's death, one of her cousins, the Miss Cecilia Winter of Washington Square to whom my mother had referred, had died also, and left Mrs. Hazeldean a handsome legacy. And a year or two later Charles Hazeldean's small estate had undergone the favourable change that befell New York realty in the 'eighties. The property he had bequeathed to his wife had doubled, then tripled, in value; and she found herself, after a few years of widowhood, in possession of an income large enough to supply her with all the luxuries which her husband had struggled so hard to provide. It was the peculiar irony of her lot to be secured from temptation when all danger of temptation was over; for she would never, I am certain, have held out the tip of her finger to any man to obtain such luxuries for her own enjoyment. But if she did not value her money for itself, she owed to it—and the service was perhaps greater than she was aware—the power of mitigating her solitude, and filling it with the trivial distractions without which she was less and less able to live.

She had been put into the world, apparently, to amuse men and enchant them; yet, her husband dead, her sacrifice accomplished, she would have preferred, I am sure, to shut herself up in a lonely monumental attitude, with thoughts and pursuits on a scale with her one great hour. But what was she to do? She had known of no way of earning money except by her graces; and now she knew no way of filling her days except with cards and chatter and theatre-going. Not one of the men who approached her passed beyond the friendly barrier she had opposed to me. Of that I was sure. She had not shut out Henry Prest in order to replace him—her face grew white at the suggestion. But what else was there to do, she asked me;

what? The days had to be spent somehow; and she was incurably, disconsolately sociable.

So she lived, in a cold celibacy that passed for I don't know what licence; so she lived, withdrawn from us all, yet needing us so desperately, inwardly faithful to her one high impulse, yet so incapable of attuning her daily behaviour to it! And so, at the very moment when she ceased to deserve the blame of society, she found herself cut off from it, and reduced to the status of the "fast" widow noted for her jolly suppers.

I bent bewildered over the depths of her plight. What else, at any stage of her career, could she have done, I often wondered? Among the young women now growing up about me I find none with enough imagination to picture the helpless incapacity of the pretty girl of the 'seventies, the girl without money or vocation, seemingly put into the world only to please, and unlearned in any way of maintaining herself there by her own efforts. Marriage alone could save such a girl from starvation, unless she happened to run across an old lady who wanted her dogs exercised and her *Churchman* read aloud to her. Even the day of painting wild-roses on fans, of colouring photographs to "look like" miniatures, of manufacturing lamp-shades and trimming hats for more fortunate friends —even this precarious beginning of feminine independence had not dawned. It was inconceivable to my mother's generation that a portionless girl should not be provided for by her relations until she found a husband; and that, having found him, she should have to help him to earn a living, was more inconceivable still. The self-sufficing little society of that vanished New York attached no great importance to wealth, but regarded poverty as so distasteful that it simply took no account of it.

These things pleaded in favour of poor Lizzie Hazeldean, though to superficial observers her daily life seemed to belie the plea. She had known no way of smoothing her husband's last years but by being false to him; but once he was dead, she expiated her betrayal by a rigidity of conduct for which she asked no reward but her own inner satisfaction. As she grew older, and her friends scattered, married, or were kept away from one cause or another, she filled her depleted circle with a less fastidious hand. One met in her drawing-room dull men, common men, men who too obviously came there because they were not invited elsewhere, and hoped to use her as a social stepping-stone. She was aware of the difference— her eyes said so whenever I found one of these newcomers installed in my arm-chair—but never, by word or sign, did she admit it. She said to me once: "You find it duller here than it used to be. It's my fault, perhaps; I think I knew better how to draw out my old friends." And another day: "Remember, the people you meet here now come out of kindness. I'm an old woman, and I consider nothing else." That was all.

She went more assiduously than ever to the theatre and the opera; she performed for her friends a hundred trivial services; in her eagerness to be always busy she invented superfluous attentions, oppressed people by offering assistance they did not need, verged at times—for all her tact—on the officiousness of the desperately lonely. At her little suppers she surprised us with exquisite flowers and novel delicacies. The champagne and cigars grew better and better as the quality of the guests declined; and sometimes, as the last of her dull company dispersed, I used to see her, among the scattered ash-trays and liqueur decanters, turn a steathy glance at her reflection in the mirror, with haggard eyes which seemed to ask: "Will even *these* come back tomorrow?"

I should be loth to leave the picture at this point; my last vision of her is more satisfying. I had been away, travelling for a year at the other end of the world; the day I came back I ran across Hubert Wesson at my club. Hubert had grown pompous and heavy. He drew me into a corner, and said, turning red, and glancing cautiously over his shoulder: "Have you seen our old friend Mrs. Hazeldean? She's very ill, I hear."

I was about to take up the "I hear"; then I remembered that in my absence Hubert had married, and that his caution was probably a tribute to his new state. I hurried at once to Mrs. Hazeldean's; and on her door-step, to my surprise, I ran against a Catholic priest, who looked gravely at me, bowed and passed out.

I was unprepared for such an encounter, for my old friend had never spoken to me of religious matters. The spectacle of her father's career had presumably shaken whatever incipient faith was in her; though in her little-girlhood, as she often told me, she had been as deeply impressed by Dr. Winter's eloquence as any grown-up member of his flock. But now, as soon as I laid eyes on her, I understood. She was very ill, she was visibly dying; and in her extremity, fate, not always kind, had sent her the solace which she needed. Had some obscure inheritance of religious feeling awaked in her? Had she remembered that her poor father, after his long life of mental and moral vagabondage, had finally found rest in the ancient fold? I never knew the explanation—she probably never knew it herself.

But she knew that she had found what she wanted. At last she could talk of Charles, she could confess her sin, she could be absolved of it. Since cards and suppers and chatter were over, what more blessed barrier could she find against solitude? All her life, henceforth, was a long preparation for that daily hour of expansion and consolation. And then this merciful visitor, who understood her so well, could also tell her things about Charles: knew where he was, how he felt, what exquisite daily attentions could still be paid to him, and how, with all unworthiness washed away, she might at last hope to reach him. Heaven could never seem strange, so interpreted; each time that I saw her, during the weeks of her slow fading, she was more and more like a traveller with her face turned homeward, yet smilingly resigned to await her summons. The house no longer seemed lonely, nor the hours tedious; there had even been found for her, among the books she had so often tried to read, those books which had long looked at her with such hostile faces, two or three (they were always on her bed) containing messages from the world where Charles was waiting.

Thus provided and led, one day she went to him.